Anderson Crow, Detective

George Barr McCutcheon

A NIGHT TO BE REMEMBERED

Two events of great importance took place in Tinkletown on the night of May 6, 1918. The first, occurring at half-past ten o'clock, was of sufficient consequence to rouse the entire population out of bed—thereby creating a situation, almost unique, which allowed every one in town to participate in all the thrills of the second. When the history of Tinkletown is written, —and it is said to be well under way at the hands of that estimable authoress, Miss Sue Becker, some fifty years a resident of the town and the great-granddaughter of one of its founders, —when this history is written, the night of May 6, 1918, will assert itself with something of the same insistence that causes the world to refresh its memory occasionally by looking into the encyclopedia to determine the exact date of the Fall of the Bastile. The fire-bell atop the town hall heralded the first event, and two small boys gave notice of the second.

Smock's grain-elevator, on the outskirts of the town, was in flames, and with a high wind blowing from the west, the Congregational and Baptist churches, the high school, Pratt's photograph gallery and the two motion-picture houses were threatened with destruction. As Anderson Crow, now deputy marshal of the town, declared the instant he arrived at the scene of the conflagration, nothing but the most heroic and indefatigable efforts on the part of the volunteer fire-department could save the town—only he put it in this way: "We'll have another Chicago fire here, sure as you're born, unless it rains or the wind changes mighty all-fired sudden; so we got to fight hard, boys."

Mr. Crow, also deputy superintendent of the fire-department, was late in getting to the engine-house back of the town hall—so late that the hand-engine and hose-reel, manned by volunteers who had waited as long as advisable, were belabouring the fire with water some time before he reached the engine-house. This irritated Mr. Crow considerably. He was out of breath when he got to the elevator, or some one would have heard from him. Another cause of annoyance was the fact that his rubber coat and helmet went with the hose-reel and were by this time adorning the person of an energetic fire-fighter who had no official right to them. After a diligent search Mr. Crow located his regalia and commanded the wearer, one Patrick Murphy, to hand 'em over at once. What Patrick Murphy, a recent arrival at Tinkletown, said in response to this demand was lost in the roar of the flames; so Anderson put his hand to his ear and shouted:

"What say?"

Patrick repeated his remark with great vigour, and Mr. Crow, apparently catching no more than the final word in the sentence, moved hastily away, but not before agreeing with Mr. Murphy that it *was* as hot as the place he mentioned.

Ed Higgins, the feed-store man, was in charge of the fire-fighters, who were industriously throwing a single stream of water from the fire-cistern into the vast and towering conflagration. It was like tossing a pint of water into the Atlantic Ocean.

"Got her under control?" roared Anderson, bristling up to Ed.

"Sure!" shouted Ed. "She's workin' beautiful. Just look at that stream. You—"

"I mean the fire," bellowed Anderson.

"Oh, I thought you meant the engine. I don't think we'll get the fire under contral till the derned warehouse is burned down. Gee whiz, Chief, where you been? We waited as long as we could for you, and then—"

"Don't blame me," was Anderson's answer. "I'd ha' been the first man at the engine-house if I hadn't waited nigh onto half an hour trying to get the chief of the fire-department out of bed and dressed. I argued—"

"What's the matter with you? Ain't you chief of the fire-department? Are you crazy or what?"

"Ain't you got any brains, Ed Higgins? My wife's been chief ever since she was elected marshal last month, an' you know it. That's what we get fer lettin' the women vote an' have a hand in the affairs of the nation. She just wouldn't get up—so I had to come off without her. Where's my trumpet? We got to get this fire under control, or the whole town will go. Gosh, if it'd only rain! Looked a little like rain this evenin'—an' this wind may be bringin' up a storm or—"

"Here's your trumpet, Mr. Crow," screeched a small boy, bursting through the crowd.

Half of the inhabitants of Tinkletown stood outside of the rim of heat and watched the fire, while the other half, in all stages of deshabille, remained in their front yards training the garden hose on the roofs and sides of their houses and yelling to every speeding passer-by to telephone to the commissioner of water-works to turn on more pressure. Among his other offices, Mr. Crow was commissioner of water-works, having held over in that office because the board of selectmen forgot to appoint any one else in his place after the last election. And while a great many citizens carried the complaint of the garden-hose handlers to the commissioner, it is doubtful if he heard them above the combined sound of his own voice and the roar of the flames.

Possessed of his trumpet, the redoubtable Mr. Crow took his stand beside the old hand-pumping "fire-engine" and gave orders right and left in a valiant but thoroughly cracked voice.

"Now, we'll git her out," panted Alf Reesling, the town drunkard, speaking to Father Maloney, the Catholic priest, who was taking a turn with him at the pumping apparatus. "Ed.'s all right, but it takes Anderson to handle a fire as she ought to be handled."

Father Maloney, perspiring copiously and breathing with great difficulty, grunted without conviction.

"Leetle more elbow-grease there, men!" shouted Anderson, directing his command to the futile pumpers. "We got to get water up to that second-story winder. More steam, boys— more steam!"

"Aw, what's the use?" growled Bill Jackson, letting go of the pump to wipe his dripping forehead. "We couldn't put her out with Niagary Falls in flood-time."

"Bring your hose over here, men—lively, now!" called out the leader. "Every second counts. Lively! Git out o' the way, Purt Throcker! Consarn you fool boys! Can't you keep back where you belong? Right over here, men! That's the ticket! Now, shoot her into that winder. Hey! One of you boys bust in that winder glass with a rock. All of you! See if you c'n hit her!"

A fusillade of stones left the hands of a score of small boys and clattered against the walls of the doomed warehouse, some of them coming as near as ten feet to the objective, two of them being so wide of the mark that simultaneous ejaculations of surprise and pain issued from the lips of Miss Spratt and Professor Smith, both of the high school.

The heat was intense, blistering. Reluctantly the crowd, awed and fascinated by the greatest blaze it had ever seen,—not even excepting the burning of Eliphalet Loop's straw-ricks in 1897,—edged farther and farther away, pursued by the relentless heat-waves. The fire-fighters withdrew in good order, obeying the instinct of self-preservation somewhat in advance of the command of their superior, who, indeed, had anticipated such a man[oe]uvre by taking a position from which he could *lead* the retreat. By the time the fire was at its height, "lighting the way clear to heaven," according to Miss Sue Becker, who had to borrow Marshal Crow's pencil and a piece of paper from Mort Fryback so that she could jot down the beautiful thought before it perished in the "turmoil of frightfulness!"

"More elbow-grease, men!" roared Anderson, "She'll get ahead of us if we let up for a second! Pump! Pump!"

And pump they did, notwithstanding the fact that the stream of water from the nozzle in the hands of Ed Higgins and Petey Cicotte was now falling short of the building by some twenty or thirty feet.

"Serves old man Smock right!" declared Anderson in wrath, addressing the town clerk and two selectmen who by virtue of office retained advantageous positions in the front rank of spectators "If he'd done as I told him an' paid fer havin' water-mains extended as fer out as his warehouse, we could have saved it fer him. It looks to me now as if she's bound to go. Where's Harry?"

Harry Squires, the reporter for The *Banner*, notebook in hand, came up at that instant.

"Looks pretty serious, doesn't it, Chief?" he remarked.

"The fire-company deserves all the credit, Harry," said Anderson magnanimously. "I want you to put it in the paper, just that way, as comin' from me. If it hadn't been for the loyal, heroic efforts of the finest fire-department Tinkletown has ever had, the—Hey! Pull that hose back here, you derned fools! Do you want to get it scorched an' ruined so's it won't be fit fer anything agin? Fetch that engine over here across the road too! Do you hear me?" Turning again to the reporter, he resumed: "Yes sir, if it hadn't been fer them boys, there wouldn't have been a blessed thing saved, Harry."

Harry Squires squinted narrowly. "I can't say that anything *has* been saved, Chief. Just mention something, please."

Anderson looked at him in amazement. "Why, ain't you got any eyes? Hain't they saved the engine and every foot of hose the town owns?"

"They could have saved that much by staying at home in bed," said Mr. Squires dryly. "I've just seen Mr. Smock. He says there were fifty thousand bushels of wheat in the bins, waiting for cars to take it down to New York. Every bushel of it was going abroad for the Allies. Does that put any sort of an idea into your nut, Anderson?"

"What?"

"Into your bean, I should say. Or, in other words, hair-pasture."

"He means head, Mr. Crow," explained Miss Sue Becker.

"Well, why don't he say head—that's what I'd like to know."

"Do you deduce anything from the fact that the grain was to go to the Allies, Anderson?" inquired Harry.

The harassed marshal scratched his head, but said: "Absolutely!"

"Well, what do you deduce, Mr. Hawkshaw?"

"I deduce, you derned jay, that old man Smock won't be able to deliver it. Move back, will you? You're right in my way, an'—"

"I suppose you know that the Germans are still fighting the Allies, don't you? Fighting 'em here as well as over in France? Now does that help you any?"

Mr. Crow's jaw fell—but only for a second. He tightened it up almost immediately and with commendable dignity.

"My sakes alive, Harry Squires, you don't suppose I'm tellin' my real suspicions to any newspaper reporter, do you? How do I know you ain't a spy? Still, dog-gone you, if it will set your mind at rest, I'll say this much: I have positive proof that Smock's warehouse was set on fire by agents of the German gover'ment. That's one of the reasons I was a little late in gettin' to the fire. Now, don't try to pump me any more, 'cause I can't tell you anything that would jeopardize the interests of justice. Hey! Where in thunder are you fellers goin' with that hose an' engine?"

The firemen were on a dead run.

"We're goin' a couple of hundred yards down the road, so's we won't be killed when that front wall caves in," shouted Ed Higgins, without pausing. "Better come along, Anderson. She's beginning to bulge something awful."

Anderson Crow arose to the occasion.

"Lively now!" he barked through the trumpet. "Get that hose and engine back to a safe place! Can't you see the wall's about ready to fall? Everybody fall back! Women and children first! Women first, remember!"

Down the road fled the crowd, looking over its collective shoulders, so to speak—followed by the venerable fire apparatus and the still more venerable commander-in-chief.

Harry Squires, in his two-column account of the fire in the *Banner*, dilated upon the fact that the women failed to retain the advantage so gallantly extended by the men. For the matter of about ten or fifteen yards they *were* first; after which, being handicapped by petticoats, they fell ingloriously behind. Some of the older ones—maliciously, he feared—impeded the progress of their protectors by neglecting to get out of the way in time, with the result that at least two men were severely bruised by falling over them—the case of Uncle Dad Simms being a particularly sad one. He collided head-on with the portly Mrs. Loop, and failing to budge her, suffered the temporary loss of a full set of teeth and nearly twenty minutes of consciousness. Mr. Squires went on to say that the only thing that saved Mr. Simms from being run over and killed by the fire-engine was the fact that the latter was about a block and a half ahead of him when the accident occurred.

Sparks soared high and far on the smoke-laden wind, scurrying townward across the barren quarry-lands. The vast canopy was red with the glow of flying embers and fire-lit clouds. Below, in the dusty road, swarmed the long procession of citizens. Grim, stark hemlocks gleamed in the weird, uncanny light that turned the green of their foliage and the black of their trunks into the colour of the rose on the side facing the fire, but left them dark and forbidding on the other. The telegraph-poles beyond the burning warehouse lining the railroad spur that ventured down from the main line some miles away and terminated at Smock's, loomed up like lofty gibbets in the ghastly light. Three quarters of a mile from the scene of the conflagration lay the homes of the people who lived on the rim of Tinkletown, and there also were the two churches and the motion-picture houses.

"We got to save them picture-houses," panted Anderson, and then in hasty apology, — "and the churches, too."

"You got to save my studio first," bawled Elmer K. Pratt, the photographer, trying to keep pace with him in the congested line.

"Halt!" commanded the chief, not because tactics called for such an action but because he was beginning to feel that he couldn't keep up with the engine.

The cavalcade eased down to a walk and finally came to a halt. Every eye was riveted on the burning structure which now stood out alone in all its grandeur beyond the quarries and gravel-pits. Every one waited in breathless suspense for the collapse of the towering walls.

A shrill, boyish voice broke out above the subdued, awe-struck chatter of the crowd.

"Where's Mr. Crow? Mr. Crow! Where are you?"

"Sh!" hissed Alf Reesling, glowering upon the excited boy, who had just come up at full speed from the direction of the town. "Don't you make so much noise! The walls are going to cave in, an' — "

"Where's Mr. Crow?" panted the boy, a lad of twelve. His eyes appeared starting from his head. A second boy joined him, and he was trembling so violently that he could not speak at all. All he could do was to point at the lank figure of the old town marshal, some distance back in the crowd.

Three seconds later the two youngsters had the ear of Anderson Crow, and between them they poured it full of news of the most extraordinary character. The crowd, forgetting the imminent crash of the warehouse wall, pressed eagerly forward.

"Wait a second—wait a second!" roared Anderson. "One at a time now. Don't both of you talk at oncet. You, Bud—you tell it. You keep still, Roswell Hatch. Take your time, Bud!"

"Lemme tell it, Mr. Crow," begged Roswell. "I knowed it first. It ain't fair for Bud to—"

"But I got here first," protested Bud, and there might have been something more sanguinary than mere words if Marshal Crow had not interfered.

"None o' that, now! What's the matter, Bud?"

"Somethin' turrible has happened, Mr. Crow—somethin' awfully turrible," wheezed the boy.

"If you derned little scalawags have run all the way from town to tell me that Smock's warehouse is on fire, you'd—"

"Oh, gee, that ain't nothin'!" gulped Bud. "Wait till you hear what I know."

"I can't wait all night. I got to save Mr. Pratt's studio, an'—"

"Well, you know them two tramps you put in the lock-up yesterday afternoon?" cried Bud.

"Desperit characters, both of 'em. I figgered they was up to some devilment an—"

"Well, they ain't in any more; they're out. Ros an' me seen the whole business. We wuz—"

"Geminy crickets! What's this? A jail-break? Out of the way, everybody! Two desperit villains are loose in town, an—"

"Hold on, Mr. Crow," cried the other lad, seizing his

opportunity. "There's more'n two. Three or four more fellers from the outside come up an' busted in the door an' *let* 'em out. Then they all run down the street to where the new bank is. Me an' Bud seen some of 'em climb into one of the winders of the bank, an' nen we struck out to find you, Mr. Crow. We thought maybe you'd like to know what—"

The rest of Roswell's narrative was lost in the hullabaloo of command and action. The fickle populace turned its back on the burning warehouse and swept down the lane in quest of new excitement. The tottering wall came down with a crash, but its fall was unwitnessed except by those infirm old ladies and gentlemen who had lagged so far behind in the first rush for safety that they were still in ignorance of the latest calamity. It was a pity, wrote Miss Sue Becker in her diary, that the gods crowded so much into a single night when there were "three hundred and sixty-four more perfectly good nights available."

The story of the two boys proved not only to be true, but also woefully lacking in exaggeration. The jail-delivery and the looting of the First National Bank of Tinkletown turned out to be but two in a long and fairly complete list of disasters.

Investigation revealed an astonishing thoroughness and impartiality on the part of the bandits. The safe in Brubaker's drugstore was missing, with something like nineteen dollars in cash; Lamson's store had been entered, and the cash-register rifled; Fryback's hardware-store, Higgins' feed-store and Rush Applegate's tailor-shop were visited, and, as Harry Squires said in the *Banner*, "contents noted." Two brand-new "shoes" and a couple of inner tubes were missing from Gillespie's Universal Garage, and Ed Higgins' dog was slain in cold blood by the "remorseless ravagers."

Nobody went to sleep that night. Everybody joined in the search for the robbers. Citizens hurried home after the first alarm and did their part by looking under every bed in their houses, after which the more venturesome visited garrets, cellars and woodsheds.

Anderson Crow, after organizing a large posse and commandeering several automobiles, suddenly remembered that he had left his silver watch and a wallet containing eleven dollars under his pillow. He drove home as rapidly as possible in John Blosser's 1903 Pope-Toledo and was considerably aggravated to find his wife sound asleep. He awoke her with some rudeness.

"Wake up, Eva! Consarn it, don't you know the town's full of highwaymen? It'd be just like you to sleep here like a log and let 'em come in an' nip my watch an' purse right out o' your own bed. I wouldn't 'a' been a bit surprised to find 'em gone—an' you chloryformed and gagged. I—"

"Burglars, did you say?" cried his wife, sitting up in bed and staring at him in alarm.

"Dozens of 'em," he declared, pocketing his watch and wallet. "Get up and help me search the house. Where's my revolver?"

"Oh, Lordy, Anderson! Your—your revolver? You're not going to shoot it off, are you?"

"I certainly am—if the derned thing's loaded. Where's it at?"

She sank back with a sigh of relief. "Thank heavens, I just remembered that Milt Cupples borrowed it last winter to—"

"Borrowed my revolver?" roared Anderson. "Why—"

"To loan to a friend of his'n who was going down to New York on business."

"An' he never brought it back?"

"He never did."

Anderson's opinion of Milt Cupples was smothered in a violent chorus of automobile horns. Mrs. Crow promptly covered her head with the bed-clothes and let out a muffled shriek.

"It's only the posse," he shouted, pulling the covers from her face. "Don't be scairt, Evy. Where's your courage? Remember who you are. Rememb—"

"I'm only a poor, weak woman—"

"I know that," he agreed, "but that ain't all. You are marshal o' Tinkletown, an' if you're goin' to cover up your head every time a horn toots, you'll—"

"Oh, go on away and leave me alone, Anderson," she cried. "I don't want to be marshal. I never did. I resign now—do you hear me? I resign this instant. I was a fool to let the women elect me—and the women were worse fools for voting for me. That's what comes of letting women vote. We had a good, well-trained marshal—because that's what you are, Anderson. And —"

The door flew open. Alf Reesling burst into the room, followed by both of Anderson Crow's daughters.

"Come on, Anderson!" shouted Alf, gasping with excitement. "Good even', Mrs. Crow. Howdy do? Hurry up, Ander—"

"We tried to keep him out, Ma," broke in Caroline Crow, glaring at Alf. "We told him you were in bed, but he—"

"Well, gosh a'mighty," cried Alf in exasperation, "we can't wait all night. We got track o' them fellers, but if we got to set around out here till mornin' just because your ma's in bed, I

—I—well, that's all I got to say." He turned to Anderson for support, and catching the look in his eye, bawled: "No, I ain't been drinkin', Anderson Crow! I'm as sober as a—"

"Get out of my bedroom this minute, Alf Reesling," cried Mrs. Crow. "I'll tell your wife how you're behavin' if you—"

"Go ahead an' tell her," snorted Alf, goaded beyond endurance. "She ain't had a good laugh since the time Anderson had his pocket picked up at Boggs City, fair-week. Go ahead an'—"

"Come on, Alf—lively now," broke in Mr. Crow hastily. "We got to be on the jump. Gosh, listen to them dogs! Never heard so much barkin' in all my life."

Out of the house rushed the two men. Anderson immediately began issuing orders.

"Ed Higgins, you take a squad o' men and go back to the fire. We got our hands full tonight. Now, all you fellers as has got pistols an' shotguns go home an' get 'em at oncet. Come back here as quick as you can an'—what say, Harry?"

He turned to the reporter.

"I said the first thing to do is to shoot about thirty or forty of these infernal dogs."

"We can't afford to waste ca'tridges, Harry Squires," said Anderson severely. "We got to tackle a desperate gang 'fore we're through."

"Where is your daughter Caroline, Mr. Crow?" inquired the reporter irrelevantly.

"She's in the house tryin' to quiet her ma. A drunk man bust into her room a little while ago an'—"

"Well, tell her to get on the job at once. She's chief telephone operator down at the exchange, and she ought to be there now sending out warnings to every town within twenty miles of—"

"Carrie! Car-ree!" shouted Anderson, racing up the path. "How many times have I got to tell you to 'tend to that telephonin'? Go down to the office this minute an' call up Boggs City an'—"

"I'm not the *night* operator," snapped Caroline, appearing in the window. "What's the matter with Jane Swiggers and Lucy Cummings? They're supposed to be on duty all night."

"Don't sass back! Do as I tell you. Telephone every town in the county to be on the lookout fer an automobile with two tires and a couple of inner tubes—"

"Two *new* tires, Caroline," amended Harry Squires.

"And carrying a tin safe with George W. Brubaker's name on it in red letters. Say that a complete description of the robbers will follow. Is your ma still in bed?"

"Yes, she is."

"Well, you tell her I'll be home soon as I capture them desperadoes." He was moving toward the front gate. Caroline's paraphrase pursued him and left a sting:

"What is home without a father!"

Followed now a lengthy and at times acrimonious argument as to the further operations of the marshal's posse.

"We're losing valuable time," protested Harry Squires at the end of a half-hour's fertile discussion. *Fertile* is here employed instead of *futile*, for never was there a more extensive crop of ideas raised by human agency.

"We can't do anything till we find out which way the derned rascals went, can we?" said Mr. Crow bitingly. "We got to find somebody that seen 'em start off in that automobile. We—"

"Stuff and nonsense!" cried Harry. "We've got to split up into parties and follow every road out of Tinkletown."

"How in thunder do you expect me to lead five or six different posses?" demanded Anderson.

"Yes, an' what in thunder would we do if we caught up with 'em unexpected-like if we didn't have Anderson with us?" said Alf Reesling, loyal to the core. "In the first place, we wouldn't have any legal right to capture 'em, and in the second place we couldn't do it anyhow."

By this time there were a dozen shotguns on the scene, to say nothing of a most impressive collection of antiquated revolvers, "Flobert" rifles, Civil War muskets and baseball bats.

"I move we move," was the laconic but excellent speech of Mr. Henry Plumb. He already had his forefinger on the trigger of his "single-barrel."

"Second the motion," cried out Ed Higgins loudly.

"I thought I told you to go an' 'tend to that fire, Ed Higgins," said Anderson, in some surprise.

An extremely noisy dog-fight put an end to the discussion for the time being, and it was too late to renew it after Situate Jones' mongrel Pete had finished with Otto Schultz's dachshund Bismarck. So vociferous was the chorus put up by the other dogs that no one noticed the approach of an automobile, coming down the Boggs City pike. The car passed at full speed. Three dogs failed to get out of the way in time, and as a result, the list of casualties was increased to four, including Ed Higgins' previously mentioned black and tan.

The speeding car, a big one loaded with men, was a hundred yards away and going like the wind before the startled group regained its senses.

"There they go!" yelled Harry Squires.

"Exceedin' the speed limit, dog-gone 'em!" roared Anderson. "They ought to be locked up fer ten days an' fined—"

"Come on, men!" shouted Harry. "After 'em! That's the gang! They've been headed off at Boggs City—or something like that."

"Did anybody ketch the number of that car?" shouted Anderson. "I c'n trace 'em by their license number if—"

The rest of the speech was lost in the rush to enter the waiting automobiles, and the shouting that ensued. Then followed a period of frantic cranking, after which came the hasty backing and turning of cars, the tooting of horns and the panic of gears.

Loaded to the "gunnels," the half-dozen machines finally got under way, and off they went into the night, chortling with an excitement all their own.

A lone figure remained standing in front of Anderson Crow's gate—a tall, lank figure without coat or hat, one suspender supporting a pair of blue trousers, the other hanging limp and useless. He wore a red undershirt and carried in his left hand the trumpet of a fire-fighting chieftain.

"Well, I'll be dog-goned!" issued from his lips as the last of the cars rattled away. Then he started off bravely on foot in the wake of the noisy cavalcade. "Now, all of 'em are breakin' the speed laws; an' it's goin' to cost 'em somethin', consarn 'em, when I yank 'em up 'fore Justice Robb tomorrow, sure as my name's Anderson Crow."

Presently he heard a car approaching from behind. It was very dark in the outskirts of the town, and the lonely highway that reached down into the valley was a thing of the imagination rather than of the vision. Profiting by the catastrophes that attended the passing of the big touring-car Anderson hastily leaped to the side of the road. A couple of small headlights veered around a curve in the road and came down the slight grade, followed naturally and somewhat haltingly by an automobile whose timorous brakes were half set. There was a single occupant.

Anderson levelled his trumpet at the driver and shouted:

"Halt!"

"Oh-h!" came in a shrill, agitated voice from the car, but the machine gave no sign of halting.

"Hey! Halt, I say!"

"I—I don't know how!" moaned the voice. "How do you stop it?"

"Good gracious sakes alive! Is—is it *you*, Eva?"

"Oh, Anderson! Thank goodness! I thought you was a highwayman. Oh, dear—oh, dear! Ain't there any way to stop this thing?"

"Shut off the power, an' it'll stop when you start up the grade."

Anderson was trotting along behind, tugging at one of the mud-guards.

"How do you shut it off?"

"The same way you turned it on."

"Goodness, what a fool way to do things!"

The little car came to a stop on the rise of the grade, and Anderson side-stepped just in time to avoid being bumped into as it started back again, released.

"It's Deacon Rank's car," explained Mrs. Crow in response to a series of bewildered, rapid-fire questions from her husband. "He offered to sell it to me for fifty dollars, and I've been learnin' how to run it for two whole days—out in Peters' Mill lane."

"How does it happen I never knowed anything about this, Eva?" demanded he, regaining in some measure his tone of authority.

"I wanted to surprise you."

"Well, by gosh, you have!"

"Deacon Rank's been giving me lessons every afternoon. I know how to start it and steer it, goin' slow-like—but of course I've got a lot to learn."

"Well, you just turn that car around an' skedaddle for home, Eva Crow," was his command. "What business have you got runnin' around the country like this in the dead o' night, all alone—"

"Ain't I the Marshal of Tinkletown?" she broke in crossly. "What right have all you men to be going off without me in this—"

"The only official thing you've done, madam, since you got to be marshal, was to resign while you was in bed not more'n an hour ago. I accepted your resignation, so now you go home as quick as that blamed old rattletrap will take you."

"Besides, I saw the ornery fools go off an' leave you behind, Anderson, and that made me mad. I run over to Deacon Rank's and got the car. Now, you hop right in, and I'll take you wherever you want to go. Get in, I say. I hereby officially withdraw my resignation. I'm still marshal of this town, and if you don't do as I tell you, I'll discharge you as deputy."

So Anderson got up beside her and pulled desperately at his chin-whiskers, no doubt to assist the words that were struggling to escape from his compressed lips.

After considerable back-firing, the decrepit machine began to climb the grade. Presently Mr. Crow found his voice.

"Didn't I tell you to turn around, Eva?"

"Don't talk to me when I'm driving," said she, gripping the wheel tightly with the fingers of death.

"You turn the car around immediately, woman. I'm your husband, an' I order you to do as I tell ye!"

"I'll turn it around when I get good and ready," said she in a strained voice. "Can't you see there ain't room enough to turn around in this road?"

"Well, it don't get any wider."

"Besides, I don't know how to turn it around," she confessed.

"Why, you just back her, same as anybody else does, an' then reverse her, an'—"

"You old goose, how can I back her when she keeps on going for'ard?"

Anderson was silent for a moment.

"Well, if I may be so bold as to ask, madam, where are you going?" he asked, with deep sarcasm in his voice.

"You leave it to me, Anderson Crow. I know what I am doing."

They went on for about a quarter of a mile before she spoke again.

"There's only one way to turn around, and I'm taking it. How far is it to Fisher's lane?"

"You can't turn her around in Fisher's lane, Eva. It's all a good-sized dog c'n do to turn around in that road."

"I asked you how far is it?"

"'Bout a mile an' a half."

"I ain't going to turn around in Fisher's lane, Anderson. I'm going to foller it straight to the Britton toll-road, and then I'm going to turn into that and head for Tinkletown. That's how I'm going to turn this plagued car around."

"Well, of all the—why, geminently, Eva, it's—it's nigh onto nine mile. You shorely can't be such a fool as to—"

"I'm going to turn this car around if it takes twenty miles," she said firmly.

There was another long, intense silence.

"I wonder if the boys have got that fire out yet?" mumbled Anderson. "Course, there ain't no use worryin' about them robbers. They got away. If I'd been along with that posse, we'd 'a' had 'em sure by this time, but—oh, well, there ain't no use cryin' over spilt milk."

In due time they came to Fisher's lane. Mrs. Crow made a very sharp but triumphant turn, and the second leg of the course was before them. Half an hour later the valiant machine sneaked out of the narrow byway into the Britton pike and pointed its nose homeward.

"Let her out a little, Eva," said Anderson, taking a long breath. "It's four mile to town, an'—"

"Oh, goodness!" squeaked the driver, giving the wheel a perilous twist. "Look! There comes a car behind us. Help! They'll run into us! They'll—"

"Pull off to the side of the road—no, this side! Gosh! Hurry up, Eva. They're comin' like greased lightnin'! Look out! Not too fer over! There's a ditch alongside—"

The remainder of the sentence was lost in the wild shriek of a siren, shriek after shriek succeeding each other as a big car, with far-reaching acetylene lamps, roared down upon them. Like a mighty whirlwind it swept by them, careening perilously on the sloping edge of the road. Suddenly the grinding of brakes assailed the ears of the thanksgiving Crows, and to their astonishment the big machine came to a standstill a hundred yards or more down the road. Mrs. Crow promptly "put on" the accelerator, and but for a vehement warning from her husband would have gone full tilt into the rear end of the mighty stranger. She managed to stop the little car when its faithful nose was not more than two yards from the little red light ahead.

"Hey, Ford!" called out a man who had arisen in the tonneau of the big car and was looking back at them.

"Hey, yourself!" responded Anderson.

"Is this the road to Albany?"

"No, it ain't."

"We've lost our way. Where does this road take us?"

"Into the city of Tinkletown."

Three or four voices in the car were guilty of saying things in the presence of a lady.

"Well, where in hell are we?" demanded the spokesman.

"You ain't in hell yet, but you will be pretty soon if you keep up that reckless driving, lemme tell you that."

"Where do we get the Albany road?" called out another voice from the car.

"The quickest way is to go into Tinkletown an' take the first turn to the left after—"

"But we don't want to go to Tinkletown, you damned old hayseed. We—"

"Shut up, Joe!" cried one of the men. "He's excited, Mister. His wife's sick, and we're trying to get him home before she—before she croaks."

"Oh, I'm so sorry," cried Mrs. Crow before Anderson could speak. She also kicked him violently on the ankle-bone. "The quickest way to get to the Albany road," she went on, "is by cuttin' through back of Cole's sawmill an' crossin' the river at Goose's Ferry. That's about seven miles from here. Take the first lane to your left, half a mile further on."

"Much obliged, ma'am."

"You're entirely welcome," said she, this time poking her elbow into Anderson's ribs. He grunted.

"Is the road pretty good all the way?"

"It's a good dirt road."

"We're in a great hurry, ma'am. Is it safe to hit it up a little on the dirt-road? His wife specially wanted to see him before she died."

"Perfectly safe, as long as you keep *in* it."

"Nightie!" called the spokesman, and the big car leaped forward as if suddenly unchained.

"Well, of all the—" began Anderson wrathfully.

"Get out and crank this car, Anderson," she broke in excitedly.

"You know as well as I do that that dirt road ends at Heffner's farm. It don't go nowheres near the river. What ails you, Eva Crow? That poor feller's wife—"

"Crank, I tell you!"

He got out and cranked the car, grumbling all the while. As he got back in the seat beside her, he exploded:

"An' what's more, there's that soldiers' camp at Green Ridge. They won't be allowed to go through it without a pass. There must be a thousand men there. They're marchin' to some'eres in America, the feller told me this mornin' when he come in at Jackson's to get some smokin' terbaccer. Camp at Green Ridge fer two days, he says, an' then—Hey! Don't drive so blamed reckless, Eva! Can't you get her under control? Put on your brakes, woman! She'll— "

"Hush up, Anderson. You let me alone."

The little old car was sailing along at a speed that caused every joint to rattle with joy unconfined. To Anderson's amazement, and to a certain extent consternation, Mrs. Crow swung into the dirt-road over which the big car was now whizzing a mile or so ahead.

"Here! Where you going?" barked Anderson, arising from the seat.

"There's going to be hell to pay before you know it, Anderson Crow," said she, her voice high and squeaky.

"Wha-what was that you said?" gasped her husband, flopping back in the seat. He couldn't believe his ears.

"I learned that from my predecessor in office," she replied somewhat guiltily. "I've heard you say it a million times."

"But I ain't no woman. I—"

"Set still! Do you want to fall out and break your neck?"

And Anderson sat still, dazed and helpless in the direful presence of a woman who, to his utter horror, had gone violently insane. He began silently but urgently to pray that the gasoline would give out, when he would find himself in a position to reason with her, gently or forcibly as the situation demanded. He broke into a profuse and chilly perspiration. His wife crazy! His wife of forty years! His old comrade!

He was aroused from these horrifying, sickening reflections by a hoarse but imperative word coming from nowhere out of the darkness of the road ahead.

"Halt!"

Mrs. Crow put on the brakes.

"Who goes there?"

"Friends!" faltered Mrs. Crow.

"The marshal of Tinkletown," added Anderson, vastly relieved by her singularly intelligent answer.

"Advance and give the countersign!"

"All right. What is it?" inquired Mrs. Crow.

A couple of non-commissioned officers joined the sentry at this moment. They were but half dressed.

"What the devil's the meaning of all this?" exclaimed one of them, planting himself beside the car and flashing a light in Mrs. Crow's face. "Don't you hayseeds know any better than to bust into a military camp—"

His companion interrupted him. "Keep your shirt on, Bill. Didn't I hear the man say he was the marshal of Tinkletown?"

"No, sir, you didn't! I said *we* are the marshal of Tinkletown. I—"

"All right, all right. Do you happen to be chasin' a gang of joy-riders?"

"We do—we are!" cried Mrs. Crow.

"They zipped through this camp like a rifle-shot about ten minutes ago. They've raised a lovely row. Officer of the day bawlin' everybody out, and—Here, hold on!"

"We've just got to catch them men," pleaded Mrs. Crow.

"One of 'em's got a sick wife," added Anderson, "an' we've got to tell him he's on the wrong road."

"Well, you just sit right where you are," spoke the top

sergeant. "They'll be back this way in a few minutes. This road ends about a mile above here, and they'll have to come back. The sentries say they went through here so fast they couldn't see anything but wind."

"Are you going to stop them?" cried Mrs. Crow eagerly.

"We sure are," said the other non-com. "See that bunch of men forming over there? Well, they've got real guns and real bullets, and they're mad, Mrs. Marshal. You can't blame 'em."

Off at one side of the road a little distance away a company of soldiers was lining up. The sharp command of an officer rang out.

"Thank goodness!" cried Mrs. Crow.

"Look here, Eva," said Anderson nervously. "I guess you'd better pull off to one side of the road, just in case them soldiers don't stop 'em. We're right smack in their way, an' gosh only knows where we'd land if they smashed into us. It'd take a week to find us, we'd be so scattered about."

"Don't be uneasy," said the top sergeant. "They'll stop, all right, all right."

"Let me whisper something to you, Mr. Officer," said Mrs. Crow. "It's very important."

He obligingly held up an ear, and she leaned down and spoke rapidly, earnestly into it.

"You don't say so!" he cried out. "Excuse *me*!" And off he dashed, calling out to his companion to follow.

A minute later the most extraordinary activity affected the group of soldiers over the way. Commands were now issued in lowered tones, and men marched rapidly away, dividing into squads.

"What did you say to that feller?" demanded Anderson.

"I told him who those men are, Anderson Crow."

"You couldn't. They're perfect strangers. If they wasn't, how'd they happen to miss the road?"

"They are the very men I'm looking for," said she. "They're the robbers,—and the men who set fire to Smock's warehouse, I'll bet you—and everything else!"

"Jumpin' Jehoshaphat!"

An officer rushed up.

"Turn that flivver around in the middle of the road and jump out quick. That will stop them. Let 'em smash it up if necessary. It isn't worth more than ten dollars."

While a half-dozen men were dragging the car into position as a barricade, Mrs. Crow exclaimed to her husband:

"That old skinflint! He said it was cheap at fifty dollars. Thank goodness, I—"

But Anderson was hustling her out of the car. In the distance the headlights of the bandits' car burst into view as it swung around a bend in the road.

Soldiers everywhere! They seemed to have sprung out of the ground. On came the big car, thundering into the trap. Bugle-calls sounded; a couple of guns blazed into the air as the car flew past the outposts, lights flared suddenly in the path of bewildered occupants, and loud imperative commands rang out on the air.

Into the gantlet of guns the big car rushed. The man at the wheel bent low and took the reckless chance of getting through.

Then, a hundred feet ahead, his lights fell upon the dauntless abandoned flivver. He jerked frantically at the brakes.

"Halt!" shouted Anderson Crow from the top of the roadside bank. "Surrender in the name of the Law!"

He spoke just in time.

Crash! They halted!

Deacon Rank's little car died a glorious, spectacular death. (Harry Squires, in his account, placed it all alone in the list of "unidentified dead.")

Three minutes after the collision, brawny soldiers were bending over the stretched-out figures of five unconscious men.

Mr. and Mrs. Crow stood on the edge of the group, awestruck and silent.

"They're coming around, all right," said some one at Anderson's elbow. "He was slowing down when they struck. But there's no hope for the poor old flivver."

Anderson found his voice—a quavering, uncertain voice—and exclaimed:

"Stand aside, men! I am the marshal of Tinkletown, an' them scoundrels are my prisoners."

His progress was barred by a couple of soldiers. An officer approached.

"Easy, Mr. Marshal—easy, now. This is our affair, you know. I guess you'd better come with me to the colonel. Don't be alarmed. They shan't escape."

"They're mighty desperit characters—" began Anderson.

"Step this way, please," said the other shortly.

It was four o'clock in the morning when Mr. and Mrs. Crow were deposited at their front door by the colonel's automobile. The robbers, under heavy guard, remained in the camp, pending action on the part of the civic authorities. They were very much alive and kicking when Anderson left them, after a pompous harangue on the futility of crime in that neck of the woods.

"Yes, sir, Colonel," he said, turning to the camp commander, "a crook ain't got any more chance than a snowball in—you know—when he tries to pull the wool over my eyes. I've been ketchin' thieves and bandits an' the Lord knows what-all for forty years er more, an' so forth. I want to thank you, sir, an' your brave soldier boys—an' the United States Government also—fer the assistance you have given me tonight. I doubt very much whether I could 'a' took 'em single-handed—handicapped as I was by havin' a woman along. An' when you git over to France with these brave troops of yours, I c'n tell you one thing: the Kaiser'll know it, you bet! Never mind about the old car. It's seen its best days. An' it ain't mine, anyhow. I'll be out here bright and early tomorrow morning with my posse, an' we'll take them fellers off'm your hands. If you'll excuse me now, I guess I'll be movin' along to'ards home. I've still got a fire to put out, an' a lot of other things to do besides. I've got to let the bank know I have recovered their money an' left it in good hands, an' I've got to send a posse out to see if they c'n locate George Brubaker's safe along the road anywheres. An' what's more, I've got to repair the jail, and officially notify Deacon Rank he's had an accident to his car."

Mrs. Crow had little to say until she was snugly in bed. Her husband was getting into his official garments.

"I think you're foolish to go out again, Anderson," she said. "It's not daylight yet. There won't be anybody around, this time of day, to listen to how you captured those robbers,—and —"

"Don't you believe it," said he. "I bet you fifty cents you are the only person in Tinkletown that's in bed at this minute. They're all *afraid* to go to bed, Eva, an' you can't blame 'em.

Nobody knows I've got them desperadoes bound hand and foot and guarded by a whole regiment of U. S. troops, specially deputized for the occasion."

"YOU ARE INVITED TO BE PRESENT"

Anderson Crow sat on the porch of the post-office, ruminating over the epidemic that had assailed Tinkletown with singular virulence, and, in a sense, enthusiasm. Not that there was anything sinister or loathsome about the plague. Far from it, he reflected, because it had broken out so soon after his bitter comments on the prolonged absence of the slightest symptom, or indication that a case was even remotely probable. And here he was, holding in his hand four fresh and unmistakable signs that the contagion was spreading. In short, he had just received and opened four envelopes addressed to Mr. and Mrs. A. Crow, and each contained an invitation to a wedding.

Alf Reesling, commonly known as the town drunkard, sat on the top step, whittling.

"No law against gittin' married, is there, constable?" he inquired.

"I don't know much about this new eugenric law," mused Mr. Crow, gingerly pulling at his whiskers. "So fer as I know, it ain't been violated up here."

"What's the harm, anyway? You was sayin' yourself only the other day that it's a crime the way the young fellers in this town *never* git married. Just set around the parlour stoves all winter holdin' hands, and on the front steps all summer——"

"Like as not the gosh-derned cowards heard what I said and got up spunk enough to tackle matrimony," interrupted the venerable town marshal. "June seems to be a good month fer weddin's everywhere else in the world except right here in Tinkletown. The last one we had was in December, and that was two years ago. Annie Bliss and Joe Hodges. Now we're goin' to have 'em so thick and fast there won't be an unmarried man in the place, first thing you know. Up to date, me and Mrs. Crow have had seventeen printed invitations, and I don't know how many by word o' mouth. Fellers that never even done any courtin', so fer as I know, are gittin' married to girls that ain't had a beau since the Methodist revival in nineteen-ten. They all got religion then, male and female, and there's nothin' like religion to make people think they ought to have somebody to share their repentance with."

"George Hoover's been goin' with Bessie Slayback ever sence McKinley beat Bryan in 'ninety-six. Swore he'd never git married till we had another democratic president. We've had one fer more'n four years and now he says he never dreamed there'd be another one, so he didn't think it was worth while to save up enough to git married on. You don't happen to have a bid there fer his weddin', have you, Anderson? That would be too much to expect, I guess."

"How old do you make out Bessie is, Alf?" asked Mr. Crow, shuffling the envelopes until he found the one he wanted. He removed the card, printed neatly by the *Tinkletown Banner* Press, and squinted at it through his spectacles.

"Forty-nine," said Alf, promptly. "Twenty-sixth of last January."

"Well, poor old George'll have to do his settin' in Sofer's store after the third o' June," said the other, chuckling. "She has threw him over, as my daughter would say."

"What's that?"

"Yep. Bessie's goin' to be married next Sunday to Charlie Smith."

"Fer the Lord's sake!" gasped Alf. "How c'n that be? Charlie's got a wife an' three grown children."

"'Tain't old Charlie. It's young Charlie," said Anderson, looking hard at the invitation. "'Charles Elias Smith, Junior,' it says."

Alf was speechless. He merely stared while the town marshal made mental calculations.

"She's twenty-six years older'n he is, Alf."

"There must be some mistake," muttered Alf.

"Not if you're sure she's forty-nine," said Anderson. "Subtract twenty-three from forty-nine and you have twenty-six, with nothin' to carry. Besides, old Charlie's middle name is Bill."

"Well, I'll be dog-goned," said Alf, in a weak voice.

"And here's another'n'," said Anderson, passing a card to his companion.

Alf read: "'The son and daughter of Mrs. Ellen Euphemia Ricketts request the pleasure of your company at the marriage of their mother to Mr. Pietro Emanuel Cocotte, on June 1, 1917, at twelve o'clock noon at the family residence, No. 17 Lincoln Street, Tinkletown, New York.' Well, I'll be—" Alf interrupted himself to repeat one of the names. "Who is this Pietro Emanuel Cocotte? I never heard of—"

"Petey Sickety," said Anderson.

"The sprinklin'-cart driver?"

"The same," said the marshal, his lips tightening. He had once tried to arrest the young man for "disturbing the peace," and had been obliged to call upon the crowd for help.

"Why, good gosh, he don't earn more'n ten dollars a week and he sends half of that back to Sweden," said Alf.

"Europe," corrected Anderson, patiently. He had put up with a good deal of ignorance on the part of Alf during a long and watchful acquaintanceship.

"Anyhow," said the town drunkard, arising in some haste, "I guess I'll be gittin' home. Maybe I ain't too late." He was moving off with considerable celerity.

"Too late for what?" called out Anderson.

"That measley, good-fer-nothin' Gates boy dropped in to see my girl Queenie last night. First time he's ever done it, but, by criminy, the way they're speedin' things up around here lately there's no tellin' what c'n happen in twenty-four hours."

"Hold on a minute, Alf. I'll walk along with you. Now, see here, Alf,"—Mr. Crow laid a kindly, encouraging hand on the other's shoulder as they ambled down the main street of the village—"no matter what happens, you mustn't let it git the best of you. Keep straight, old feller. Don't touch a drop o'—"

Mr. Reesling stopped short in the middle of the sidewalk. "Dog-gone it, Anderson—leggo of my arm. Do you want everybody to think you're takin' me to jail, or home to my poor wife, or somethin' like that? It'll be all over town in fifteen minutes if you—"

"'Tain't my fault if you've got a reputation, Alf," retorted the town marshal sorrowfully.

"Well, it ain't my fault either," declared Alf. "Look at me. I ain't had a drink in twenty-three years, and what good does it do me? Every time a stranger comes to town people point at me an' say, 'There goes the town drunkard.' Oh, I've heerd 'em. I ain't deef. An' besides, ain't they always preachin' at me an' about me at the Methodist an' Congregational churches? Ain't they always tellin' the young boys that they got to be careful er they'll be like Alf Reesling? An' what's it all come from? Comes from the three times I got drunk back in the fall of 'ninety-three when my cousin was here from Albany fer a visit. I *had* to entertain him, didn't I? An' there wasn't any other way to do it in this jerk-water town, was there? An' ever since then the windbags in this town have been prayin' fer me an' pityin' my poor wife. That's what a feller gits fer livin' in a—"

"Now, now!" admonished Anderson soothingly. "Don't git excited, Alf. You deserve a lot o' credit. Ain't many men, I tell you, could break off sudden like that, an'—"

"Oh, you go to grass!" exclaimed Alf hotly.

Anderson inspected him closely. "Lemme smell your breath, Alf Reesling," he commanded.

"What's the use?" growled Alf. "Wouldn't last fer twenty-three years, would it?"

"Well, you talk mighty queer," said the marshal, unconvinced. He couldn't imagine such a thing as a strictly sober man telling him to go to grass. He was the most important man in Tinkletown.

Further discussion was prevented by the approach of Mr. Crow's daughter, Susie, accompanied by a tall, pink-faced young man in a resplendent checked suit and a dazzling red necktie. They came from Brubaker's popular drugstore and ice-cream "parlour," two doors below.

"Hello, Pop," said Susie gaily, as the couple sauntered past their half-halting seniors.

"H'are you, Mr. Crow?" was the young man's greeting, uttered with the convulsive earnestness of sudden embarrassment. "Fine day, ain't it?"

Mr. Crow said that it was, and then both he and Alf

stopped short in their tracks and gazed intently at the backs of the young people. Even as they stared, a fiery redness enveloped the ears of Susie's companion. A few steps farther on he turned his head and looked back. Something that may be described as sheepish defiance marked that swift, involuntary glance.

Mr. Reesling broke the silence. There was a worried, sympathetic note in his voice.

"Got on his Sunday clothes, Anderson, and this is only Wednesday. Beats the Dutch, don't it?"

"I wonder—" began Mr. Crow, and then closed his lips so tightly and so abruptly that his sparse chin whiskers stuck out almost horizontally.

He started off briskly in the wake of the young people. Alf, forgetting his own apprehensions in the face of this visible manifestation, shuffled along a few paces behind.

Miss Crow and her companion turned the corner below and were lost to view.

"By gosh," said Alf, suddenly increasing his speed until he came abreast of the other; "you better hurry, Anderson. Justice Robb's in his office. I seen his feet in the winder a little while ago."

"They surely can't be thinkin' of—" Mr. Crow did not complete the sentence.

"Why not?" demanded Alf. "Everybody else is. And it would be just like that Schultz boy to do it without an invitation. Ever since this war's been goin' on them Schultzes have been blowin' about always bein' prepared fer anything. German efficiency's what they're always throwin' up to people. I bet he's been over to the county seat an' got a license to—"

Anderson interrupted him with a snort. He put his hand

on his right hip pocket, where something bulged ominously, and quickened his pace.

"I been watchin' these Schultzes fer nearly a year," said he, "an' the whole caboodle of 'em are spies."

They turned the corner. Susie and her companion were on the point of disappearing in a doorway fifty yards down Sickle Street.

Anderson slowed up. He removed his broad felt hat with the gold cord around it, and mopped his forehead.

"That's the tin-type gallery," he said, a little out of breath.

"Worse an' more of it," said Alf. "That's the surest sign I know of. It never fails. Mollie an' me had our'n taken the day before we was married an'—an'—why, it's almost the same as a certificat', Anderson."

"Now, you move on, Alf," commanded the marshal. "How many times I got to tell you not to loiter aroun' the streets? Move on, I say."

"Aw, now, Anderson—"

"I'll have to run you in, Alf. The ord'nance is very p'ticular, an' that notice stuck up on the telephone pole over there means you more'n anybody else. No loiterin'."

"If you need any evidence ag'in that Schultz boy, just call on me," said Alf generously. "I seen him commit an atrocity last week."

"What was it?"

"He give that little Griggs girl a lift in his butcher wagon," said Alf darkly.

Anderson scowled. "The sooner we run these cussed Germans out o' town the better off we'll be."

Alf ambled off, casting many glances over his shoulder,

and the marshal crossed the street and entered Hawkins's Undertaking and Embalming establishment, from a window of which he had a fair view of the "studio."

Presently Susie and young Schultz emerged, giggling and snickering over the pink objects they held in their hands. They sauntered slowly, shoulder to shoulder, in the direction of Main Street.

Mr. Hawkins was in the middle of one of his funniest stories when Anderson got up and walked out hurriedly. The undertaker had a reputation as a wit. He was the life of the community. He radiated optimism, even when most depressingly employed. And here he was telling Anderson Crow a brand-new story he had heard at a funeral over in Kirkville, when up jumps his listener and "lights out" without so much as a word. Mr. Hawkins went to the door and looked out, expecting to see a fight or a runaway horse or a German airplane. All he saw was the marshal not two doors away, peering intently into a show-window, while from across the street two young people regarded him with visible amusement. For a long time thereafter the undertaker sat in his office and stared moodily at the row of caskets lining the opposite wall. Could it be possible that he was losing his grip?

Miss Crow and Mr. Otto Schultz resumed their stroll after a few moments, and the marshal, following their movements in the reflecting show-window, waited until they were safely around the corner. Then he retraced his steps quickly, passed the undertaker's place, and turned into the alley beyond. Three minutes later, he entered Main Street a block above Sickle Street, and was leaning carelessly against the Indian tobacco sign in front of Jackson's cigar store, when his daughter and her companion bore down upon his left flank.

Mr. Alf Reesling was a few paces behind them.

As they came within earshot, young Schultz was saying in a suspiciously earnest manner:

"You better come in and have anodder sody, Susie."

Just then their gaze fell upon Mr. Crow.

"Goodness!" exclaimed Susie, startled.

"By cheminy!" fell from Otto's wide-open mouth. He blinked a couple of times. "Is—is that you?" he inquired, incredulously.

"You mean *me*?" asked Anderson, with considerable asperity.

"Sure," said Otto, halting.

"Can't you see it's me?" demanded Mr. Crow.

"But you ain'd here," said the perplexed young man, getting pinker all the time. "You're aroundt in Sickle Street."

"Alf!" called out Anderson. "Look here a minute. Is this me?" He spoke with biting sarcasm.

Mr. Reesling regarded him with some anxiety.

"You better go home, Anderson," he said. "This sun is a derned sight hotter'n you think."

"Didn't we see you a minute ago around in Sickle Street, Pop?" inquired Susie. "Looking in that hair-dresser's window?"

"Maybe you did and maybe you didn't," replied Mr. Crow, shrewdly. Then, with thinly veiled significance: "I'm purty busy lookin' into a good many things nowadays." He favoured Otto with a penetrating glance. "Ever sence the U. S. A. declared war on Germany, Mr. Otto Schultz."

"How aboudt that sody, Miss Susie?" said Otto, in a pained sort of voice.

"You'd better be saving your money, Otto," she advised, with such firmness that her father looked at her sharply.

"Oh, spiffles!" said Otto, getting still redder.

Mr. Crow was all ears. Alf Reesling burned his fingers on a match he held too long in the hot, still air some six or eight inches from the bowl of his pipe.

"Well, getting married is no joke," said Susie, shaking her pretty head solemnly.

Otto took a deep breath. "You bet you it ain'd," he said, with feeling. That seemed to give him courage. He took off his straw hat, and, as he ran his finger around the moist "sweat-band," he blurted out: "I don't mind if you tell your fadder, Susie. Go and tell him."

"Tell him yourself," said Susie.

"As I was saying a few minutes ago," said Otto ingenuously, "the only obchection I had to your tellin' your fadder was that I didn't want everybody in town to know it before I could get home and tell my mother yet."

"Don't go away, Alf," said Mr. Crow, darkly. "I'll need you as a witness. I hereby subpoena you as a witness to what's goin' to happen in less'n no time. Now, Mr. Otto Schultz, spit it out."

Otto disgorged these cyclonic words:

"I'm going to get married, Mr. Crow, that's all."

Mr. Crow was equally explicit and quite as brief.

"Only over my dead body," he shouted, and then turned upon Susie. "You go home, Susan Crow! Skedaddle! Get a move on, I say. I'll nip this blamed German plot right in the beginning. Do you hear me, Susan—"

Susan stared at him. "Hear you?" she cried. "They can

hear you up in the graveyard. What on earth's got into you, Pop? What—"

"You'll see what's got into me, purty derned quick," said Anderson, and pointed his long, trembling forefinger at the amazed Mr. Schultz, who had dropped his hat and was stooping over to retrieve it without taking his eyes from the menacing face of the speaker.

It had rolled in the direction of Mr. Alf Reesling. That gentleman obligingly stopped it with his foot. After removing his foot, he undertook to return the hat without stooping at all, the result being that it sped past Otto and landed in the middle of the street some twenty feet away.

"So you think you c'n git married without my consent, do you?" demanded Anderson, witheringly. "You think you c'n sneak around behind my back an'—"

"I ain'd sneakin' aroundt behind anybody's back," broke in Otto, straightening up. "I don't know what you are talking aboud, Mr. Crow,—and needer do you," he added gratuitously. "What for do I haf to get your consent to get married for? I get myself's consent and my girl's consent and my fadder's consent —Say!" His voice rose. "Don't you think I am of age yet?"

"If you talk loud like that, I'll run you in fer disturbin' the peace, young feller," warned Anderson, observing that a few of Tinkletown's citizens were slowly but surely surrendering squatter's rights to chairs and soap-boxes on the shady side of the block. "Just you keep a civil tongue in—"

"You ain'd answered my question yet," insisted Otto, with increased vigour.

"Here's your hat, Otto," said Alf Reesling in a conciliatory voice. He was brushing the article with the sleeve of

his coat. "A horse must'a' stepped on it or somethin'. I never see
— "

"Ain'd I of age, Mr. Crow?" bellowed Otto. "Didn't I
vote for you at the last— "

"That ain't the question," interrupted Anderson sharply.
"The question is, is the girl of age?" He favoured his sixteen-
year-old daughter with a fiery glance.

Otto Schultz's broad, flat face became strangely pinched.
There was something positively apoplectic in the hue that spread
over it.

"Oh, Pop!" shrieked Susie, a peal of laughter bursting
from her lips. Instantly, however, her two hands were pressed to
her mouth, stifling the outburst.

Otto gave her a hurt, surprised—and unmistakably
horrified—look. Then a silly grin struggled into existence.

"Maybe she don'd tell the truth aboud her age yet, Mr.
Crow," he said huskily. "Women always lie aboud their ages.
Maybe she lie aboud hers."

Anderson flared. "Don't you dare say my daughter lies
about her age—or anything else," he roared.

"Whose daughter?" gasped Otto.

"Mine!"

"But she ain'd your daughter."

"*What!* Well, of all the— "

Words failed Mr. Crow. He looked helplessly, appealingly
at Alf Reesling, as if for support.

Mr. Reesling rose to the occasion.

"Do you mean to insinuate, Otto Schultz, that— " he
began as he started to remove his coat.

By this time Susie felt it was safe to trust herself to speech.

She removed her hands from her mouth and cried out:

"He isn't talking about me, Pop," she gasped. "It's Gertie Bumbelburg."

"Sure," said Otto hastily.

Mr. Crow still being speechless, Alf suspended his belligerent preparations, and cocking one eye calculatingly, settled the matter of Miss Bumbelburg's age with exasperating accuracy.

"Gertie's a little past forty-two," he announced. "Born in March, 1875, just back o' where Sid Martin's feed-store used to be."

The marshal had recovered his composure.

"That's sufficient," he said, accepting Alf s testimony with a profound air of dignity. "There ain't no law against anybody marryin' a woman old enough to be his mother."

"Everybody in town give Gertie up long ago," added Alf, amiably. "Only goes to show that while there's life there's hope. I'd 'a' swore she was on the shelf fer good. How'd you happen to pick her, Otto?"

"She's all right," growled Otto uncomfortably. Then he added, with considerable acerbity: "I'm goin' to tell her you said she was forty-two, Alf Reesling."

"Well, ain't she?" demanded Alf, bristling.

"No, she ain'd," replied Otto. "She's twendy-nine."

"Come, come," put in Anderson sternly. "None o' this now! Move on, Alf! No scrappin' on the public thoroughfares o' Tinkletown. You're gettin' more and more rambunctious every day, Alf."

"He ought to be ashamed of himself, speakin' by a lady when he knows he's in such a condition," said Otto, turning from the unfortunate Alf to Miss Crow. "Ain'd that so, Susie?"

"Don't answer, Susie," said Mr. Crow, quickly. "This is no time to side in with Germany."

"I'm as good an American as you are already," cried Otto, goaded beyond endurance.

Mr. Crow smiled tolerantly. "Git out! Let's hear you say 'vinegar'."

"Winegar," said Otto triumphantly. "I can say it as good as you can yet."

Anderson nudged Mr. Reesling, and chuckled.

"That's the way to spot 'em," he said significantly.

"There's a better way than that," said Alf.

"How's that?"

Alf whispered in the marshal's ear.

Anderson shook his head. "But where are you goin' to get the weenywurst, Alf?"

"Come on, Otto," said Susie, impatiently. "I have an engagement."

They moved off rapidly, passing the ice-cream parlour without hesitating.

"D'you hear that?" said Alf, after a moment. "She said she was engaged."

That night Anderson Crow, town marshal, superintendent of streets, chief of the fire department, post-commander of the G. A. R., truant officer, dog-catcher, member of the American Horse-thief Detective Association, member of the Universal Detective Bureau, chairman of Tinkletown Battlefield Society, etc., lay awake until nearly nine o'clock, seeking a solution to the astonishing problem that confronted Tinkletown and its environs.

Late reports, received by telephone just before retiring, ran the number of prospective marriages up to twenty-eight. His daughters, Susie and Caroline—the latter the eldest of a family of six and secretly approaching the age of thirty-two—confided to him that they had had eleven and three proposals respectively. A singular feature of the craze was the unanimity of impulse affecting men between the ages of twenty and thirty, and the utter absence of concentration on the part of the applicants. It was of record that some of them proposed to as many as five or six young women before being finally accepted. Rashness appeared to be the watchword. The matrimonial stampede swept caution and consequences into a general heap, and delivered a community of the backwardness that threatened to become a menace to posterity.

As Anderson Crow lay in his bed, he tried to enumerate on his fingers the young men who remained unpledged. Starting with his thumb he got as far as the third finger of his left hand and then, being sleepy and the effort a trying one, he lost track of those already counted and had to begin all over again, with the maddening result that he could go no further than the second finger. One of the eligibles had slipped his mind completely. The whole situation was harrowing.

"Fer instance," he ruminated aloud, oblivious of the fact that his wife was sound asleep, "what is a feller like Newt Blossom goin' to keep a wife on, I'd like to know. He c'n hardly keep himself in chewin' tobaccer as it is, an' as fer the other necessities of life he wouldn't have any of 'em if his mother wasn't such a dern' fool about him. The idee of him tryin' to get our Susie to marry him—an' Carrie too, fer that matter—w'y, I git in a cold sweat every time I think of it."

He shook his wife vigorously.

"Say, Ma," he said, yawning, "I just thought o' somethin' I want you to remember in the mornin'. Wake up."

"All right," she mumbled, sleepily. "What is it?"

But Mr. Crow was now fast asleep himself.

Early the next morning he entered the kitchen, where he found Caroline helping her mother with the breakfast.

Mrs. Crow paused in the act of paring slices from a side of bacon. She eyed her husband inimically.

"See here, Anderson, you just got to put a stop to all this foolishness."

"Don't bother me. Can't you see I'm thinkin'?" said he.

"Well, it's time you did somethin' more than think. That Smathers boy was here about ten minutes ago, red as a beet, askin' fer Susie. Carrie told him she wasn't up yet, and what do you think the little whipper-snapper said?"

Anderson blinked, and shook his head.

"He said, 'Well, I guess you'll do, Caroline. Would you mind steppin' outside fer a couple of minutes? I got somethin' I want to say to you in private.'"

Caroline sat down and laughed unrestrainedly.

"Well, by geminy crickets!" gasped Anderson, aghast. Then he added anxiously: "You—you didn't go an' do anything foolish, did you, Carrie?"

"Not unless you'd call throwing a pail of cold water on him foolish," said Carrie, wiping her eyes.

"Somethin's got to be done, Anderson," said his wife, compressing her lips.

Susie came in at that juncture. She was the apple of

Anderson's eye—the prettiest girl in town. Mr. Crow hurried to the kitchen door.

"Go back upstairs," he ordered, casting a swift, uneasy glance around the back yard.

"What's the matter, Pop?"

Mr. Crow did not respond. His keen, roving eye had descried a motionless figure at the mouth of the alley.

Caroline explained.

"Can you beat it?" cried Susie, inelegantly, but with a very proper scorn. "I told him yesterday he ought to be ashamed of himself, trying to coax Fanny Burns away from Ed Foster."

"Ed Foster?" exclaimed Mr. Crow sharply, turning from the doorway. "Why, he's not goin' to be married till after the war, an' that's a long ways off. Ed's around in his uniform an' says the National Guard's likely to be called 'most any day now. He—"

"That's one of the arguments Joe Smathers put up to Fanny," said his youngest daughter. "He said maybe the war would last five years, and he thought she was a fool to wait that long. What's more, he said, if Ed ever does get to France he's likely to be killed—or fatally wounded—and then where would she be?"

Anderson suddenly lifted his right leg and slapped it with great force.

"By the great Jehoshaphat!" he shouted. "I've got it! I've solved the whole derned mystery. Come to me like a flash. Of all the low-down, cowardly—"

Mrs. Crow interrupted him. "Do you mean to say, Anderson Crow, that you never suspected what's got into all these gay Lotharios?"

He was instantly on his guard. "What are you talkin' about, Ma?" he demanded querulously. "You surely can't mean to insinuate that I—"

"What is this mystery you've just been solvin'?" she asked relentlessly.

He met this with a calm intolerance.

"Nothin' much. Just simply got to the bottom of a German plot to stuff the young men of America so full of weddin' cake they won't be able to git into the trenches, that's all."

"My goodness!" exclaimed Mrs. Crow, who, as a dutiful wife, never failed to be impressed by her husband's belated discoveries.

"Eggin' our boys into gittin' married, so's they can't be drafted," went on Anderson, expanding with his new-found idea. "It's a general pro-German plot—world-wide, as the sayin' is. Now, I'll tell you somethin' else. Shut the door, Susie. Like as not some spy's listenin' outside this very minute. They know I'm onto 'em." He lowered his voice. "You'd be surprised if I was to tell you that the whole derned plot originated right here in Tinkletown, wouldn't you? Well, that's exactly what I'm goin' to tell you. Started right here and spread from one end of the land to the other. Sort of headquarters here. I don't know as there is any more prominent or influential Germans in the whole United States than Adolph Schultz, the butcher on Main Street, and Heiney Wimpelmeyer, the tanyard man, and Ben Olson, the contractor, and—"

"Ben Olson is a Swede," interrupted Carrie.

"He *claims* to be a Swede," said her father severely. "Don't try to tell me anything, Carrie. I guess I know what I'm talkin' about." He paused to mentally repair the break in his chain of thought. "Um—ah—what *wuz* I talkin' about?"

"About the Swedes," said Carrie, snickering.

"Breakfast's ready, Pa," said Mrs. Crow. "Call the boys, Susie."

"How are you going to stop it, Pop?" inquired Susie, after they were all seated.

"Never you mind," said he. "I've got the thing all worked out. I'll stop it, all right."

"You can't keep people from gittin' married, Anderson, if they're set on doin' it," said his wife.

"You bet if I was old enough I wouldn't be gittin' married," said fourteen-year-old Hiram, in a somewhat ambiguous burst of patriotism.

Immediately after breakfast Mr. Crow set out for the town hall. He was deep in thought. His whiskers were elevated to an almost unprecedented level, so tightly was his jaw set. He had made up his mind to preserve the honour of Tinkletown. Meeting Alf Reesling in front of the post office, he unburdened himself in a flood of indignation that left the town drunkard soberer than he had been in years, despite his vaunted abstemiousness.

"But you can't slap all the Germans in jail, Anderson," protested Alf. "In the first place, it ain't legal, and in the second place—in the second place—" He paused and scratched his head, evidently to some purpose, for suddenly his face cleared. "In the second place, the jail ain't big enough."

"That ain't my fault," said the marshal grimly. "We've got to nip this thing in the bud if we have to—"

"What proof have you got that the Germans are back of

all this? Got to have proof, you know."

"Gosh a'mighty, Alf, ain't you got any sense at all? What are all these fellers gittin' married for if there ain't somethin' behind it? They ain't—"

"They're gittin' married because every blamed one of 'em is a slacker," said Alf forcibly.

"A what?"

"Slacker. They don't want to fight, that's what it means."

Anderson pondered. He tugged at his whiskers.

"They don't want to fight *who*?" he demanded abruptly.

"W'y—w'y—nobody," said Alf.

"They don't want to fight the *Germans*," said Mr. Crow triumphantly. "That ought to settle the matter, Alf. What better proof do you want than that? That shows the Germans are back of the whole infernal plot. They are corruptin' our young men. Eggin' 'em into gittin' married so's—"

"Well," said Alf, "there's only one way to put a stop to that. You got to appeal to the women and girls of this here town. You simply got to talk to 'em like a Dutch uncle, Anderson. These boys of our'n have just got to remain single fer the duration of the war."

"That puts an idee in my head," said Anderson. "S'posin' I put up an official notice from Washin'ton that all marriages contracted before the draft are fer the duration of the war only. How's that?"

"Thunderation! No! That's just what the boys would like better'n anything."

"But it ain't what the *girls* would like, it is?"

Mr. Reesling was silent for a long time, letting the idea crystallize, so to speak.

"Supposin' they hear about it in Washin'ton," said he doubtfully, but still dazzled by the thought.

"President Wilson don't know this town's on the map," said Anderson, a most surprising admission for him. "An' even if he does hear about it, he'll back me up, you c'n bet your boots on that—even if I am a Republican. Come on, Alf; let's step around to the *Banner*printin' office."

Shortly before noon a hastily printed poster, still damp and smelling of ink, appeared on the bulletin-board in front of the town hall. A few minutes later a similar decoration marred the façade of the Fairbanks scales in front of Higgins's Feed Store, and still another loomed up on the telephone pole in front of the post office.

With the help of the editor, who was above all things an enterprising citizen and a patriot, the "official notice" was drafted, doctored and approved in the dingy composing-room of the *Tinkletown Banner*. The lone compositor, with a bucket of paste, sallied forth and, under the critical eye of the town marshal, "stuck up" the poster in places where no one could help seeing it.

The notice read:

<   h4 style="text-align: center;">OFFICIAL!!!
War Proclamation No. 7!!!

The Undersigned by Virtue of the Authority
vested in him by his fellowmen hereby
gives
DUE NOTICE
to the citizens of Tinkletown that the

President of These United States
and
Congress in solemn conclave
have uttered the following decree, to become
effective immediately upon publication
thereof:

 All marriages entered into by Male Citizens of the United States of America between the ages of twenty-one and thirty-one on and after this date, the 21st of May, 1917, shall be in force for the duration of the War only. This measure is taken at this time for the purpose of making things as easy as possible for our young heroes, who, in the grave hour of battle, must not be worried with thoughts of the future.

Men so marrying shall have precedence over all others in the
SELECTIVE DRAFT
for the National Army Immediately to
be Called.
Such men shall be the first called to the
Colours.
TEMPORARY WIDOWS
of any and all such Soldiers shall not be
entitled to
PENSIONS
in the Event of the Death of said Provisional Husbands, and
 shall revert upon notice thereof, to the State of Single-blessedness

from which they were
LURED!!!

By order of
Anderson Crow,
Marshal.

As the first of these desolating posters was put in place, the Rev. Mr. Maltby, pastor of the Congregational Church, happened to be passing the town hall. He halted and, in astonishment, read the notice.

"My dear man," said he to Mr. Crow, "this cannot be true."

"Does seem a little high-handed, don't it?" said Anderson guiltily.

"Can it be possible that the President has issued such a revolutionary—"

"Listen a minute, Mr. Maltby," said the marshal, taking him by the arm and furtively glancing over his own shoulder. "It ain't true—not a derned word of it. Now, wait a minute. Don't fly off the—Mornin', Father Maloney, mornin' to you."

The sunny-faced Catholic priest had joined them. He adjusted his spectacles and peered at the notice.

"Well, well, bless my soul!" he exclaimed, staring blankly at the Congregationalist. "What's all this I see?"

"Come inside," said Anderson hastily. "Alf, if you happen to see Mr. Downs, the Methodist preacher, and Justice Robb, bring 'em here right away, will you?"

"Shall I go ahead and paste any more of these, Anderson?" inquired the compositor, shifting his quid.

"Certainly," said the marshal.

Later on the marshal left the town hall, followed by several smiling gentlemen of the cloth, Justice Robb, and the editor of the *Banner*.

"Bless your heart, Marshal Crow," said Father Maloney, "we're with ye to a man. It's a glorious lie ye're telling, and ye've got the church solid behind ye."

"Naturally *we* shall not be obliged to falsify," said the Rev. Mr. Maltby, still a bit shaken. "We can simply say that the matter is news to us. Eh, brothers?"

"Sure," said Father Maloney. "We can do that much for the good of the country. Indeed, if I'm closely pressed I may go as far as to say that I caught a glimpse of the official despatch from Washington. This is no time to deny the President, gentlemen, no matter who issues his proclamation." He added the last with a whimsical smile and a wink that rather shocked his Methodist brother. "Especially when the whole matter is vouched for by our respected town marshal, who, to my certain knowledge, possesses the veracity of a George Washington. Have you ever been caught chopping down a cherry tree, Mr. Marshal?"

"No, *sir*," said Anderson promptly.

Father Maloney beamed. "There ye are!" he exclaimed heartily. "I told ye so. The epitome of veracity. There isn't another man of his age in America who would have answered no to that question, with no one in a position to contradict him."

The editor had his notebook. "Gentlemen, would you object to being interviewed on this important message from

Washington? Giving your views on the situation and anything else—"

"You may say for me, Harry, that I warmly indorse the President of the United States in any act which he may deem wise and expedient," said Rev. Mr. Maltby, rising nobly to the occasion. Father Maloney and Rev. Mr. Downs promptly acquiesced.

"And also that I am prepared to issue marriage certificates for the duration of the war to all females so desirin' 'em," said Justice of the Peace Robb. "It ain't cuttin' me out of any fees," he went on, addressing the marshal. "Fer as I c'n make out, they all want to git married fer nothin'."

"I will be very careful how I word your remarks, gentlemen," said Editor Squires, putting up his notebook. "Now, I'll start out and interview a few of the prospective brides. It ought to make good reading."

Long before nightfall the sleepy village of Tinkletown was in a state of agitation unsurpassed by anything within the memory of the oldest inhabitant.... . Along about supper time one could have heard animated arguments rising above the clear stillness of the air, penetrating even to the heaven which was called upon to witness the unswerving fidelity of two opposing sexes. There was a distinct difference, however, in the duration of this professed fidelity. Masculine voices pleaded for the immediate justification of undying constancy, while those of a feminine quality preferred a prolongation of the exquisite agony of suspense. In short, the brides-elect were obdurate. They insisted on waiting, even to the end of time, for the realization of their fondest, dearest hopes. Several heartbroken gentlemen, preferring anything to procrastination, threatened to shoot themselves.

"What's the sense of doing that?" argued one middle-aged widow of a practical turn of mind. "You can save funeral expenses by letting the Germans do it for you."

The next day the merchants of Tinkletown—notably the Five and Ten Cent Store and Fisher's Queensware Store—did a thriving business. From one end of the town to the other came people returning presents that fortunately had not been delivered, and others asking to have their accounts credited with presents already received.

Of the twenty-odd weddings announced for the week ending June 3, 1917, only one took place.

Mr. Otto Schultz was married on Saturday to Miss Bumbelburg. He was the only candidate in town who was worth suing for breach of promise. Miss Bumbelburg, having waited many years for her chance, was not to be frightened by a Presidential proclamation. The duration of the war meant nothing to her. She had unlimited faith in the Kaiser. When the war was over he would come over to the United States and revoke all the silly old laws. And she was so positive about it that, after a rather heated interview in the home of Mr. Schultz, senior, that gentleman admitted it would be cheaper for her to come and live with them after the wedding than to present her with the thousand dollars she demanded in case Otto preferred war to peace.

Mr. Crow, on the 5th of June, strode proudly, efficiently, up and down Main Street, always stopping at the registration booth to slap former fiancés on the back and encourage them with such remarks as this:

"That's right, son. If you've *got* to fight, fight for your country."

To Mr. Alf Reesling he confided:

"I tell you what, Alf, when this here Kaiser comes up ag'inst me he strikes a snag. He couldn't 'a' started his plot in a worse place than here in Tinkletown. Gosh, with all you hear about German efficiency, you'd 'a' thought he'd 'a' knowed better, wouldn't you?"

THE PERFECT END OF A DAY

Anderson Crow Gets One on the Kaiser

A long, low-lying bank of almost inky-black clouds hung over a blood-red horizon. The sun of a warm, drowsy September day was going to bed beyond the scallop of hills.

Suddenly the red in the sky, as if fanned by an angry wind, blazed into a rigid flame; catching the base of the coal-black cloud it turned its edges into fire; and as the flame burnt itself out, the rich yellow of gold came to glorify the triumphant cloud. The nether edge seemed to dip into a lake, the shores of which were molten gold and upon whose surface craft of ever-changing colours lay moored for the coming night.

Anderson Crow, Marshal of Tinkletown, leaned upon his front-yard fence and listened to the rhapsodic comments of Miss Sue Becker on the passing panorama. Miss Becker, who had contributed several poems to the columns of the Tinkletown *Banner*, and more than once had exhibited encouraging letters from the editors of *McClure's*, *Scribner's*, *Harper's*, and other magazines, was always worth listening to, for, as every one knows, she was the first, and, so far as revealed, the only literary genius ever created within the precincts of Tinkletown.

"You'll have to write a piece about it, Sue," said Anderson, shifting his spare frame slightly.

"No mortal pen, Mr. Crow, could do justice to the grandeur, the overpowering splendour of that vista," said she.

Anderson took another look at the sunset,—a more or less stealthy one, it must be confessed, out of the corner of his eye. Sunsets were not much in his line.

"It's a great vister," he acknowledged. "I don't know as I can think of a word that will rhyme with it, though."

"There is such a thing as blank verse, Mr. Crow," said Miss Becker, smiling in a most superior way.

Mr. Crow was thinking. "Blister wouldn't be bad," he announced. "Something about the vister causin' a blister. I don't know as you are aware of the fact, Sue, but I wrote consider'ble poetry when I was a young feller. Mrs. Crow's got 'em all tied up in a pink ribbon. It's a mighty funny thing that she won't even show 'em to anybody."

"Oh, but they are sacred," said Miss Becker feelingly, as she looked over the rims of her spectacles at a spot in the sky some forty-five degrees above the steeple of the Congregational Church down the street.

"I don't know as I meant 'em to be sacred at the time," said he; "but there wasn't anything in 'em that was unfittin' for a young lady to read."

"You don't understand. What could be more sacred than the outpourings of love? What more—"

"'Course it was a good many years ago," Mr. Crow was quick to explain.

"Love's young dream," chided Miss Becker coyly.

Mr. Crow twisted his sparse grey beard with unusual tenderness. "Beats all, don't it, Sue, what a poet'll do when he's tryin' to raise a moustache?"

"I am sure I don't know," said Miss Becker stiffly.

"Speakin' about sunsets," said he hastily, after a quick

glance at her shaded upper lip, "how's your pa? I heard he had a sinkin' spell yestiday."

"He's better." A moment later, with fine scorn: "His sun hasn't set yet, Mr. Crow."

"Beats all how he hangs on, don't it? Eighty-seven last birthday, an' spry as a man o' fifty up to—" He broke off to devote his attention to a couple of strangers farther down the tree-lined street: two men who approached slowly on the plank sidewalk, pausing every now and then to peer inquiringly at the front doors of houses along the way.

Miss Sue Becker, whose back was toward the strangers, allowed her poetic mind to resume its interest in the sunset.

"Golden cloudlets float upon a coral—What did you say, Mr. Crow?"

"Ever see 'em before, Sue?"

"Hundreds of times. They remind me of the daintiest, fleeciest puffs of—"

"I'm talkin' about those men comin' up the street," said the old town marshal sharply.

Miss Becker abandoned the transient sunset for something more durable. Forty-odd summers had passed over her head.

For one professedly indifferent to the opposite sex, Miss Becker went far toward dislocating her neck when Anderson Crow mentioned the approach of a couple of strange men.

"I've never seen either of them before, Mr. Crow," she said, a little jump in her voice.

"That settles it," said Anderson, putting on his spectacles.

"Settles what?"

"Proves they ain't been in Tinkletown more'n twenty

minutes," he replied, much too promptly to suit Miss Becker, who favoured him with a look he wouldn't have forgotten in a long time if he had had eyes in the back of his head. "They must be lookin' for some one," he went on, squinting narrowly. "Good-bye, Sue. See you tomorrer, I suppose."

"I'm not going yet, Mr. Crow," she said, moving a little closer to the fence. "You don't suppose I'm going to let those men pursue me all the way home, do you?"

"They don't look like kidnappers," he said. "Besides, it ain't dark enough yet."

"Just what do you mean by that, Anderson Crow?" she snapped.

"What do I mean by what?" he inquired in some surprise.

"By what you just said."

"I mean you're perfectly safe as long as it's daylight," he retorted. "What else could I mean?"

The two strangers were quite near by this time—near enough, in fact, to cause Miss Becker to lower her voice as she said:

"They're awfully nice looking gentlemen, ain't they?"

Evidently Mr. Crow's explanation had satisfied her, for she was smiling with considerable vivacity as she made the remark. Up to that instant she had neglected her back hair. Now she gracefully, lingeringly fingered it to see if it was properly in place. In doing so, she managed to drop her parasol.

To her chagrin, Marshal Crow took that occasion to behave in a most incredible manner. It is quite probable that he forgot himself. In any case, he picked up the parasol and returned it to her, snatching it, in fact, almost from beneath the foot of the nearest stranger.

"Oh, thank you—thank you kindly, Mr. Crow," she giggled, and proceeded to let it slip out of her fingers again. "Oh, how stupid! How perfectly clumsy—"

"Did I hear you addressed as Mr. Crow?" inquired the foremost of the two strangers, halting abruptly. He was a tall, florid man of forty or thereabouts, with a deep and not unpleasant voice. His companion was also tall but very gaunt and sallow. He wore huge round spectacles, hooked over his ears. Both were well dressed, one in grey flannel, the other in blue serge.

"You did," said the town marshal, straightening up. "You dropped your umbrell' ag'in, Sue," he added. "Yes, sir, my name's Crow."

Miss Becker waited a few seconds and then picked up the parasol.

"The celebrated Anderson Crow?" asked the man with the glasses, opening his eyes a little wider.

Mr. Crow suddenly remembered that he was in his shirt-sleeves. His faded blue sack-coat—"undress," he called it—hung limp and neglected on the gate-post.

"More or less," he admitted, wishing to goodness he had on his best pair of "galluses" instead of the ones he was wearing.

"Marshal of Tinkletown, I believe?" said the florid stranger, raising his eyebrows slightly.

"Excuse me," said Anderson, conscious of a certain disparaging note in the speaker's voice, which he quite naturally laid to the "galluses." Without turning his back toward them he retrieved his coat from the gate-post, remembering in time that those "plaguey" suspenders had played him false that day and Alf Reesling had volunteered to "tie a knot in 'em," somewhere in the back. "I could fine myself five dollars fer goin' without my uniform," said he, as he slipped an arm into one sleeve. "It's one of my hide-boundest rules," and his other arm went in—not without a slight twinge, for he had been experiencing a touch of rheumatism in that shoulder. "Yes, sir, I'm the Marshal o' Tinkletown," he added, indicating the bright nickel star that gleamed resplendent among an assortment of glittering and impressive dangling emblems.

The man with the spectacles peered intently at the collection on Mr. Crow's breast.

"You appear to be almost everything else as well, Mr. Crow," said he, respectfully.

"Well, I guess I'll have to be going," put in Miss Becker at this juncture. "Give my love to the girls, Mr. Crow."

She moved off up the board-walk, her back as stiff as a ramrod. Any one with half an eye could see that she was resolved not to drop the parasol again. No savage warrior on battle bent ever gripped his club with greater determination.

"So long," was all that Marshal Crow could spare the time to say. "Yes sir," he went on, making a fine show of stifling a yawn, "yes, sir, I've had a few triflin' honours in my day. You gentlemen lookin' fer any one in partic'lar?"

"Not now," said the florid one. "We've found him."

The spectacled man had his nose quite close to Mr. Crow's badges. He read them off, in the voice and manner of one tremendously impressed. "Grand Army of the Republic. Sons of the American Revolution. Sons of Veterans. Tinkletown Battlefield Association. New York Imperial Detective Association. Bramble County Horse-Thief Detective Association. Chief of Fire Department. And what, may I ask, is the little round button at the top?"

The marshal was astonished. "Don't you know what that is?"

"It doesn't appear to have any lettering—"

"It don't have to have any. That's an American Red Cross button."

"So it is,—so it is," cried the other hastily. "How stupid of me."

"And this one on the other lapel is a Liberty Loan button, —one hundred dollars is what it represents, if anybody should ast you."

"I recognized it at once, sir. I have one of my own." He raised his hand to his own lapel. "Why, hang it all, I forgot to remove it from my other coat this morning."

"Well," said Anderson drily, "there 'pears to be some advantage in havin' only one coat."

"Mr. Marshal," cut in the larger man brusquely, "we came to see you in regard to a matter of great importance—and, I may add, privacy. Having heard of your reputation for cleverness and infallibility—"

"As everybody in the land has heard," put in the other.

"—we desire your co-operation in an undertaking of considerable magnitude. Quite frankly, I do not see how we can succeed without your valuable assistance. You—"

"Hold on! If you're tryin' to get me to subscribe to a set of books, so's my name at the head of the list will drag other suckers into—"

"Not at all, sir—not at all. We are not book-agents, Mr. Marshal."

"Well, what are ye?"

"Metallurgists," said the florid one.

"I see, I see," said Anderson, who didn't see at all. "You started off just like a book-agent, er a lightnin'-rod salesman."

"My name is Bacon,—George Washington Bacon,—and my friend bears an even nobler moniker, if that be possible. He is Abraham Lincoln Bonaparte—a direct descendant of both of those illustrious gentlemen."

"You don't say! I didn't know Lincoln was any connection of Bonaparte's."

"It isn't generally known," the descendant informed him, with becoming modesty.

"Well, I'm seventy-three years old an' I never heard—"

"Seventy-three!" gasped Mr. Bonaparte, incredulously. "I don't believe it. You can't be more than fifty, Mr. Crow."

"Do you suppose I fought in the Union Army before I was born?" demanded Mr. Crow. "Where'd I get this G. A. R. badge, lemme ast you? An' you don't think the citizens of this here town would elect a ten-year-old boy to the responsible position of town marshal, do you? Why, gosh snap it, I been Marshal o' Tinkletown fer forty years—skippin' two years back in the nineties when I retired in favour of Ed Higgins, owin' to a misunderstandin' concernin' my health—an'—"

"It is incredible, sir. You are the youngest-looking man for your years I've ever seen. But we are digressing. Proceed, Mr. Bacon. Pardon the interruption."

Marshal Crow had drawn himself up to his full height,—a good six feet,—and, expanding under the influence of a just pride, his chest came perilously near to dislodging a couple of brass buttons. His keen little grey eyes snapped brightly in their deep sockets; his sparse chin whiskers, responding to the occasion, bristled noticeably. Employing his thumb and forefinger, he first gave his beard a short caress, after which he drew it safely out of line and expectorated thinly between his teeth with such astounding accuracy that both of the strangers stared. His objective was a narrow slit in the tree-box across the sidewalk.

"I couldn't do that in a thousand years," said Mr. Bacon, deeply impressed.

"You could do it in half that time if you lived in Tinkletown," was Anderson's cryptic return. "You ought to see Ed Higgins. He's our champeen. His specialty is knot-holes. Ed c'n hit—"

"Are you interested in metallurgy, Mr. Crow?" broke in Mr. Bacon, a little rudely.

Anderson pondered a few seconds, squinting at the tree-tops. The two strangers waited his reply with evident concern.

"Sometimes I am, an' sometimes I ain't," said he at last, very seriously. He even went so far as to shake his head slowly, as if to emphasize the fact that he had made a life-long study of the subject and had not been able to arrive at a definite conclusion.

"Good!" exclaimed Mr. Bonaparte. "That proves, Mr. Crow, that you are a man of very great discernment, very great discernment indeed."

Mr. Crow brightened perceptibly. "I have to know a little of everything in my line of work, Mr. Lincoln."

Mr. Bonaparte made no attempt to correct him. As a matter of fact, for a moment or two he was in some doubt himself; it was only after indulging in a hasty bit of mental jugglery that he decided his friend couldn't possibly have introduced him as Bonaparte Abraham Lincoln, or Abraham Bonaparte Lincoln. He wished, however, that he had paid a little closer attention when Mr. George Washington Bacon arranged his names for him.

"We should like to have a few minutes' private conversation with you, Mr. Marshal," said Bacon, lowering his voice.

"Fire away, gents."

"I—ahem!—I said private, Mr. Crow."

"Well, if it's anything you don't want the birds to hear, I guess we'd better go up to the house. If you don't mind that woodpecker up yander an' them two sparrers out there in the road, I guess this is about as private a place as you'll find in Tinkletown."

"Haven't you—an office, Mr. Crow?" demanded Mr. Bacon.

"Yes, but it ain't private. Whenever I've got anything private to 'tend to—er even *think* about—I allus go out in the middle of the street. Shoot ahead; nobody'll hear you."

"It will take some little time," explained Mr. Bonaparte, anxiously. "Have you had your dinner?"

Anderson looked at him keenly. "What's that got to do with it?"

"Mr. Bonaparte means supper," explained Mr. Bacon. "He is a bit excited, Mr. Crow."

"He *must* be," agreed Anderson, glancing at his watch. "Half-past six. Go ahead. We won't be interrupted now till it's time to go to bed."

The two strangers in Tinkletown drew still closer—so close, indeed, that the town marshal, having had his pocket picked once or twice at the County Fair, fell back a little from the fence.

"You must be careful to show no sign of surprise, Mr. Crow," said Bacon. "What I am about to say to you may startle you, but you—"

Anderson reassured him with a gesture.

"Perceed," he said.

Whereupon the spokesman, Mr. Bacon, did a tale unfold that caused the town marshal to lie awake nearly all night and to pop out of bed the next morning fully an hour earlier than usual. For the time being, however, he succeeded so admirably in simulating indifference that the men themselves were not only surprised but a trifle disturbed. He wasn't conducting himself at all as they had expected. At the conclusion of this serious fifteen minutes' recital,—rendered into paragraphs by Anderson's frequent interruptions,—the eager Mr. Bonaparte exclaimed:

"Well, Mr. Crow, doesn't it completely bowl you over?"

"What's that? Bowl me over? I should say not! Why, I knowed fer I can't tell you how long that there's gold up yander in my piece of timberland on Crow's Mountain. Knowed it ever since I was a boy."

His hearers blinked rapidly for a few seconds.

"Really?" murmured Mr. Bacon.

"Do you mean to say there actually *is* gold—" began Mr. Bonaparte, but he got no farther. Whether accidentally or otherwise, Mr. Bacon's foot came sharply into contact with the speaker's shin, and the question terminated in a pained look of surprise, directed with some intensity and a great deal of fortitude at nothing in particular.

"Well, you *are* a wonder, Mr. Crow," said Mr. Bacon

hastily. "I am immensely relieved that you *do* know of its existence. It simplifies matters tremendously. It has been there all the time and you've never known just how to go about getting it out of the ground—isn't that the case, Mr. Crow?"

"Exactly," said Mr. Crow.

Mr. Bacon shot a significant look at Mr. Bonaparte, and that worthy put his hand suddenly to his mouth.

"Well, that's what we're here for, Mr. Crow—to get that gold out of the earth. If our estimates are correct—or, I should say, if our investigations establish the fact that it is a real vein and not merely a little pocket, there ought to be a million dollars in that piece of land of yours. Now, let me see. Just how much land do you own up there, Mr. Crow?"

"I own derned near all of it," said the marshal promptly. "'Bout seventy-five acres, I should say."

"Nothing but timberland, I assume—judging from what we have been able to observe."

"All timber. Never been cleared, 'cept purty well down the slope."

"And it is about five miles as the crow flies from Tinkletown, eh?"

"I ginerally say as the wild goose flies," said Mr. Crow, somewhat curtly.

"Well, you have heard the proposition I bring from my employers in New York City. Think it over tonight, Mr. Crow. Then, we will meet tomorrow morning at your office to complete our plans. I shall be prepared to hand you a draft for two hundred dollars to bind the bargain. What time do you reach your office?"

"Ginerally some'eres between six and a quarter-past."

"My God!" muttered Mr. Bonaparte.

"We will be there at six-fifteen," said Mr. Bacon firmly. "Good evening, Mr. Crow."

Far in the night, Mrs. Crow peevishly mumbled to her bedfellow: "What ails you, Anderson Crow? Go to sleep!"

"Never mind, never mind. I can't tell you, so don't pester me. All I ast of you is to wake me at five if I happen to oversleep."

"Well, of all the—do you suppose I'm goin' to lay awake here all night waitin' for five o'clock to——"

"How in thunder do you expect me to go to sleep, Eva, if you keep jabberin' away to me all night long like this? Ding it all to gosh, here it is after one o'clock an' you still talkin'. Don't do it, I say. Don't ast another question till five o'clock, an' then all you got to do it to ast me if I'm awake."

"Umph!" said Mrs. Crow.

Messrs. Bacon and Bonaparte were an hour and forty minutes late.

It was nearly eight o'clock when the two gentlemen came hurrying around the corner into Sickle street, piloted by Alf Reesling, the town drunkard.

A long, important-looking cigar propitiated Mr. Crow, and after Mr. Reesling and other citizens had been given to understand that the strangers were figuring on buying all the timber on Crow's Mountain, the three principals set forth in Anderson's buckboard.

In due time they arrived at the top of the "Mountain." Now Crow's Mountain was no mountain at all. It was a thickly wooded hill that had achieved eminence by happening to be a scant fifty feet higher than the knolls surrounding it. From the low-lying pastures and grain-fields to the top of the outstanding pine that reared its blasted storm-stripped tip far above its fellows, the elevation was not more than three hundred feet. Nevertheless, it was the loftiest hill in all that region and capped Anderson Crow's agricultural possessions.

Just before the Boggs City National Bank at the county seat closed that afternoon Mr. Crow appeared at the receiving-teller's window. He deposited two hundred dollars in currency. Mr. Bacon had decided that a draft on New York might excite undue curiosity.

"If people were to get wise to what we are really after up here on this mountain, Mr. Crow," said he, "it would play hob with everything. If it gets out that we are after gold—why, the price of land would be so high we couldn't—"

"Lot of these hayseeds been wantin' to sell fer years, the derned rubes," broke in Anderson, pityingly.

"Well, you get me, don't you? Keep our eyes open and our mouths closed, and we will be millionaires inside of a year—or two, at the outside."

"Mum's the word, as the feller said," agreed Mr. Crow.

"And of course you see the advisability of having our articles of incorporation filed secretly in New Jersey. This contract we have signed will be ratified by our employers in New York, and the regular articles drawn up at once. Wait till you see the names of the men who are behind this enterprise. The first meeting of the board of directors will bring together a dozen of the greatest—"

"Where will the meetin' be held?" broke in Anderson, somewhat anxiously.

"New York City, of course. It wouldn't surprise me in the least to see you elected President of the Corporation, Mr. Crow."

"Oh, gosh-a-mighty! I—I can't accept the honour, Mr. Bacon. It's too much of a responsibility. Besides, I don't see how I'm goin' to be able to get away from Tinkletown this fall to attend the meetin'. The County Fair opens next week at Boggs City, an' the second week in October there's to be a Baptist revival—"

"You can send in your proxy, Mr. Crow," explained Mr. Bacon. "It will be all the same to us, you know."

"Well, I guess I better," said Anderson thoughtfully.

A fortnight went by. Crow's Mountain had become the scene of sharp but stealthy activity. Anderson went about the streets of Tinkletown as if in a daze. Acting upon the stern, almost offensive, advice of his new partners, he did not go near the "Mountain" after the first couple of days. They made it very plain to him that *everything* depended on his shrewdness in staying away from the "Mountain" altogether.

The Tinkletown *Banner*, in reporting the vast transaction, incorporated an interview with Mr. G. W. Bacon, who announced that the syndicate he represented had in mind a project to erect a huge summer hotel on top of the "most beautiful mountain east of the Rockies," in the event that satisfactory terms could be arranged with Mr. Crow. As a matter of fact, explained Mr. Bacon, he had been instructed to make certain preliminary investigations in regard to construction, and so forth—such as ascertaining how far down they would have to go to bed-rock, and all that sort of thing.

Practically all of the syndicate's preparatory work on Crow's Mountain was done under cover of night. Motor-trucks that were said to have been driven all the way from Pittsburgh—on account of the dreadful congestion on the railroads—delivered machinery, tools, drills, rods, bolts, rivets and thin jangling strips of structural steel.

Marshal Crow, assuming an importance he did not feel, strutted about Tinkletown.

His abstraction had a good deal to do with the accident to old Mrs. Twiggers. He was dreamily cogitating at the time she was run down by Schultz's butcher-wagon, and as the catastrophe took place almost under his nose, more than one citizen called him names he wouldn't forget. The old lady had her spectacles smashed and lost a dozen eggs in the confusion. Moreover, Ed Higgins's hen-roost was robbed; and three tramps spent as much as half a day on Main Street before Anderson took any notice of them. Ordinarily, he was death on tramps. Crime, as Mr. Harry Squires put it in a caustic editorial in the *Banner*, was rampant in Tinkletown. It was getting so rampant, he complained, that it wasn't safe to cross the street—especially while eggs were retailing at forty-two cents a dozen.

It remained for Alf Reesling, the town drunkard, to bring order out of chaos. Not that he seized the opportunity to go on a spree while Anderson was moon-gazing,—not at all. Alf loathed intoxicating liquors. He did not drink himself, and he had a horror of any one who did. He had been drunk just three times in his life, but as he had managed to crowd the three exhibitions into the space of one week—some twenty years before—Tinkletown elected him forthwith for life to the office of town sot.

Now, Alf had a grievance. He finally got the ear of

Marshal Crow and let loose in a way that startled the old man out of his daze.

"Here you been watchin' me, an' trailin' me, an' lecturin' me for twenty years, dern ye,—an' pleadin' with me to keep sober fer the sake of Tinkletown's fair name, an' you let this feller Bonyparte git full an' keep people awake half the night. He's been drunk more times in the last three weeks than I ever was in all my life. He—"

"What's that? Did you say drunk?" demanded Anderson, blinking. "Who told you he was drunk?"

"*He* did," said Alf. "He don't make any bones about it. He tells everybody when he is drunk. He's proud of it."

"An' I suppose everybody believes him," said Anderson scathingly. "The people of this here town will believe *any* thing if —"

"Las' night that pardner of his'n an' two other fellers from up the hill had to take him up to his room an' lock him in. He was tryin' to sing the Star Spangled Banner in *Dutch*. Gosh, it was awful! He orter be arrested, same as anybody else, Anderson Crow. You got me under suspicion every minute o' the time—night *and* day—"

"That'll do, that'll do, now Alf. No more back talk out o' you," exclaimed Anderson menacingly. "You might as well *be* drunk as to *act* drunk. Don't you know any better'n—"

"Are you goin' to arrest this Bonyparte feller?"

Anderson eyed him sternly for a moment. "I got half a notion to run you in, Alf Reesling, fer interferin' with an officer."

"How'm I interferin'?"

"You're preventin' me from arrestin' a violater of the law,

dern you. Can't you see I'm on my way over to Justice Robb's to swear out a warrant against Abraham Lincoln Bonaparte for bein' intoxicated? What do you mean by stoppin' me an'—"

"I'll go along, Andy," broke in Alf, suddenly affable. "I'll swear to it if you—"

"'Tain't necessary," announced Anderson loftily. "I c'n attend to my own business, if you can't. Nobody c'n sing the Star Spangled Banner in Dutch without havin' a charge of intoxication filed ag'in him, lemme tell you that. Git out o' my way, Alf."

Mr. Crow's pride had been touched. The shaft of criticism had gone home. He would arrest Mr. Abraham Lincoln Bonaparte, no matter what came of it. He did not like Mr. Bonaparte anyway. It was Mr. Bonaparte who had ordered him off Crow's Mountain—his own mountain, mind you—and told him not to come puttering around there any more.

On second thoughts, he accepted the nominal town sot's offer to make affidavit against a real offender, but declined his company and assistance in effecting the arrest. Down in the old Marshal's heart lurked the fear that his new partners would put up such strenuous objections to the arrest that he would have to give way to them. It was this misgiving that caused him to make the trip to Crow's Mountain instead of confronting his man that evening at the hotel or in the street, in the presence of an audience.

Arriving at the cross-roads half a mile from the foot of Crow's Mountain, he encountered two men tinkering with the engine of a big automobile. They stopped him and inquired if there was a garage nearby. While he was directing them to Pete Olsen's in town, he espied two more men reposing in the shade of a tree farther up the lane.

As he drove on, leaving them behind, he found himself possessed of the notion that the two men were strangely nervous and impatient. He decided, after he had gone a half mile farther that they had, as a matter-of-fact, acted in a very suspicious manner,—just as automobile thieves might be expected to act in the presence of an officer of the law. He made up his mind that if they were still there when he returned with his prisoner, he would yank 'em up for investigation.

He went through the motions of hitching old Hip and Jim to a sapling near the top of the "Mountain." They went to sleep almost instantly.

In the little clearing off to the left, a couple of hundred yards away, Marshal Crow observed several men at work constructing a "shanty." Closer at hand, almost lost to view among the pines, rose the thin, open-work steel tower from which the "drill" was to be operated. Standing out among the tree-tops were the long cross-bars of steel, and from them ran the "guy" wires to the ground below. Mr. Crow had never seen a "drill" before, but he had been told by Mr. Bacon that this was the newest thing on the market.

The Marshal started off in the direction of the "shanty" and suddenly a most astonishing thing happened. Mr. Crow disappeared from view as if by magic!

In order to give the drill as wide a berth as possible, he had deployed widely to the left of the path, making his way somewhat tortuously through a rough lot of underbrush. Without the slightest warning, the earth gave way beneath him and down he shot, clawing frantically at the edges of a well-camouflaged hole in the ground, taking with him a vast amount of twigs, branches and a net-work of sapling poles.

Not only did he drop a good twelve feet, but he landed squarely upon the stooping person of Mr. Bacon, who emitted a startling sound that began as a yell and ended as a grunt. He then crumpled up and spread himself out flat, with Mr. Crow draped awkwardly across his prostrate form. For the time being, Mr. Bacon was as still as the grave. He was out.

Anderson scrambled to his feet, pawing the air with his hands, his eyes tightly shut. He was yelling for help.

Now, it was this yelling for help that deceived the astonished Mr. Bonaparte. He jumped at once to the conclusion that the Marshal was calling for assistance from the *outside*.

So he threw up his hands!

"I—surrender! I give in!" he yelled. "Keep them off! Don't let them get at me!"

Anderson opened his eyes and stared.

He found himself in a small, squat room lighted by a lantern which stood upon a crudely made table in the corner beyond Bonaparte. There was a board floor well littered with soil and shavings. In another corner stood a singular looking contraption, not unlike a dynamo.

Marshal Crow bethought himself of his mission. Although the breath had been jarred out of his body, he managed to say,—explosively:

"I—I got a warrant for your arrest. Come along now! Don't resist. Don't make a fuss. Come along peaceably. I—"

"I'll come, Mr. Crow. I was dragged into this thing against my will. *Gott in Himmel! Gott!*—"

"Never mind what you got," exclaimed Anderson sharply. "You come along with me or you'll get something worse'n that."

"Is—is he dead!" groaned Bonaparte, his eyes almost starting from his head.

Anderson backed away from the sprawling, motionless figure on the floor.

"I—I—gosh, I hope not. I—I was as much surprised as anybody. Say, you see if he's breathin'. We got to git him out o' this place right away an' send for a doctor. The good Lord knows I didn't intend to light on him like that. It was an accident, I swear it was. You know just how it happened, an'—you'll stand by me, won't you, if—"

Just then a loud voice came from above.

"Hey, down there!" A second's pause. Then: "We've got you dead to rights, so no monkey business. Come up out o' that, or we'll pump enough lead down there to—"

"Don't shoot,—don't shoot!" yelled Mr. Bonaparte shrilly. "Tell your men not to fire, Mr. Crow!"

"Tell—tell *who*?" cried Anderson blankly. Suddenly he sprang to his companion's side; seizing him by the arm, he whispered hoarsely: "By gosh, I thought there was somethin' queer about that gang. Have you got any of the gold here? I recollect that feller's voice, plain as day. They're after the gold. They've heard about—"

"Are you coming up?" roared the voice from the outer world.

"Who are you?" called back Anderson stoutly.

"Oh, I guess you'll recognize United States marshals when you see 'em. Come on, now."

Abraham Lincoln Bonaparte faced Marshal Crow, the truth dawning upon him like a flash.

"You damned old rube!" he snarled, and forthwith planted his fist under Anderson's chin-whiskers, with such surprising force that the old man once more landed heavily on the prostrate form of the unfortunate Bacon.

"O-oh, gosh!" groaned Anderson, and as his eyes rolled upward he saw a million stars chasing each other around the ceiling.

"I'll get *that* much satisfaction out of it anyhow," he heard some one say, from a very great distance.

Sometime afterward he was dimly aware of a jumble of excited voices about him. Some one was shouting in his ear. He opened his eyes and everything looked green before them. In time he recognized pine trees, very lofty pine trees that slowly but surely shrank in size as he gazed wonderingly at them.

There were a lot of strange men surrounding him. Out of the mass, he finally selected a face that grew upon him. It was the face of Alf Reesling.

"By jinks, Anderson, you done it *this* time," Alf cried excitedly. "I told 'em you was on your way up here to arrest these fellers, an' by jinks, I knowed you'd get 'em."

"Le—lemme set down, please," mumbled Anderson, and the two men who supported him lowered him gently to the ground, with his back against a tree trunk. "Come here, Alf," he called out feebly.

Alf shuffled forward.

"Who are these men?" whispered Anderson.

"Detectives—reg'lar detectives," replied Alf. "United States detectives—what do you call 'em?"

"Scotland Yard men," replied Anderson, who had done a good deal of reading in his time.

"I started out after you on my wheel, Andy, thinkin' maybe you'd have trouble. Down the road I met up with these fellers in a big automobile. They stopped me an' said I couldn't go up the hill. Just then up comes another car full of men. They all seemed to be acquainted. I told 'em I was a deputy marshal an' was goin' up the hill to help you arrest a feller named Bonyparte. Well, by jinks, you oughter heard 'em! They cussed, and said the derned ole fool would spile everything. Then, 'fore you could say Joe, they piled into one o' the cars an' sailed up the hill. I didn't get up here till after they'd hauled you an' your prisoners out o' that hole, but I give 'em the laugh just the same. You captured the two ringleaders. By gosh, I'm glad you're alive, Andy. I bet the Kaiser'll hate you fer this."

"The—the what?"

"Ole Kaiser Bill. Say, you was down there quite a little spell, an' they won't let me go down. What does a wireless plant look like, Anderson?"

That evening Marshal Crow sat on the porch in front of Lamson's store, smoking a fine cigar, presented to him by Harry Squires, reporter for the *Banner*. He had a large audience. Indeed, he was obliged to raise his voice considerably in order to reach the outer rim.

He had been called a hero, a fearless officer, and a lot of other pleasant things, by the astonished United States marshals, and he had been given to understand that he would hear from Washington before long. Mr. Bacon (Kurt von Poppenblitz) and Mr. Bonaparte (Conrad Bloom) had also called him something, but he didn't mind. His erstwhile partners, with their four or five henchmen, were now well on their way to limbo, and Mr. Crow was regaling his hearers with the story. During the first recital (this being either the ninth or tenth), Alf Reesling had been obliged to prompt him—a circumstance readily explainable when one stops to consider the effect of the murderous blow Mr. Crow had received.

"'Course," said Anderson, "they *did* fool me at first. But I wasn't long gittin' onto 'em. I used to sneak up there and investigate ever' now an' ag'in. Finally I got onto the fact that they was German spies—I got positive proof of it. I can't tell you just what it is, 'cause it's government business. Then I finds out they got a wireless plant all in order, an' ready to relay messages to the coast o' Maine, from some'eres out west. So today, I goes over to Justice Robb's and gits a warrant for intoxication. That was to make it legal fer me to bust into their shanty if necessary. Course, the drunk charge was only a blind, as I told the U. S. marshal. I went right straight to that underground den o' their'n, an' afore they knowed what was up, I leaped down on 'em. Fust thing I done was to put the big and dangerous one horse de combat. He was the one I was worried about. I knocked him flat an' then went after t'other one. He let on like he was surrenderin'. He fooled me, I admit—'cause I don't know anything 'bout wireless machinery. All of a sudden he give me a wireless shock—out o' nowhere, you might say—an' well, by cracky, I thought it was all over. 'Course, I realize now it was foolish o' me to try to go up there an' take them two desperadoes single-handed, but I—What's that, Bud?"

"Mrs. Crow sent me to tell you if you didn't come home to supper this minute, you wouldn't git any," called out a boy from the outskirts of the crowd.

"That's the second wireless shock you've had today,

Anderson," said Harry Squires, drily, and slowly closed one eye.

THE BEST MAN WINS!

Anderson Crow Meets His Waterloo and His Marne

For sixteen consecutive years Anderson Crow had been the Marshal of Tinkletown. A hiatus of two years separated this period of service from another which, according to persons of apparently infallible memory, ran through an unbroken stretch of twenty-two years. Uncle Gid Luce stoutly maintained—and with some authority—that anybody who said twenty-two years was either mistaken or lying. He knew for a positive fact that it was only twenty-one for the simple reason that at the beginning of the Crow dynasty a full year elapsed before Anderson could be convinced that he actually had been victorious at the polls over his venerable predecessor, ex-marshal Bunker, who had served uninterruptedly for something like thirty years before him.

It took the wisest men in town nearly a year to persuade the incredulous Mr. Bunker that he had been defeated, and also to prove to Mr. Crow that he had been elected. Neither one of 'em would believe it.

It was the consensus of opinion, however, that Anderson Crow had served, all told, thirty-eight years, the aforesaid hiatus being the result of a decision on his part to permanently abandon public life in order to carry on his work as a private detective. Mr. Ed. Higgins held the office for two years and then retired, claiming that there wasn't any sense in Tinkletown having *two* marshals and only paying for one. And, as the salary and perquisites were too meagre to warrant a division, and the duties of office barely sufficient to keep *one* man awake, he arrived at the only conclusion possible: it was only fair that he should split even with Anderson.

After thinking it over for some time, he decided that about the best way to solve the problem was for him to take the pay and allow Anderson to do the work,—an arrangement that was eminently satisfactory to the entire population of Tinkletown.

Elections were held biennially. Every two years, in the spring, as provided by statute, the voters of Tinkletown—unless otherwise engaged—ambled up to the polling place in the rear of Hawkins's Undertaking Emporium and voted not only for Anderson Crow, but for a town clerk, a justice of the peace, and three selectmen. No one ever thought of voting for any one except Mr. Crow. Once, and only once, was there an opposition candidate for the office of Town Marshal. It is on record that he did not receive a solitary vote.

Republicans and Democrats voted for Anderson with persistent fidelity, and while there were notable contests for the other offices at nearly every election, no one bothered himself about the marshal-ship.

The regular election was drawing near. Marshal Crow was mildly concerned,—not about himself, but on account of the tremendous battle that was to be waged for the office of town clerk. Henry Wimpelmeyer, the proprietor of the tanyard, had come out for the office, and was spending money freely. The incumbent, Ezra Pounder, had had a good deal of sickness in his family during the winter, and was in no position to be bountiful.

Moreover, Ezra was further handicapped by the fact that nearly every voter in Tinkletown owed money to Henry

Wimpelmeyer. Inasmuch as it was just the other way round with Ezra, it may be seen that his adversary possessed a sickening advantage. Mr. Wimpelmeyer could afford to slap every one on the back and jingle his pocketful of change in the most reckless fashion. He did not have to dodge any one on the street, not he.

Anderson Crow was a strong Pounder man. He was worried. Henry Wimpelmeyer had openly stated that if he were elected he would be pleased to show his gratitude to his friends by cancelling every obligation due him!

He was planning to run on what was to be called the People's ticket. Ezra was an Anderson Crow republican. Tinkletown itself was largely republican. The democrats never had a chance to hold office except when there was a democratic president at Washington. Then one of them got the post-office, and almost immediately began to show signs of turning republican so that he could be reasonably certain of reappointment at the end of his four years.

Anderson Crow lay awake nights trying to evolve a plan by which Henry Wimpelmeyer's astonishing methods could be overcome. That frank and unchallenged promise to cancel all debts was absolutely certain to defeat Ezra. So far as the marshal knew, no one owed Henry more than five dollars—in most cases it was even less—but when you sat down and figured up just how much Henry would ever realize in hard cash on these accounts, even if he waited a hundred years, it was easy to see that the election wasn't going to cost him a dollar.

For example, Alf Reesling had owed him a dollar and thirty-five cents for nearly seven years. Alf admitted that the obligation worried him a great deal, and it was pretty nearly certain that he would jump at the chance to be relieved. Other items: Henry Plumb, two dollars and a quarter; Harvey Shortfork, ninety cents; Ben Pickett, a dollar-seventy-five; Rush Applegate, three-twenty; Lum Gillespie, one-fifteen,—and so on, including Ezra Pounder himself, who owed the staggering sum of eleven dollars and eighty-two cents. There was, after all, some consolation in the thought that Ezra would be benefited to that extent by his own defeat.

Naturally, Mr. Crow gave no thought to his own candidacy. No one was running against him, and apparently no one ever would. Therefore, Mr. Crow was in a position to devote his apprehensions exclusively to the rest of the ticket, and to Ezra Pounder in particular.

He could think of but one way to forestall Mr. Wimpelmeyer, and that was by digging down into his own pocket and paying in cash every single cent that the electorate of Tinkletown owed "the dad-burned Shylark!" He even went so far as to ascertain—almost to a dollar—just how much it would take to save the honour of Tinkletown, finding, after an investigation, that $276.82 would square up everything, and leave Henry high and dry with nothing but the German vote to depend upon. There were exactly twenty-two eligible voters in town with German names, and seven of them professed to be Swiss the instant the United States went into the war.

Mr. Crow was making profound calculation on the back of an envelope when Alf Reesling, the town drunkard, came scuttling excitedly around the corner from the *Banner* office.

"Gee whiz!" gasped Alf, "I been lookin' all over fer you, Anderson."

"Say, can't you see I'm busy? Now, I got to begin all over ag'in. Move on, now—"

"Have you heard the latest?" gulped Alf, grabbing him by the arm.

"What ails you, Alf? Wait a minute! No, by gosh, it's more like onions. For a second I thought you'd—"

"I'm as sober as ever," interrupted Alf hotly.

"That's what you been sayin' fer twenty years," said Anderson.

"Well, ain't I?"

"I don't know what you do when I'm not watchin' you."

"Well, all I got to say is I never felt more like takin' a drink. An' you'll feel like it, too, when you hear the latest. Maybe you'll drop dead er somethin'. Serve you right, too, by jiminy, the way you keep insinyating about—"

"Go on an' tell me. Don't talk all day. Just *tell* me. That's all you're called on to do."

"Well," sputtered Alf. "Some one's come out ag'in you fer marshal. I seen the item they're printin' over at the *Banner* office. Seen the name an' everything."

Anderson blinked two or three times, reached for his whiskers and missed them, and then roared:

"You must be crazy, Alf! By thunder, I hate to do it, but I'll have to put you in a safe—"

"You just wait an' see if I'm—"

"—safe place where you can't harm nobody. You oughtn't to be runnin' round at large like this. Here! Leggo my arm! What the dickens are you tryin' to—"

"Come on! I'll *show* you!" exclaimed Alf. "I'll take you right around to the *Banner* office an'—say, didn't you know the People's Party nominated a full ticket las' night over at Odd Fellers' Hall?"

Anderson submitted himself to be led—or rather dragged—around the corner into Sickle Street.

Several business men aroused from mid-morning lassitude allowed their chairs to come down with a thump upon divers mercantile porches, and fell in behind the two principal citizens of Tinkletown. Something terrible must have happened or Marshal Crow wouldn't be summoned in any such imperative manner as this.

"What's up, Anderson?" called out Mort Fryback, the hardware dealer, wavering on one leg while he reached frantically behind him for his crutch. Mort was always looking for excitement. He hadn't had any to speak of since the day he created the greatest furor the town had experienced in years by losing one of his legs under an extremely heavy kitchen stove.

"Is there a fire?" shouted Mr. Brubaker, the druggist, half a block away.

Mr. Jones, proprietor of the *Banner* Job Printing office, obligingly produced the "galley-proof" of the account of the People's Convention, prepared by his "city editor," Harry Squires, for the ensuing issue of the weekly. Mr. Squires himself emerged from the press-room, and sarcastically offered his condolences to Anderson Crow.

"Well, here's a pretty howdy-do, Anderson," he said, elevating his eye-shade to a position that established a green halo over a perfectly pink pate.

"Howdy-do," responded Anderson, with unaccustomed politeness. He was staring hard at the dirty strip of paper which he held to the light.

"Didn't I *tell* you?" exclaimed Alf Reesling triumphantly. "There she is, right before your eyes."

Mr. Reesling employed the proper gender in making this assertion. "She" was right before the eyes of every one who cared to look. Anderson slowly read off the "ticket." His voice cracked deplorably as he pronounced the last of the six names that smote him where he had never been smitten before.

Clerk—Henry Wimpelmeyer

Justice of the Peace—William Kiser

Selectman, First District—Otto Schultz

Selectman, Second District—Conrad Blank

Selectman, Third District—Christopher Columbus Callahan

Marshal—Minnie Stitzenberg.

A long silence followed the last syllable in Minnie's name, broken at last by Marshal Crow, who turned upon Harry Squires and demanded:

"What do you mean, Harry Squires, by belittlin' a woman's name in your paper like this? She c'n sue for libel. You got no right to make fun of a respectable, hard-workin' woman, even though she did make a derned fool of herself gittin' up that pertition to have me removed from office."

"Well, that's what she's still trying to do," said Harry.

"What say?"

"I say she's still trying to remove you from office. She's going to get your hide, Anderson, for arresting her when she tried to make that Suffrage speech in front of the town hall last fall."

"I had a right to arrest her. She was obstructin' the public thoroughfare."

"That's all right, but she said she had as much right to block the street as you had. You made speeches all over the place."

"Yes, but I made 'em in good American English, an' she spoke half the time in German. How in thunder was I to know what she was sayin'? She might 'a' been sayin' somethin' ag'in the United States Government, fer all I knew."

"Well, anyhow, she's going to get your scalp for it, if it's in woman's power to do it."

"I'm ag'in any female citizen of this here town that subscribes to a German paper printed in New York City an' refuses to read the *Banner*," declared Anderson loudly—and with all the astuteness of the experienced politician. "An' what's more," pursued Anderson scornfully, "I'm ag'in that whole ticket. There's only one American on it, an' he was a Democrat up to las' Sunday. Besides, it's ag'in the law to nominate Minnie Stitzenberg."

"Why?" demanded Harry Squires.

"Ain't she a woman?"

"Certainly she is."

"Well, ain't *that* ag'in the law? A woman ain't got no right to run for nothin'," said Anderson. "She ain't—"

"She ain't, eh? Didn't you walk up to the polls last fall and vote to give her the right?" demanded Harry. "Didn't every dog-goned man in this town except Bill Wynkoop vote for suffrage? Well, then, what are you kicking about? She's got as much right to run for marshal as you have, old Sport, and if what she says is true, every blessed woman in Tinkletown is going to vote for her."

Marshal Crow sat down, a queer, dazed look in his eyes.

"By gosh, I—I never thought they'd act like this," he murmured.

Every man in the group was asking the same question in the back of his startled brain: "Has *my* wife gone an' got mixed up in this scheme of Minnie's without sayin' anything to me?" Visions of feminine supremacy filled the mental eye of a suddenly perturbed constituency. The realization flashed through every mind that if the women of Tinkletown stuck solidly together, there wasn't the ghost of a chance for the sex that had been in the saddle since the world began. An unwitting, or perhaps a designing, Providence had populated Tinkletown with at least twenty more women than men!

Alf Reesling was the first to speak. He addressed the complacent Mr. Squires:

"I know one woman that ain't goin' to vote for Minnie Stitzenberg," said he, somewhat fiercely.

"What are you going to do?" inquired Harry mildly. "Kill her?"

"Nothin' as triflin' as that," said Alf. "I'm goin' to tell my wife if she votes for Minnie I'll pack up and leave her."

"Minnie's sure of *one* vote, all right," was Harry's comment.

Fully ten minutes were required to convince the marshal that Minnie Stitzenberg was a bona fide candidate.

Anderson finally arose, drew himself to his full height, lifted his chin, and faced the group with something truly martial in his eye.

"Feller citizens," he began solemnly, "the time has come for us men to stand together. We got to pertect our rights. We got to let the women know that they can't come between us. For the last million years we have been supportin' an' pertectin' and puttin' up with all sorts of women, an' we got to give 'em to understand that this is no time for them to git it into their heads they can support and perfect us. Everybody, includin' the women, knows there's a great war goin' on over in Europe. Us men are fightin' that war. We're bleedin' an' dyin' an' bein' captured by the orneriest villains outside o' hell—as the feller says. I'm not sayin' the women ain't doin' their part, mind you. They're doin' noble, an' you couldn't git me to say a thing ag'in women *as* women. They're a derned sight better'n we are. That's jest the point. We got to *keep* 'em better'n we are, an' what's more to the point, we don't want 'em to find out they're better'n we are. Just as soon as they git to be as overbearin' an' as incontrollable as we are, then there's goin' to be thunder to pay. I'm willin' to work, an' fight, an' die fer my wife an' my daughters, but I'm derned if I like the idee of them workin' an' fightin' ag'in *me*. I'm willin' the women should vote. But they oughtn't to run out an' vote ag'in the men the first chance they git. When this war's over an' there ain't no able-bodied men left to run things, then you bet the women will be derned glad we fixed things so's *they* won't never have to worry about goin' to war with the ding-blasted ravishers over in Germany. If the time ever comes—an' it may, if they keep killin' us off over there— when the women have to run this here government, they'll find it's a man-sized job, an' that we took care of it mighty well up to the time we got all shot to pieces preservin' humanity, an' civilization, an' all the women an' children the Germans didn't git a chance to butcher because we wouldn't let 'em. Now, I'm ready any time to knuckle under to a man that's better'n I am. But I'm dog-goned if I'm willin' to admit that Minnie Stitzenberg's that man! Yes, sir, gentlemen, we men have got to stand together!"

"'Sh!" hissed Mort Fryback, jerking his head in the direction of Main Street. With one accord the men on the porch turned to look.

Miss Minnie Stitzenberg had come into view on the opposite side of the street, and was striding manfully in their direction. The Higgins dog trotted proudly, confidently, a few feet ahead of her. She waved a friendly hand and called out, in a genial but ludicrous effort to mimic the lordly Mr. Crow:

"Move on there, now. Don't loiter."

A little later, the agitated town marshal, flanked by the town drunkard and the one-legged Mr. Fryback, viewed with no little dismay a group of women congregated in front of Parr's drygoods store. In the centre of this group was the new candidate for town marshal. Alf Reesling stopped short and said something under his breath. His wife was one of Miss Stitzenberg's most attentive listeners.

Marshal Crow was not disheartened. He knew that Minnie Stitzenberg could not defeat him at the polls. The thing that rankled was the fact that a woman had been selected to run against him. It was an offence to his dignity. The leaders of the People's Party made it quite plain that they did not consider him of sufficient importance to justify anything so dignified as masculine opposition!

On the day of the Republican Convention, which was to be held in the town hall in the evening, Anderson went in despair and humility to Harry Squires, the reporter.

"Harry," he said, "I been thinkin' it over. I can't run ag'in a woman. It goes ag'in the grain. If I beat her, I'd never be able to look anybody in the face, an' if she beats me—why, by gosh, I couldn't even look myself in the face. So I'm goin' to decline the nomination tonight."

He was rather pathetic, and Harry Squires was touched. He had a great fondness for the old marshal, notwithstanding his habit of poking fun at him and ridiculing him in the *Banner*. He laid his hand on the old man's arm and there was genuine warmth in his voice as he spoke to him.

"Anderson, we can't allow you to withdraw. It would be the vilest thing the people of this town could do if they turned you out of office after all these years of faithful service. We—"

"Can't be helped, Harry," said Anderson firmly. "I won't run ag'in a woman, so that's the end of it."

Harry looked cautiously around, and then, leaning a little closer, said:

"I know something that would put Minnie in the soup, clean over her head. All I've got to do is to tell what I know about—"

"Hold on, Harry," broke in the marshal sternly. "Is it somethin' ag'in her character?"

"It's something that would prevent every man, woman and child in Tinkletown from voting for her," said Harry.

"Somethin' scand'lous?" demanded Anderson, perking up instantly.

"Decidedly. A word from me and—"

"Wait a second. Is—is there a man in the case?"

"A *man*?" cried Harry. "Bless your soul, Anderson, there are fifty men in it."

Anderson fell back a step or two. For a moment or two he was speechless.

"Sakes alive! *Fifty?* For goodness' sake, Harry, are you sure?"

"Not exactly. It may be sixty," amended Harry. "We could easily find out just how many—"

"Never mind! Never mind!" cried Anderson, recovering himself. "If it's as bad as all that, we just got to keep still about it. I wouldn't allow you to throw mud at her if she's been carryin' on with only *one* man, but if there's fifty or—But, gosh a' mighty, Harry, it ain't possible. A woman as homely as Minnie— why, dog-gone it, a woman as homely as she is simply couldn't be bad no matter how much she wanted to. It ain't human nature. She—"

"Hold your horses, Anderson," broke in Harry, after a perplexed stare. "I guess you're jumping at conclusions. I didn't say—"

"There ain't going to be no scandal in this campaign. If Minnie Stitzenberg—German or no German—has been—"

"It isn't the kind of scandal you think it is," protested Harry. "What I'm trying to tell you is that it was Minnie Stitzenberg who got that guy up here from New York two years ago to sell stock in the Salt Water Gold Company, and stung fifty or sixty of our wisest citizens to the extent of thirty dollars apiece. I happen to know that Minnie got five dollars for every sucker that was landed. That guy was her cousin and she gave him a list of the easiest marks in town. If I remember correctly, you were one of them, Anderson. She got something like two hundred dollars for giving him the proper steer, and that's what I meant when I said there were fifty or sixty men in the case."

"Well, I'll be ding-blasted!"

"And do you know what she did with her ill-gotten gains?"

Anderson could only shake his head.

"She went up to Boggs City and took singing lessons. Now you know the worst."

The marshal found his voice. "An' it went on for nearly six months, too—people had to keep their windows shut so's they couldn't hear her yellin' as if somebody was tryin' to murder her. An' when I went to her an' respectfully requested her to quit disturbin' the peace, she—do you know what she said to me?"

"I've got a sneaking idea."

"Well, you're wrong. She said I was a finicky old jackass." The memory of it brought an apoplectic red to his face.

"And being a gentleman, you couldn't deny it," said Harry soberly.

"What's that?"

"I mean, you couldn't call her a liar. What did you say?"

"I looked her right in the eyes an' I said I'd been neutral up to that minute, but from then on I'd be derned if I'd try any longer. By gosh, I guess she knowed what I meant all right."

"Well, as I was saying, all you've got to do is to tell the voters of this town that she helped put up that job on them, and —"

Anderson held up his hand and shook his head resolutely.

"Nope! I'm through. I'm not goin' to run. I mean to withdraw my name tonight."

Considering the matter closed, he sauntered to the middle of the street where he held up his hand and stopped a lame and venerable Ford driven—or as Mr. Squires was in the habit of saying, urged—by Deacon Rank.

"What's your speedo-*meter* say, Deacon?" inquired the marshal blandly.

"It don't say anything," snapped the deacon.

Anderson saw fit to indulge in sarcasm. "Well, by gum, I'd 'a' swore your old machine was movin'. Is it possible my eyes deceived me?"

"Course it was movin'—movin' strictly accordin' to law, too. Six miles an hour. What you holdin' me up for?"

"So's I could get in and take a little joy ride with you," said Mr. Crow affably. "Drop me at the post office, will you?" He stepped up beside the deacon and calmly seated himself.

The deacon grumbled. "'Tain't more'n a hundred yards to the post office," he said. "Stoppin' me like this an'—an' makin' me get out and crank the car besides. An' I'm in a hurry, too. Couldn't you—"

"Well, I ain't in no hurry. If I was, don't you suppose I'd 'a' walked?"

That evening the town hall was filled with discouraged, apprehensive Republicans. A half-dozen newly enfranchised women occupied front seats. Ed. Higgins confided to those nearest him that he felt as though he was in church, and Alf Reesling loudly advised the convention to be careful, as there were ladies present.

Mr. Hud Lamson, as usual, was the chairman of the "Convention." No one else ever had a chance to be chairman for the reason that Hud did not insist upon having the honour thrust upon him. He simply *took* it.

Following the usual resolutions condemning the Democratic Party to perdition and at the same time eulogizing the Democratic Administration at Washington, Mr. Ezra Pounder was nominated by acclamation for the responsible post of town clerk. In swift succession, Ed. Higgins, Abner Pickerell and Situate M. Jones were chosen for selectmen. Justice Robb was unanimously chosen to succeed himself.

Then ensued a strange, significant silence—a silence fraught with exceeding gravity and the portentous suggestion of something devastating about to overtake the assemblage. Some one in the back of the hall cleared his throat, and instantly, with one accord, every eye was turned in his direction. It was as if he were clearing the way for action.

Harry Squires, the perennial secretary of all conventions held by all parties in Tinkletown, by virtue of his skill with the pencil, arose from his seat—and stepped to the front of the platform.

"Order!" called out Marshal Crow, in his most authoritative voice, sweeping the convention with an accusing eye.

"Mr. Chairman, fellow Republicans and voters of the opposite sex," began Harry, in a distinctly lugubrious tone, "we have now come to the most critical moment in the history of Tinkletown. It is with ineffable sorrow and dismay that I stand before you this evening, the bearer of sad tidings. On the other hand, I expect to derive great joy in offsetting this sad news later on in my humble speech. I am now, gentlemen—and ladies—speaking of our most noted and most cherished citizen, Mr. Anderson Crow, known to you all, I believe, without exception. I—"

At this juncture, up jumped Alf Reesling and shouted:

"Three cheers for Anderson Crow!"

And three cheers were given with a vim. Uncle Dad Simms, a patriot of long-standing but of exceedingly short memory, took the convention by storm by crying out in a cracked but penetrating voice:

"Three cheers for the President of the United States! I don't keer if he is a Democrat! Come on, now, men! Three cheers for President Cleveland!"

A roar of laughter went up and Uncle Dad, being quite deaf, followed it with two squeaky cheers, all by himself, and then looked about in triumph. Alf Reesling proposed three cheers for President Wilson, and again the welkin rang. Having established a success as a promoter of enthusiasm, Alf mounted a chair and roared:

"Now, let's give three cheers for General Pershing an' the boys over in France, includin' the four noble young men from Tinkletown who are with him in the trenches, killin' the botches! Now, hip—hip—"

And once more the air shivered under the impact of vocal enthusiasm.

Mr. Squires held up his hands and checked what might have become a habit by thanking the convention for the timely and admirable interruption, explaining that the digression had given him an opportunity to regain command of his emotions.

"It is, however, with pain that I am authorized to announce, not only to the glorious Republican Party, but to the City of Tinkletown, that—Hold on, Alf! We can get along without three cheers for Tinkletown! To announce that the name of Anderson Crow is hereby withdrawn from the consideration of this convention for the—er—the nomination for Town Marshal. Mr. Crow positively declines to make the race. It is not necessary for me to dilate upon the manifold virtues and accomplishments of our distinguished marshal. His fame extends to the uttermost corners of the earth. For nearly half a century he has kept this town jogging along in a straight and narrow path, and I for one—and I feel that I voice the sentiment of every citizen here and elsewhere—I for one do not resent the frequent reproaches and occasional arrests he has heaped upon me in the discharge of his duty. It was all for the good of the community, and I am proud to say that I have been arrested by Marshal Crow more times than I have fingers and toes. And, I am further proud to add, that on not a single occasion did Marshal Crow hesitate to admit that he was mistaken. Gentlemen, it takes a pretty big man to admit that he is mistaken. But, if you will read the next issue of the *Banner*, you will see that I can write about him much more eloquently than I can speak. He has positively decided not to be a candidate for re-election. While we are thereby plunged into grief of the darkest hue, I am here to tell you that our grief is mitigated by the most gorgeous ray of light that ever beamed upon the human race. It is my pleasure, gentlemen of the Republican Party—and ladies of the same sect —to present for your—"

Alf Reesling's voice was heard in plaintive protest. He spoke to his elbow neighbour, but in a tone audible to every one, far and near.

"I'll be dog-goned if I'll stand for that. It's an insult to every man here to say they are of the same sex. We give 'em the vote and, by gosh, they claim our sex. I—"

"Order!" commanded Marshal Crow.

The orator resumed. "It is my privilege to present for your consideration the name of one of our most illustrious citizens for the honourable office of Town Marshal. A name that is a household word, second only to that of the present incumbent. Circumstances over which we have no control—

although we did have it up to a short time ago—make it possible for me to present to you a name that will go down in history as one of the grandest since the bonny days of good Queen Bess. Gentlemen—and at the same time, ladies—I have the honour to put in nomination for Town Marshal our distinguished fellow voter, Mrs. Anderson Crow!"

A silence even more potential than the one preceding Mr. Squire's peroration ensued. It was broken this time by Uncle Dad Simms, who proceeded to further glorify his deafness by squeaking:

"And he'll be elected, too, you bet your boots. We don't want no gosh-blamed woman fer—eh? What say, Alf?" And Alf, making a cup of his hands, repeated with great vigour an inch or so from Uncle Dad's ear the timely remark that had caused the ancient to hesitate. It is not necessary to quote Alf, but Uncle Dad's rejoinder is important.

"Well, *Jee*-hosaphat!" he gasped.

"Is there a second to the nomination?" inquired the chairman.

Marshal Crow arose. "I second the nomination," he said, taking a sudden tug at his whiskers. "Before we take a ballot, Mr. Chairman, I want to say right here an' now that Mrs. Crow will have my full an' undivided support, just as she has always had. I have allus maintained that a woman's place is in the home. Therefore, when it comes time fer Mrs. Crow to assume the responsibilities of this here office, I am goin' to see to it that she *stays* home an' tends to her household duties. I am goin' to be deputy marshal durin' her term of office, without pay, ladies an' gentlemen, an' I am goin' to lift every bit o' the work off'n her shoulders. I believe in equal sufferin'. If she'll do the woman's share o' the work, I'll do the man's, an' nothin' could be fairer than that. Between us we'll give the city o' Tinkletown the best administration the office of marshal has ever had. My wife ain't here tonight to accept the honour you are goin' to heap on her, but I think I can safely promise she'll consent to make the race. She may kick like a bay steer at first, but when she sees it's her *duty* to run, you bet she'll do it! It's a case of woman ag'in woman, feller Republicans, an' man ag'in man. All I got to say is that the best woman's bound to win. I almost forgot to say that if the voters o' Tinkletown don't jump at the chance to git a marshal an' a experienced deputy for the price o' one salary, it's because there's more derned fools in the town than I thought there was."

Mr. Ed Higgins sprang to his feet.

"I move, Mr. Chairman, that we make the nomination unanimous without a dissenting vote," he cried out. "We got a chance to get the best deputy marshal in the United States of America without it costin' us a red cent, an' besides that, we get the best cook in all Tinkletown for marshal. If there's anybody here, male or female, who c'n deny that Mrs. Crow is the best cook alive I'd like to hear him say so. I've eat a hundred meals in her house an' I know what I'm talkin' about. I defy anybody—"

"I call for a vote!" cried out one of the women, bridling a little. "And I want to say to you, Ed Higgins, that while I think Mrs. Crow will make the best marshal we've ever had, I wouldn't go so far as to say she's the best cook in Tinkletown. You haven't been invited to eat in *every* house in this town, don't forget that."

"All in favour of making the nomination of Mrs. Crow unanimous signify by holding up their hands," said the chairman.

Every hand went up. Then a rousing cheer was given for the "next Marshal of Tinkletown," followed by the customary mumbling of "The Star Spangled Banner."

Three full days were devoted by Anderson and the leaders of the Republican Party to the task of inducing Mrs. Crow to make the race against Minnie Stitzenberg. At first she refused point-blank. She didn't intend to neglect her household duties for all the offices in Tinkletown!

"But, consarn it, Eva!" Anderson protested for the hundredth time, "nobody's askin' you to neglect your household duties. Ain't I agreein' to handle the job for you?"

"Well, I posi-*tive*-ly refuse to wear a star—or carry a pistol."

"You don't have to. I'll wear the star."

"And if you think I'll traipse the streets of Tinkletown from morning till night, you're very much—"

"That ain't any respectable woman's job," said her husband stiffly. "You're not expected to do it as long as you got a deputy."

"And as for snooping around putting my nose into other people's business,—why—"

"Now, don't let that worry you, Eva. That's part o' my job."

"Who's going to tend jail when there's anybody locked up in it?"

"I am, o' course."

"And who's going to be street commissioner, truant officer, chief of the fire depart—"

"You are, Eva,—but I'm going to look after *everything*,

mind you. All you got to do is to see that I git somethin' to eat whenever I need it, an' a bed to sleep in at night, an' I'll—"

"A bed to sleep in, you ninny!" she cried. "You're going to sleep in the same bed you've been sleeping in for forty years. What are you talking about? Ain't you going to sleep with me if I appoint you deputy marshal?"

"Certainly," Anderson made haste to assure her. "Unofficially, o' course," he went on, with profound regard for the ethics involved.

"Well, I'll think it over," she said wearily. "Don't bother me now, you two; can't you see I'm making apple butter?"

"I hope you will consent to run, Mrs. Crow," put in the wily Mr. Squires, "if only for the sake of showing Minnie Stitzenberg that it won't do her any good to be saying things about—well, about anybody in particular." He concluded very lamely.

"Has that woman been saying things about me?" demanded Mrs. Crow.

"I ought to have sense enough to keep my mouth shut," said Harry, scowling darkly. Catching the astonished look on Anderson's face, he hastily suggested that they "beat it."

Out in the front yard Anderson halted him. "Has Minnie been saying anything about my wife, Harry Squires?"

Harry first looked over his shoulder and then winked. "Not that I know of," he said, chuckling. "But I guess it's safe to go ahead and print the ticket with Mrs. Crow's name on it."

Never in all its sedentary existence had Tinkletown experienced a livelier campaign.

"If you vote for Minnie Stitzenberg, I'll never speak to you again," was the common argument of the Crowites, and

"Don't you ever try to look me in the face again if you vote for that old Mrs. Crow," was the slogan of the opposition.

Mrs. Crow conducted her own campaign.

Anderson discovered to his great dismay that his meals were not only irregular in the matter of time, but frequently did not materialize at all. His wife and daughters neglected him completely. On three separate occasions after waiting until nearly eight o'clock for his supper, he strolled disconsolately over to the equally abandoned home of Alf Reesling.

"I'm a mighty poor cook," confessed Alf on the first occasion, a hungry, harassed look in his eyes. "But anything's better'n starvin', ain't it?"

"It shore is," said Anderson with feeling.

"I ain't seen a petticoat around my house since half-past nine this mornin'," lamented Alf, upsetting a pan of milk while trying to get a plate of cold ham out of the icebox. "It's terrible."

"Lemme take your knife, Alf. I'll peel the pertatoes—if you'll tell me where they are."

"I don't know where anything is," said Alf, leaning dejectedly against the kitchen sink.

"Well," said Anderson, "let's look."

"If the election was a week further off, I'd give up an' go to drinkin' again," said Alf on another occasion. "I'd sooner drink myself to death than starve. Starvation is a terrible end, Anderson. Worse than hangin', they say."

"Only four days more," sighed Anderson, clipping off a hunk of bologna. "My wife says if I'll hold out till after election, she won't never leave the kitchen ag'in long as she lives."

"That's what mine says. Sherman was only half right. War may be hell for men, but, by gosh, women are hell for war. An' that's what it is—war, Anderson, war to the hilt. Every woman in town's got her knife out an', my God, how they're slashin' each other! There won't be a whole woman left."

"Well, I'd be satisfied with half a one," mused Anderson, a faraway look in his eyes.

The day before the election, Mrs. Crow played her trump card. She had treasured an open boast made years before by the disappointed old maid who now opposed her. Minnie, before attaining years of discretion and still smarting under the failures of youth, had spitefully announced that she was a spinster from choice. With great scorn she had stated, while sitting on Mrs. Crow's porch, that she would die an old maid a hundred times over sooner than marry any one in Tinkletown. And, she added, the best proof that she meant what she said was the fact that nearly every man in town had asked her to marry him before he asked any one else!

The news spread like wildfire the instant Mrs. Crow released it. Mrs. Crow's veracity was not a thing to be questioned.

When the returns were all in, Mrs. Crow was found to have received 573 votes (women included), out of a total of 601 cast. Miss Stitzenberg held the German vote solid, including seven from her own sex who could afford to disregard the slander because they had been safely married in Germany long before coming to Tinkletown.

The day after the new marshal's induction into office Anderson appeared with his star glittering so brightly that it dazzled the eye. His shoes were polished, his clothes brushed and—shocking to relate—his trousers creased. In all his career as marshal he had never gone to such extremes as this. He was, however, not in a happy frame of mind. His customary aplomb was missing.

"Well, of all the—" began Alf Reesling. Then, before Anderson could put in a word of warning, he shouted to the group in front of Lamson's store: "Hey! Look at the dude!"

Anderson, very red in the face, declined a seat on a soap box.

"If I'd knowed she was goin' to act like this, I'd a voted ag'in her myself," he said rather wanly. "She started in bossin' me the very minute she got my place as marshal. She's laid down the law to me, an', by crickety, she says if I'm goin' to be her deputy I've got to look like this every day. Look at them shoes! And these pants! No, I can't set down. I don't dare risk sp'ilin' the creases my daughter Susie put in 'em 'fore I was up this mornin'."

VICIOUS LUCIUS

Lucius Fry lived up back of the Power-house on the outskirts of Tinkletown. He had a wife, two children and a horse and buggy. For a great many years he had led a quiet, peaceful, even suppressed existence. Being a rather smallish, bony sort of man, with a large Adam's apple and bow legs, he was an object of considerable scorn not only to his acquaintances but to his wife and children, and after a fashion, to his horse.

The latter paid absolutely no attention to him when he said "Get-ap," or when he applied the "gad"; she neither obeyed the command nor resented the chastisement. She jogged along in her own sweet way quite as if he were nowhere in the vicinity. His wife abused him, and his children ignored him. No one, it would appear, had the slightest use or respect for Lucius Fry.

He was, by profession, a well-digger. The installation of a water-works system in Tinkletown had made him a well-digger in name only. For a matter of five or six years, barring the last six months, he had been in the employ of his wife. She took in washing, and it was his job to collect and deliver the "wash" three times a week. In return for this he received board and lodging and an occasional visit to the moving-picture theatre. One of his daughters clerked in the five-and-ten-cent store, and the other, aged twelve, was errand girl to Miss Angie Nixon, the fashionable dressmaker.

Lucius had married very much above him, so to speak. That is to say, his wife was something like nine or ten inches the taller of the two. When they appeared on the street together,— which was seldom,—you could see him only if you chanced to be on *that* side of her. Mrs. Fry was nearly six feet tall and very wide, but Lucius was not much over five feet two. He had a receding chin that tried to secrete itself behind a scant, dun-colored crop of whiskers, cultivated by him with two purposes in view; first, to provide shelter for his shrinking chin, and second, to avoid the arduous and unnecessary task of shaving.

Roughly speaking, Lucius was a shiftless creature. It had long been the consensus of opinion—freely expressed throughout Tinkletown—that he did not amount to a tinker's dam.

However that may be, some six or seven months prior to the incidents about to be related, Mr. Fry himself wrought a tremendous and unbelievable change in the foregoing opinion. Almost in the wink of an eyelash he passed through a process of transmogrification that not only bewildered him but caused the entire community to sit up and take notice of him.

It all came about in the oddest sort of way. For a number of years Lucius had been in the habit of currying the old grey mare on Saturday mornings. Away back in his mind lurked an hereditary respect for the Sabbath. He wanted old Peggy to be as clean as possible on Sunday—observing the same principle, no doubt, that induces a great many people to take a bath on Saturday night. Moreover, he changed the bedding in her stall on Saturdays, employing a pitchfork and a spade.

For a number of years Peggy had put up with these attentions, responding amiably to his directions—such as "Get over, dern ye," or "Whoa, back," "Stan' still, can't ye?" and so on.

One never-to-be-forgotten Saturday morning in the spring of the year, Peggy happened to be peevish. The cause of her peevishness was a swarm of intensely active flies. Mr. Fry was accustomed to an occasional swish of her tail across his face. He even welcomed it, for the flies bothered him almost as much as they did Peggy. On mornings when he felt unusually tired, he was rather grateful to Peggy for including him in the sweep of her tail.

But on this particular morning the exasperated nag planted one of her hoofs on Mr. Fry's toes while he was engaged in brushing out the kinks in her mane.

Mrs. Fry happened to be in the stable at the time, seeing if the hens had mislaid anything in the hay. She was astonished by the roar of a mighty oath, followed almost instantly by a thunderous thump on the barrel-like anatomy of the family horse. A second or two later Peggy's head came in for a resounding whack, and the stream of profanity increased to a torrent.

Springing to her feet, the surprised lady cast a startled glance over the manger into the stall. Her husband had old Peggy backed up against the partition and was preparing to deliver a third blow with the spade when she called out to him: "Stop it, you little fool!"

Mr. Fry's attention was diverted. Peggy was spared the impending blow. Instead, the outraged hostler charged around the partition, through a narrow passage and into the presence of his wife. He hobbled painfully. Inarticulate sounds issued from his compressed lips. He gripped the spade-handle so tightly that cords stood out on his rather formidable forearms.

Mrs. Fry got as far as "You ugly little—" and then, as he bore down upon her, turned to flee. He altered his course, and as she passed him on the way to the open door, the flat of the spade landed with impelling force upon the broadest part of her person. The sound was not so hollow as that which resulted from the wallop on Peggy's ribs, but its echo was a great deal more far-reaching. Indeed, Mrs. Fry's howl could have been heard a quarter of a mile away. She passed through the door into the barnyard on the wing, as it were.

Lucius blindly took another swing at her with the spade as she made her exit. Missing her by several feet, he spun completely around several times with the momentum; then, not to be deprived of the full measure of triumph, he hurled the implement after her retreating figure. Rage improved the accuracy as well as the force of his effort. The spade caught Mrs. Fry below the waistline and for nearly a month thereafter she was in the habit of repairing with female visitors to an upstairs bedroom where she proudly revealed to them the extensive welt produced by her husband's belated return to power.

Not completely satisfied, however, he set out in pursuit of her, principally on one foot, but with a swiftness that surprised both of them. Overtaking her near the barnyard gate, he pulled up suddenly, realizing the peril of being too precipitate. He was rushing into disaster. She was likely to turn and snatch the offensive away from him. But just as he was on the point of turning to run the other way, she flopped down on her knees and began begging him for God's sake to spare her! Her eyes were tightly closed, and her arms were raised to shield her face.

Seizing this fine opportunity, he edged around in front of her, took the most careful, deliberate aim, and forthwith planted his fist solidly upon her unprotected nose.

He had always wanted to do it, but never before had the opportunity presented itself. He couldn't remember when he had caught her with her eyes closed before. She invariably stayed awake longer than he did at night, telling him the same thing she had told him the night before, and in the morning she kicked him out of bed before his eyes were open. Now here was the golden, long-desired chance. It might never occur again. So he swung with all his might and main.

Mrs. Fry involuntarily arose from her knees, balanced on her heels for a second or two and then sat down some distance away with the same heels in the air.

Then and there Lucius Fry ceased to be a person of no consequence.

Two or three neighbours, bent on rescuing Mrs. Fry, got no nearer than the barn-lot fence. Lucius, still hopping around on one foot, gathered up a stick of stove-wood in each hand, and let fly at them with such determination and precision that they decided to let him go ahead and murder her.

When Mrs. Fry's daughters hurried into the house a short time afterward, they found their mother dressing and bandaging Mr. Fry's foot and chokingly inquiring if she was hurting him. Between sentences she applied a wet towel to a prodigious, unrecognizable object that had once been her nose.

Juliet, the elder, planted herself in front of her father and passionately inquired if it was true that he had dared to strike her mother.

Lucius, with rare forethought, had provided himself with a stick of stove-wood before entering the house. He now held it in his right hand. He was not going to take any chances on his wife's treachery. He was ready for the slightest sign of an uprising. Without answering his daughter's question, he took a firm grip on the stick and started to arise from his chair, upsetting the pail of water that his wife had been using. Mrs. Fry screeched.

"Don't hit her! Don't kill her, Lucius! For God's— — "

"Shut up!" snarled Lucius. "I'm goin' to belt the life out of her if she comes around here disturbin' the peace. I'm peaceable now, Stella—we've got perfect peace now, ain't we? But if she tries to—Well, you'll see what'll happen, young lady. Go an' get a mop and clean up that water. D'ye hear me? Beat it!"

"For the Lord's sake, Juliet, do what he tells you," begged Mrs. Fry.

"An' do it *quick*," said Mr. Fry.

Having so suddenly—and unintentionally—gained the upper hand in his household, he was determined if possible to retain it. Temporarily at least he had his wife scared almost to death and so submissive that he couldn't think of half enough indignities to heap upon her, no matter how hard he tried; and his disdainful daughters spoke in hushed voices, and got up every morning to start the kitchen fire, and carried in the wood, and waited on him first at meals, and allowed him to read *The Banner* before any one else claimed it, and fed the chickens, and behaved as daughters ought to behave. It was too good to be true. But as long as it really appeared to be true, he couldn't afford to relax for an instant; he went about with a perpetual scowl and swore from morning till night.

Every other week he went out to the stable, and after closing the doors, proceeded to belabour an old saddle with a pitchfork handle. The sounds reaching the back porch of the house caused Mrs. Fry to cover her ears and moan: "Poor old Peggy! O-oh! My gracious! He'll—he'll kill her!"

Occasionally he threw a stove-lid or a hatchet or something else at his wife, but his aim was singularly bad, for try as he would, he did not appear to come closer than five or six feet to her with any of the missiles. Once in a while he displayed the most appalling desire to destroy everything in sight. On such occasions he smashed chairs, broke up the crockery or tramped all over the garments that Mrs. Fry had just hung out to dry. By mistake, he once picked up a hot stove-lid, and then he swore in earnest. His dutiful wife wrapped his hand up in soda and called the stove-lid a "nasty old thing!"

In a very short time everybody in Tinkletown was talking about Lucius Fry. Some one, lying with a little more enterprise than the rest, started the report that he had gone to Boggs City, the county seat, and had thrashed a bartender who refused to sell him a drink. This report grew until Lucius was credited with having polished off a whole bar-room full of men without so much as sustaining a scratch himself.

When Lucius appeared on Main Street, men who had never noticed him before went out of their way to be polite and friendly. Women who pitied Mrs. Fry looked at him with interest and called him, under their breath, a "big ugly brute." Children stopped playing and ran when they saw Lucius Fry approaching.

Harry Squires, editor of *The Banner*, in reporting one of Mr. Fry's most violent eruptions, alluded to him as "vicious Lucius." The name clung to the little man. It was some time before the general public could utter it with confidence. Haste was not conducive to accuracy. Rash assuredness frequently turned Mr. Fry into "Vooshious Lishius" or "Lishius Vooshious" or even "V'looshious Ooshious."

Mrs. Fry, in course of time, grew to be very proud of her master, the despot of Power-house Gully. She revealed her pride every time she fell in with acquaintances on the way to church. In reply to an oft-repeated question as to why Mr. Fry did not go to church with her any longer, she invariably gave the supercilious reply that nowadays when she requested her husband to go to church, he told her to go to hell instead—and that was the kind of a man she respected, she said, not one of your weak-kneed, henpecked cowards who go to church because they are more afraid of their wives than they are of the devil. And while the mountainous Mrs. Fry was no longer able to thrash her five-foot-two husband, she still inspired fear among churchgoers of both sexes and all ages. She frequently asserted that she could lick any man in Tinkletown except her husband— and moreover, if any officer of the law ever attempted to arrest Lucius for what he did to her, she'd beat his head off—that's what she'd do.

The marshal of Tinkletown, Anderson Crow, on three separate occasions organized a posse to go out to Power-house Gully to arrest Lucius on the complaint of neighbours who said they couldn't stand hearing his wife's howls any longer. On each of these occasions, the marshal got as far as the Fry front gate, backed by eight or ten of the huskiest men in town. There they were intercepted by Mrs. Fry, who told them that Lucius was upstairs peaceably reloading his double-barreled shotgun, or oiling up his trusty old horse-pistol, as the case may have been, and she didn't believe he would like to be disturbed.

"Is he ca'am an' quiet, Stella?" Marshal Crow would ask.

"As quiet as a lamb," Mrs. Fry would reply.

"Then I guess we'd better leave him alone," the Marshal

would say, adding: "But if he ever goes on the rampage again, just you send for me, Stella, an' I'll come as quick as I can."

And the wife of Vicious Lucius would say: "Don't forget to bring the undertaker with you when you come, Anderson. You won't need a doctor."

At times Lucius would feel his courage slipping. At such times he would go out to the barn and jostle old Peggy around in the stall, hoping against hope, but without the desired result. She simply *wouldn't* step on his foot.

One bitter cold night just before Christmas, a group of Tinkletown's foremost citizens sat around the big sheet-iron stove in Lamson's store. Outside, the wind was blowing a gale; it howled and shrieked around the corners of the building, banged forgotten window-shutters, slammed suspended signboards with relentless fury, and afforded unlimited food for reflection, reminiscence and prophecy. It was long past Mr. Lamson's customary hour for closing the store, but with rare tact the loungers permitted him to do most of the talking. It was nice and warm in the vicinity of the stove, and there were tubs of dried apples and prunes and a sack of hazel nuts within easy reach.

"I'll never forget the Christmas I spent out in Nebraska," Mr. Lamson was saying. He was probably the most travelled man in town. Every time he told a story, he went a little farther West. (Harry Squires disconcerted him on one occasion by asking in his most ironic manner if he didn't think it would be a good idea to settle in California when he got there, and Mr. Lamson, after thinking it over, stopped his subscription to *The Banner*.) "Yes sir; that was a terrible winter. I don't know as I ever told you about it, but we had to drive twenty-six miles in sleighs to get a tree on Christmas Eve. I mean a Christmas tree.

The thermometer registered twenty-six below zero and—"

He was interrupted by the opening of the door. An icy draft swept down the length of the store.

"Shut that door!" roared out Marshal Crow.

But the door remained open. Whereupon every one craned his neck to see who was responsible. There was no one in sight.

"That's funny," said Newt Spratt. "I shut it tight when I came in awhile ago."

"Well, go and shut it again," ordered Mr. Crow. "Do you want us to freeze our ears right here in sight o' Jim Lamson's stove?"

Newt got up and kicked the door shut, saw that it was latched, and returned to his place near the stove. Marshal Crow, during his absence, had bettered his position. He had exchanged a seat on a box of soap for the cane-bottom chair Newt had been occupying.

"As I was sayin'," resumed Mr. Lamson, "the thermometer registered—"

Again the door flew open, banging against a barrel of sugar. With one accord the assembled group arose and peered at the open door.

"Well, now, that *is* funny," said Newt. "I latched her sure that time."

"Acts like ghosts," said Elmer K. Pratt, the photographer.

"If I was a drinking man," said Alf Reesling, the town drunkard, "I'd think I had 'em."

Marshal Crow stalked to the door, pulling his coat-collar up about his throat as he encountered the furious blast of the wind.

At the top of the steps leading up to the porch stood a small figure wrapped in a shawl. The light from within shone full upon the figure. It was that of a young girl, and she was looking intently up the street.

"Well, of all the—Say, don't you know it's after nine o'clock?" exclaimed the old Marshal. "What's a young girl like you doin' out this time o' night?"

"Is—is that you, Mr. Crow?" quaked the girl without turning her head.

"It is. What's that got to do with it?"

"I—You don't see him anywheres up the street, do you?"

"Come inside if you want to talk to me. I ain't goin' to stand here in this door an' freeze to death. Come in here, I say."

"I dassent. Maybe he follered me."

"Maybe who follered you?"

"Him."

By this time several other customers had joined the Marshal.

"Why, it's Lucius Fry's girl Elfaretta," said Elmer K. Pratt. "What's the matter, Elfie?"

"You're sure he ain't follerin' me? Look hard," said the girl.

They all looked hard.

"I don't see anybody, Elfie," said Anderson Crow.

"It's a little early for Santa Claus," said Harry Squires, turning back to the stove, his eye on the only rocking-chair in the place. "Come inside and tell us all about it."

The girl entered the store, and some one closed the door. She was shivering, and not altogether from the cold. Her glance darted hither and thither, as if in quest of a more enduring protection than that exemplified by the man-power surrounding her.

"Roll that barrel of sugar over against the door," she ordered quickly. "I wouldn't have him catch me here for anything."

"You needn't be skeered," said the Marshal. "Ain't we here? Let's see: there's one, two—eight of us. I guess—"

"He'd clean this bunch up as easy as rolling off a log," said Elfaretta, edging toward the fire, but all the while casting uneasy apprehensive glances over her shoulder.

Newt Spratt and Situate M. Jones jointly took it upon themselves to roll the barrel of sugar up against the door.

"Are you referring to your estimable dad?" inquired Mr. Squires from the rocking-chair.

"Yes, I am," said Elfaretta somewhat defiantly.

"Is he a little more vicious than usual tonight?" asked the reporter.

"He never was worse," said the girl. "He's just simply awful. I had to come out to see if I couldn't get Mr. Crow to come up to the house an'—an' settle him. He seen me just as I was going out the door, and took after me. Out by the front gate he slipped on the ice and set down like a ton of bricks. Oh, I never heard such cussing. You got to come up to the house right away, Mr. Crow. He's just terrible. He—"

"Hold on a minute," interrupted the Marshal. "Go slow, now, an' answer my questions. Is he—"

"He's throwing things around something awful. Ma's in the pantry with the door locked, and Juliet's hiding up in the—"

"I know all that," broke in Mr. Crow sharply. "You needn't tell me about that. What I want to know is, is he or is he not in his own house, under his own roof?"

"He is, unless he's still setting out there in the front yard —or follerin' after me," she concluded with a terrified look at the barricaded door. "Do you think that barrel's heavy enough to stop him?"

"Well, if he's inside his own house, I can't touch him without a warrant. You'll have to go an' swear out a search-warrant for him, Elfarettie. It's against the law for me to arrest —"

"But ain't it against the law for him to be trying to murder Ma and Juliet and me?"

"There ain't no use arguing about it. I can't go an' get him without a warrant."

"You won't have to go in," said she confidently. "All you got to do is to let him know you're outside—anywheres—looking for him, and he'll come out; and he'll come without a warrant—you can bet your life on that, Mr. Crow. He says he's getting awful sick of having nothing to lick but women. He—"

"Did he say that?" demanded Marshal Crow, frowning and pulling at his whiskers.

"He put in some extra words, but I can't say 'em," said Elfaretta.

"I've a notion to—to—" began the Marshal in a somewhat bellicose manner, and then sadly shook his head. "No, it wouldn't be legal. I'm an officer of the law. But let me tell you one thing, Elfaretta Fry, if I *wasn't* an officer of the law, I'd take your dad by the back of the neck and shake him till his shoes flew off."

"We're getting away from the main issue," broke in Mr. Squires, the gadfly. "The point is, Anderson, are you going to let

Vicious Lucius beat his family to death, or are you going up to the Gully and arrest him?"

The Marshal looked at Harry reproachfully. "You know I ain't empowered by law to enter a man's house without a warrant, Harry Squires."

"But the girl says you won't have to. She says her father will be only too glad to step outside."

"How do I know she's telling the truth about all this rumpus? She ain't under oath, is she? Well, there's got to be an affidavit, properly sworn to, before I do anything. It's the law, an' you know it. She may be lyin' like all get-out."

The girl flared up. "I'm going to tell Pa you called me a liar. He'll bust your jaw if—"

"I didn't *call* you a liar," snapped Anderson. "I only said *maybe* you're lyin'. I leave it to anybody here if I said you was a liar; an' besides, your pa ain't man enough to bust my jaw anyhow. You go home an' tell him I said—"

"Let's get the facts about this present embroglio, Anderson, before we make arrangements for another," put in Mr. Squires.

"I've no objection to that," said Anderson, a note of relief in his voice. "She can't swear out a warrant till tomorrow morning anyhow, so there's no particular hurry."

"But he's killin' Ma tonight!" burst in the girl.

"Keep cool now, my girl; don't get excited," cautioned the Marshal. "What was he plannin' to kill her with? A gun?"

"No, sir. He had a hammer in one hand and a flatiron in the other, the last I saw of him."

"Well, go on—tell us all about it."

"It was awful sudden. We were all setting around the

kitchen stove, and Pa was cracking hickory-nuts, just as nice and peaceful as anything. He was joking with Ma and telling her he couldn't help it if the women up our way were going plumb crazy over him—specially that Mrs. Banks, whose husband works at the tanyard. Every time Pa goes out in the back yard, she comes and leans on her fence and talks to him, making eyes and grinning like a cat. She's worse than Mrs. Elam Crippen and Mrs. Ducker—and Ma's been noticing it too. She's worried about Pa.

"Up to three months ago there wasn't a woman in town that'd look at him, and now they can't seem to look at anybody else. Mrs. Banks came out in her back yard yesterday and gave Pa a good pair of overshoes and a fur cap that belonged to her husband. Pa didn't want to take 'em, but she said she didn't care if Mr. Banks *did* get mad; he wasn't much of a man anyhow and she wouldn't take any back talk off'n him. Juliet heard Mrs. Crippen say to Pa the other day that if he'd give her one of his photographs, she'd be the happiest mortal alive. And Mrs. Ducker calls to see Ma nearly every washday now, just when she's busiest, and so Pa has to sit and entertain her.

"Yesterday a couple of women that Ma don't even know stopped out in front of the house and giggled at everything Pa said, and one of 'em said: 'Oh, you naughty man!' When Pa came into the house, Ma asked him what he was saying to those strange women that made 'em call him a naughty man, and Pa looked awful worried and wouldn't tell her. He said it wasn't his fault if women acted like fools. He's all swelled-up, Pa is. Wears his best clothes every day and has taken to smoking cigarettes instead of a pipe when he's outside the house. Ma was counting up the other day just to see how much the cigarettes cost her, and

—But that wasn't what I started to tell you. I—"

"I seen him walkin' down Cutler Street day before yesterday with a woman," said Alf Reesling. "Fat sort of a woman with a pink hat on."

"That's Mrs. Banks. She—"

"Never mind about Mrs. Banks," interrupted the Marshal. "Confine yourself to the evidence in this case, an' nothing else."

"Well, as I was saying, Pa was peaceful and quiet, cracking nuts on the flatiron. He got hold of a tough hickor'-nut, and it wouldn't crack very easy. So he had to hit it as hard as he could. Somehow he missed it, and smack went the hammer right on his thumb. My goodness! You'd ought to have heard him yell. He hopped up and began dancing around the kitchen, sucking his thumb and trying to swear with his mouth full. Ma says,—this is all she said,—Ma says: 'Did you hit your finger, Lucius?' Pa let fly the hammer. It didn't miss her head a foot. Then he fired the flatiron at her feet. Ma screamed and started to run to'ards the back stairs. Pa knocked over the kitchen table trying to head her off. She stumbled and fell down on her hands and knees. Then while he was looking for something to beat her brains out with, she got up and run into the pantry and locked the door.

"Juliet was squealing her head off. Pa picked up the hammer and started to'ard her. Juliet made a break for the stairs, and Pa let go with the hammer. He missed her, but he knocked a big hole in the ceiling. Then he grabbed the tea-kettle off the stove and threw it at the cat. He got some of the boiling water on his legs, I guess, because he grabbed 'em in his hands and yelled like an Indian. He swore he'd kill everybody in the house. So I beat it. He was hunting for the flatiron and the hammer, and I was outside before he noticed me. I grabbed this old red tablecloth as I went out and put it around me. When I saw a light in your store, Mr. Lamson, I knowed Mr. Crow would be here, so up I came. Now, what are you going to do about it, Mr. Crow?"

The Marshal pondered. "You say your Ma's safely locked in the pantry?"

"She was—unless he busted the door down."

"And Julie is up in the attic?"

"Yes, and she's probably dead by this time. There ain't any lock on the attic door."

"Well, seems to me they're perfectly safe till morning. Julie could jump out of the attic window if the worst come to the worst. The thing that's worryin' me is you. Where are you going to sleep tonight, Elfie?"

"Right here in Mr. Lamson's rocking-chair," said the girl promptly.

"I'll take her up to my house," said Alf Reesling. "She can crawl in with my daughter Queenie."

"That's out of the question," said Harry Squires, arising and looking around for his overcoat. "We will need you, Alf. The Marshal is going to organize a posse and go up to Power-house Gully and capture Vicious Lucius dead or alive, before he's half an hour older."

"What's that?" demanded the Marshal, startled.

"You heard what I said. Get into your overcoats and goloshes, gentlemen. The Marshal instructs me to say that we will be leaving here in five minutes."

"Well, I'll be dog-goned!" oozed from Marshal Crow's lips. He was staring quite hopelessly at Harry Squires.

"Isn't that a fact, Mr. Crow?" inquired Harry, fixing him with a most disconcerting look.

Anderson indulged in a short fit of coughing. "Yes," he said, after recovering himself, "it *is* a fact, but I'd like to know how you got onto it."

"I am a mental telegrapher, Mr. Crow," said the reporter, carefully placing a hat upon Mr. Reesling's head. "There's your hat, Alf. Now be sure and pick out a good coat."

The Marshal's posse eventually resolved itself into a party of two—Anderson Crow and Harry Squires. Elmer K. Pratt remembered that his youngest child had the croup, and he couldn't leave her; Situate M. Jones complained of a sudden and violent attack of lumbago; Newt Spratt loudly demanded the flaxseed his wife had asked him to bring home so that she could make a poultice for a terrible toothache she was enjoying that evening; Alf Reesling refused to desert poor little Elfie; and two other gentlemen succeeded in sneaking out the back way while the Marshal's view was obstructed by the aforesaid slackers. Storekeeper Lamson had a perfectly sound excuse. He was a pacifist. However, he was willing to lend his revolver to the Marshal and a pair of brass "knucks" to Harry Squires.

Approaching Power-house Gully, the two adventurers observed shadowy forms moving about in the darkness at the foot of the slope. They paused.

"Mostly women, I should say," remarked the Marshal.

"Probably hoping that Lucius is a widower by this time," said the reporter.

"So's they c'n send flowers an' victuals to him all the time he's in jail," said Anderson. "S'pose you go down an' talk to 'em,

Harry, while I sneak around the back way and reconnoitre."

"That's a good idea," said Harry. "I'll just rush in through the front door, and he'll make a break to escape by the rear, so you'll be right there to head him off."

"Come to think of it," said Anderson hastily, "maybe we'd better see if he's out in the front yard first. Come on."

Eight or ten people were congregated in front of the Fry house, conversing in a hushed, excited manner. The Marshal and his companion bore down upon them. As the former had remarked, they were "mostly" women. There was but one man in the group. He turned out to be no other than Vicious Lucius himself.

"What's this I hear about you, Lucius Fry?" demanded Anderson Crow.

"Don't you dare arrest Mr. Fry, Anderson Crow," cried one of the ladies. "He ain't done anything but give her what she deserves, and— —"

"Can I speak to you private, Mr. Crow?" interrupted Vicious Lucius in a hurried manner. He was wearing an overcoat that came down to his heels, and a derby hat that rested rather firmly upon his ears.

Anderson stared at him in horror.

"Good gosh, Lucius, have you—have you had your hands cut off?" he gasped, looking hard at the flapping coat-sleeves.

"Course I ain't," said Mr. Fry, lifting his arms on high, allowing the sleeves to slip down a half a foot or more and revealing his hands. "This ain't my coat. It's Jim Banks'. A little too big fer me—and the hat too, I reckon."

"I just couldn't let him catch his death o' cold," explained the buxom Mrs. Banks.

"He just simply won't go back into the house," said Mrs. Ducker. "And I don't blame him, either. He's afraid he might throw her out of a window and—and break her neck, didn't you say, Lucius?"

"No, I didn't. I said I was afraid I'd break the winder," said Lucius, glaring at Mrs. Ducker from beneath the rim of Mr. Banks' hat.

"Where is your wife?" demanded Anderson.

"In there," said Lucius, pointing a drooping coat-sleeve in the general direction of his domicile. "Come on over here by the lamp-post, Mr. Crow. I got something important I want to say to you."

"You ain't going to give yourself up without a fight, are you, Lucius?" cried Mrs. Banks in considerable agitation.

"You leave me alone," snarled Lucius in a manner so malevolent that Mrs. Banks cried out delightedly:

"Oh, ain't he just grand? Did you hear the way he spoke to me, Emma Ducker? Goodness, what would I give if I had a man that could talk to me like—"

"You ought to heard what he said to me when I asked him to come over to our house and—" began Mrs. Ducker somewhat acrimoniously.

"Oh, cut it out—cut it out!" rasped Lucius. "Beat it! Go home, all of you! Gosh a'mighty, can't a feller lick his own wife without—Here! Leggo my arm! What in thunder are you tryin' to do, Lou Banks?"

"I'm going to take you over to my house and put your feet in a hot mustard bath, and—"

"No, you ain't! Leggo, I say! Fer the Lord's sake, Officer, chase 'em away!"

"Move on, now—move on, all of you," commanded the Marshal, waving the revolver in lieu of his well-known nightstick. "What you got to say to me, Lucius?" he asked as the women fell back.

"Do you think they c'n hear?"

"Not unless you whisper loudern' that."

"Well, say, I want you to do me a favour. I want you to take me up to the jail an' lock me in."

"You—you want to be locked in?"

"I don't care whether you put it that way er to lock all these fool women out. It's all the same to me. I ain't had a minute's peace for nearly two months. I—"

"Why don't you go in your own house an' stay there?" demanded Anderson.

"That don't seem to help any. They come to call on me so often you'd think I was a preacher or a doctor. An' what's more, my wife's beginnin' to get her dander up. I c'n see what's comin'. If she ever—gee, it will be awful!"

"Then you hain't murdered her yet? I understood you had."

Vicious Lucius looked over his shoulder and drew closer to the Marshal.

"This here strain is gittin' to be too much fer me, Mr. Crow. I can't keep it up much longer. I'm breakin' down. I been thinkin' it over, an' I can't see any way out of it except to go to jail fer a month er two."

"What's the charge?" inquired Marshal Crow.

"There won't be any. I'll do it fer nothing. It won't cost you a cent to arrest me."

"That ain't what I mean. What I mean is what offence have you committed? What law have you broke?"

"Well, it's purty hard to say."

"What charge will your wife make ag'inst you? Somebody has to make one, you know."

"That's just it. She won't make any charge against me— positively not. So I've got to do it myself. You've had a lot of experience. What fer sort of a charge would you say I ought to bring?"

"Against yourself? It ain't regular, Lucius."

"How about insanity? Wouldn't that be a safe sort of complaint? I been actin' mighty queer lately."

"I should say you had. Ain't you goin' to resist arrest?"

"No, I'm askin' fer it. If you don't want to be seen walkin' through the streets with me, I'll go on ahead an' wait fer you at the jail."

"Well, this certainly beats all! I thought sure you'd put up an awful fight, Lucius."

"I want to be locked up so's I won't commit murder," Lucius explained eagerly.

"Good gracious! You come along with me, Lucius Fry. You got to be put under lock an' key 'fore this night is over. I can't take no chances on your murderin' that pore defenceless wife of your'n. You come—"

"I ain't thinkin' of murderin' my wife," protested Lucius, holding back. "What I'm scared of is I'll murder one or two of these pesky women—that Banks woman, fer instance. It's gittin' so I can't stick my nose outside the door 'thout her droppin' everything an' runnin' out to gab with me. I don't get a minute's privacy. If it ain't one, it's another. You'd think I was Napoleon

Boneparte, the way them women act. I don't know what's come over 'em."

"Why, it's just 'cause they think you can lick any man in town. That's the way with some women. The more brutal a man is to his own wife, the more the other women seem to appreciate him. I must say, it takes a purty good man to lick that wife of your'n—she's twice as big as you are, and—"

"Why, gosh dern it, Mr. Crow, I couldn't lick Stella in a million years," whispered Lucius fiercely.

"What's that? You—you say you can't lick your wife?"

"*I should say not!*" exclaimed Mr. Fry, raising his voice in earnestness. Instantly he lowered it, standing on his tip-toes the better to impart the following information to the amazed Marshal: "She can lick me with both hands tied behind her back. Nobody knows it better'n I do. I just got to keep throwin' things at her an' cussin' an' smashin' furniture, an' all that, 'cause if she ever got an idea how scared I am of her, she'd pick me up by the seat of my pants an'—Oh, I tell you it's gettin' to be more'n I c'n stand, Mr. Crow. It's mighty hard to keep on thinkin' you got to keep on bein' brave when you're scared plumb to death all the time. Why, if Stella ever got onto the fact that I—"

"But you keep on beatin' her just the same, don't you?"

"I never beat her unless her back's turned. First I throw somethin' at her. That's the best way. But you never ought to throw anything unless you got somethin' ready in the other hand. *An' hang onto that until you're sure she's not goin' to run to'ards you 'stead of the other way.* If you're goin' to be a successful wife-beater, you got to use an awful lot of common-sense." He looked over his shoulder. "Come on up the street a little ways, Mr. Crow," he said nervously. "Them fool women are edgin' nearer all the time. Next thing you know, they'll be tryin' to sick me onto you, an'—an' I'd have to make good. They got all their husbands scared of me, an' they keep tellin' me that I'm the grandest little man in the world. You know Jim Banks? Well, he's twice as big as I am. A week or two ago he came out on his back porch an' called me a name. I started over to apologize to him, but he thought I was comin' *after*him, so he jumped back in the kitchen an' slammed the door. She told me he wanted to send fer you, Mr. Crow. I—I wish he had."

"I understand you been makin' threats about what you'd do to me if I ever tried to arrest you," said Anderson sternly. "Is that true?"

"No, it ain't. My wife's been makin' all the threats. She don't make any bones about what *she'll* do to you if you ever try to arrest me. She says she'll bust your head fer you."

Marshal Crow straightened up and glared at the Fry habitation. There was a light in the kitchen window.

"You wait here, Lucius Fry, an' don't move till I come back. I'm going in there an' talk to that wife o' yourn."

"You better take a gang o' men with you. Remember, I'm givin' you fair warnin'. She'll eat you alive."

"I'll take my friend Mr. Squires with me fer a witness— that's all. Is she out in the kitchen?"

"I don't know. I ain't been in the house since the row. She locked the door on me."

The Marshal strode away, leaving Vicious Lucius to the mercy of the women. Harry Squires was nowhere in sight. Mr. Crow looked about in some alarm. His speed noticeably decreased. Fumbling in his coat pocket, he found his police whistle and proceeded to blow a shrill blast upon it. A few moments passed, and then Harry came hurrying around the corner of the house.

"Where have you been, dern you?"

"I've been in the house chatting with Mrs. Fry," said the reporter.

"Is she conscious? Is she able to talk?"

"She certainly is. Come on. She wants to see you."

Harry Squires grasped his arm and led him toward the kitchen door. Mrs. Fry herself admitted them. She looked most formidable.

"Did my daughter Elfaretta ask you to come here and interfere with my private affairs, Anderson Crow?" she demanded.

"I am not supposed to answer questions like that, Mrs. Fry," said Anderson with dignity. "I am pleased to inform you, however, that I have succeeded in arrestin' your husband, an' I intend to see to it that he is locked up fer—"

"Oh, my goodness!" groaned the gigantic lady, dropping suddenly into a chair and lowering her face into her apron.

The Marshal looked at her in astonishment.

"You have got to release Vicious Lucius at once," said Harry Squires sternly. "We can't afford to wreck this poor little woman's life."

"Little—what's that you said?" stammered the Marshal, still gazing at the ponderous bulk in the chair.

"You heard what I said—wreck this poor but proud lady's life. Speak up, Mrs. Fry. Tell the good Marshal all about it."

Whereupon the woebegone Mrs. Fry lifted her head and her voice in lamentation.

"I knew it couldn't last. I might 'a' knowed something would turn up to spoil it. It was too much to expect. Oh, if you only wouldn't lock him up, Mr. Crow! What will people say when they find out you was able to arrest him single-handed, without a gang o' men to help you? Oh, oh, oh!"

Mr. Squires interposed a suggestion just as she was on the verge of sobs.

"I dare say we could stage a perfectly realistic struggle between Mr. Fry and Mr. Crow. Mr. Fry could trip Mr. Crow up —all in play, you know; and then I could rush in and grab Mr. Fry from behind while he was letting on as though he was kicking Mr. Crow in the face. The spectators would—"

"I won't be a party to any such monkey business!" exclaimed the Marshal in some heat. "What do you take me for? If I arrest Lucius Fry, I'll jest simply pick him up by the coat-collar and—"

"That's just it," cried Mrs. Fry. "He wouldn't fight back, and how would I feel if you carried him off to jail as if he was a lunch-basket? And I was beginning to feel so proud and happy. I was getting so I could look those cats in the face, all because my husband was the best little daredevil in the Gully. They used to pity me. Now they are so jealous of me they don't know what to do. They'd give anything if they had a husband like Lucius— little as he is. My, how they envy me, and how I have been looking down on all of 'em the last six months! And here you arrest him as easy as if he was a little girl, when I been telling everybody there wasn't anybody living that could take my man to jail. Oh, I—I wish I'd never been born!"

Anderson Crow was puzzled. He pulled at his whiskers

in the most helpless way, and stared wide-eyed.

"But—but ain't you afraid to live with him?" he mumbled. "Ain't you afraid he'll lick you to death sometime when he's in one of—"

"He couldn't lick me if I was chloroformed," blurted out Mrs. Fry, arising suddenly. She bared a huge right arm. "See that? Well, that's as big as his leg. Don't you ever get it in your head that I can't lick Lucius Fry. That ain't the point. I can do it, but I wouldn't do it for anything on earth. I want to be proud of him, and I want these other women to feel sorry for me because I've got a *man* for a husband, and not a rabbit. Where is he, Mr. Crow?"

"He's out there waitin' fer me to take him to jail—that is, he *said* he'd wait. Course, if you won't make any affidavit ag'inst him, I—I guess there's no sense in me lockin' him up. I was doin' it as a—er—as a sort of favour to him, anyhow. He seemed to be afraid he'd kill some of them women that hang around him."

"I just thought he'd act that way. I won't make any charge against him. I want him to stay just the way he is—a fine, upstanding brutal sort of feller. You go out there an' tell him to come in here. I want to go down on my knees again and forgive him."

The Marshal hesitated. He was between two fires. He couldn't very well oblige *both* of them. Lucius unquestionably was eager to go to jail for reasons of his own, and Mrs. Fry was just as eager that he should remain at large. The Marshal scratched his head.

"I feel kinder sorry fer him," he mused. "Like as not, one of them women will git so foolish over him that her husband will take it into his head to get a divorce, an'—" He paused in confusion.

"Go on—go on!" pleaded Mrs. Fry, her eyes sparkling.

"Well, from all Lucius says, he despises the whole lot of 'em. Still, that ain't goin' to help *him* any if Jim Banks er one of them other idiots gits all het up an' jealous an' goes and sues fer a divorce, namin' Lucius Fry as—"

Mrs. Fry slapped him violently on the back.

"That's just what I want!" she cried eagerly. "I'd be the proudest woman in Tinkletown."

The Marshal stared. Harry Squires covered his mouth with his hand.

"Well, of all the gosh—"

His ejaculation was cut short by the opening of the kitchen door. Lucius stood outlined in the aperture. He was clapping his arms about his body, and his teeth were chattering. The voluminous sleeves flapped like great limp wings.

"Say," he whined, "I can't wait out there all night in this kinder weather. If I got to go to jail, I want to do it right away. It's cruelty to animals to leave me standin' out there with nothing on my feet but carpet-slippers. Come on an'—"

"Come in to the fire an' get warm, Lucius dear," called out his wife, as shrinking and as timid as a whipped child. "I forgive you. Julie! Jul-ie! Come down here an' help me get some hot coffee an' something to eat fer your Pa."

"I—I guess we'd better be goin', Harry," said Marshall Crow uncomfortably. "I got to disperse that crowd o' women out there in the street. Good night, Lucius. Night, Mrs. Fry. If you ever need me, all yer got to do is just send word."

Lucius followed him to the door, and would have gone

out into the night with him if the Marshal had not deliberately pushed him back.

"You—you ain't goin' to desert me, are you?" whispered Lucius fiercely.

The Marshal leaned over and whispered to Lucius.

"If all the other men in this here town had as soft a snap as you've got, Lucius Fry, they'd hate to die worse'n ever, because they'd know they'd never git back into heaven ag'in."

THE VEILED LADY AND THE SHADOW

A veiled lady is not, in ordinary circumstances, an object of concern to anybody. Circumstances, however, are sometimes so extraordinary that a veiled lady becomes an object of concern to everybody. If the old-time novelists are to be credited, an abundantly veiled lady is more than a source of interest; she is the vital, central figure in a mystery that continues from week to week, or month to month, as the case may be, until the last chapter is reached and she turns out to be the person you thought she was all the time.

Now, the village of Tinkletown is a slow-going, somnolent sort of place in which veils are worn by old ladies who wish to enjoy a pleasant snooze during the sermon without being caught in the act. That any one should wear a veil with the same regularity and the same purpose that she wears the dress which renders the remainder of her person invisible is a circumstance calculated to excite the curiosity of even the most indifferent observers in the village of Tinkletown.

So when the news travelled up and down Main Street, and off into the side-streets, and far out beyond Three Oaks Cemetery to the new division known as Oak Park, wherein reside four lonely pioneer families, that the lady who rented Mrs. Nixon's house for the month of September was in a "perpetual state of obscurity" (to quote Mr. Harry Squires, the *Banner* reporter), the residents of Tinkletown admitted that they didn't know what to make of it.

The Nixon cottage was a quaint, old-fashioned place on the side of Battle Hill, looking down upon the maples of Sickle

Street. The grounds were rather spacious, and the house stood well back from the street, establishing an aloofness that had never been noticed before. A low stone wall guarded the lawn and rose-garden, and there was an iron gate at the bottom of the slope. The front porch was partly screened by "Dutchman's Pipe" vines. With the advent of the tenant, smart Japanese sun-curtains made their appearance, and from that day on no prying eye, no matter how well-trained it may have been, could accomplish anything like a satisfactory visit to the regions beyond.

Mrs. Nixon usually rented her house for the summer months. The summer of 1918 had proved an unprofitable season for her. It was war-time, and the people who lived in the cities proved unduly reluctant to venture far from their bases of supplies. Consequently Mrs. Nixon and her daughter Angie remained in occupancy, more heartsick than ever over the horrors of war. Just as they were about to give up hope, the unexpected happened. Joseph P. Singer, the real-estate agent, offices in the Lamson Block, appeared bright and early one morning to inquire if the cottage could be had for the month of September and part of October.

"You may ask any price you like, Abbie," he said. "The letter I received this morning was written on the paper of the Plaza Hotel in New York. Anybody who can afford to put up at the Plaza, which is right on Central Park,—and also on Fifth Avenue,—ain't going to haggle about prices. The party wants a bathroom with hot and cold water and electric lights. Well, you've got all these improvements, and—"

"I've got to have references," said Mrs. Nixon firmly.

"I guess if the Plaza is willing to rent a room to a party,

there oughtn't to be any question as to the respectability of the said party," said Mr. Singer. "They're mighty particular in them New York hotels."

"Well, you write and tell the party—"

"I am requested to telegraph, Abbie," said he. "The party wants to know right away."

As the result of this conversation and a subsequent exchange of telegrams, the "party" arrived in Tinkletown on the first day of September. Mr. Singer's contentions were justified by the manner in which the new tenant descended upon the village. She came in a maroon-and-black limousine with a smart-looking chauffeur, a French maid, a French poodle and what all of the up-to-date ladies in Tinkletown unhesitatingly described as a French gown à la mode.

Miss Angie Nixon, who had never been nearer to Paris than Brattleboro, Vermont, said to her customers that from what she had seen of the new tenant's outfit, she was undoubtedly from the Tooleries. Miss Angie was the leading dressmaker of Tinkletown. If she had said the lady was from Somaliland, the statement would have gone unchallenged.

The same day, a man cook and a "hired girl" arrived from Boggs City, having come up by rail from New York.

The tenant was a tall, slender lady. There could be no division of opinion as to that. As to whether she was young, middle-aged or only well-preserved, no one was in a position to asseverate. As a matter of fact, observers would have been justified in wondering whether she was black or white. She was never abroad without the thick, voluminous veil, and her hands were never ungloved. Mrs. Nixon and Angie described her voice as refined and elegant, and she spoke English as well as anybody, not excepting Professor Rank of the high school.

By the end of her first week in the Nixon cottage, there wasn't a person in Tinkletown, exclusive of small babies, who had not advanced a theory concerning Mrs. Smith, the new tenant. On one point all agreed; she was the most "stuck-up" person ever seen in Tinkletown.

She resolutely avoided all contact with her neighbours. On several occasions, polite and cordial citizens had bowed and mumbled "Howdy-do" to her as she passed in the automobile, but there is no record of a single instance in which she paid the slightest heed to these civilities. All of her marketing was done by the man cook, and while he was able to speak English quite fluently when objecting to the quality, the quantity and the price of everything, he was singularly unable to carry on a conversation in that language when invited to do so by friendly clerks or proprietors.

As for the French chauffeur, his knowledge of English appeared to be limited to an explosive sort of profanity. Lum Gillespie declared on the third day after Mrs. Smith's car first came to his garage for live storage, that "that feller Francose" knew more English cuss-words than all the Irishmen in the world.

The veiled lady did a good many surprising things. In the first place, she had been in the Nixon cottage not more than an hour when she ordered the telephone taken out—not merely discontinued, but taken out. She gave no reason, and satisfied the telephone-company by making the local manager a present of ten dollars. She kept all of the green window-shutters open during the day, letting the sunshine into the rooms to give the carpets the first surprise they had had in years, and at night she sat out on the screened-in porch, with a reading-lamp, until an hour when many of the residents of Tinkletown were looking out of their windows to see what sort of a day it was going to be. She paid cash for everything, and always with bright, crisp banknotes, "fresh from the mint." She slept till noon. She went out every afternoon about four, rain or shine, for long motor-rides in the country. The queerest thing about her was that she never went near the "movies."

Nearly every afternoon, directly after luncheon—they called it dinner in Tinkletown—she appeared in the back yard and put her extraordinarily barbered dog through a raft of tricks. Passers-by always paused to watch the performance. She had him walking first on his hind legs, then on his front legs; then he was catching a tennis-ball which she tossed every which way (just as a woman would, said Alf Reesling); and when he wasn't catching the ball, he was turning somersaults, or waltzing to the tune she whistled, or playing dead. The poodle's name was Snooks.

The venerable town marshal, Anderson Crow, sat in front of Lamson's store one hot evening about a week after the advent of the mystery. He was the center of a thoughtful, speculative group of gentlemen representing the first families of Tinkletown. Among those present were: Alf Reesling, the town drunkard; Harry Squires, the reporter; Ed Higgins, the feed-store man; Justice of the Peace Robb; Elmer K. Pratt, the photographer; Situate M. Jones; and two or three others of less note. The shades of night had just descended; some of the gentlemen had already yawned three or four times.

"There ain't no law against wearin' a veil," said the

Marshal, reaching out just in time to pluck a nice red apple before Lamson's clerk could make up his mind to do what he had come out of the store expressly to do—that is, to carry inside for the night the bushel basket containing, among other things, a plainly printed placard informing the public that "No. 1 Winesaps" were "2 for 5c."

Crow inspected the apple critically for a moment, looking for a suitable place to begin; then, with his mouth full, he went on: "The only thing I got ag'inst her is that she's settin' a new style in Tinkletown. In the last two-three days I've seen more'n one of our fair sex lookin' at veils in the Five an' Ten Cent Store, and this afternoon I saw somebody I was sure was Sue Becker walkin' up Maple Street with her head wrapped up in something as green as grass. Couldn't see her face to save my soul, but I recognized her feet. My daughter Caroline was fixin' herself up before the lookin'-glass last night, seein' how she'd look in a veil, she said. It won't be long before we won't any of us be able to recognize our own wives an' daughters when we meet 'em on the street."

"My girl Queenie's got a new pink one," said Alf Reesling. "She made it out of some sort of stuff she wore over her graduatin' dress three years ago."

"Maybe she's got a bad complexion," ventured Mr. Jones.

"Who? My girl Queenie? Not on your—" began Alf, bristling.

"I mean the woman up at Mrs. Nixon's," explained Mr. Jones hastily.

Harry Squires had taken no part in the conversation up to this juncture. He had been ruminating. His inevitable—you might almost say, his indefatigable—pipe had gone out four or five times.

"Say, Anderson," he broke in abruptly, "has it ever occurred to you that there might be something back of it that ought to be investigated?" The flare of the match he was holding over the bowl of his pipe revealed an eager twinkle in his eyes.

"There you go, talkin' foolishness again," said Anderson. "I guess there ain't anything back of it 'cept a face, an' she's got a right to have a face, ain't she?"

"I mean the *reason* for wearing a veil that completely obscures her face—*all the time*. They say she never takes it off, even in the house."

"Who told you that?"

"Angie Nixon. She says she believes she sleeps in it."

"How does she deduce that?" demanded Anderson, idly fingering the badge of the New York Detective Association, which for obvious reasons,—it being a very hot night,—was attached to his suspenders.

"She deduced it through a keyhole," replied Mr. Squires. "Angie was up at the cottage last night to get something she had left in an upstairs hall closet. She just happened to stoop over to pick up something on the floor right in front of Mrs. Smith's door. The strangest thing occurred. She said it couldn't occur again in a thousand years, not even if she tried to do it. Her left ear happened to stop not more than half an inch from the keyhole. She just couldn't help hearing what Mrs. Smith said to her maid. Angie says she said, plain as anything: 'You couldn't blame me for sitting up all night, if you had to sleep in a thing like this.' She didn't hear anything more, because she hates eavesdropping. Besides, she thought she heard the maid walking toward the door. Now, what do you make of that, Mr.

Hawkshaw?"

"If you don't stop callin' me Hawkshaw, I'll—"

"I apologize. An acute case of lapsus lingua, Mr. Crow. But wasn't that remark significant?"

"I am a friend of Mrs. Nixon's, an' I must decline to criticize her beds," said Mr. Crow rather loftily. "I ain't ever slept in one of 'em, but I'd do it any time before I'd set up all night."

"Granting that the bed was all right, then isn't it pretty clear that she was referring to something else? The veil, for instance?"

"Sounds reasonable," said Newt Spratt, and then, after due reflection,—"mighty reasonable."

"I'd hate to sleep in a veil," said Alf Reesling. "It's bad enough to try to sleep with a mustard poultice on your jaw, like I did last winter when I had that bad toothache. Doc Ellis says he never pulled a bigger er a stubborner tooth in all his experience than—"

"I think you ought to investigate the Veiled Lady of Nixon Cottage," said Harry Squires, lowering his voice and glancing over his shoulder. "You can't tell what she's up to, Anderson. It wouldn't surprise me if she's a woman with a past. She may be using that veil as a disguise. What's more, there may be a price on her head. The country is full of these female spies, working tooth and nail for Germany. Suppose she should turn out to be that society woman the New York papers say the Secret Service men are chasing all over the country and can't find —the Baroness von Slipernitz."

"What fer kind of a dog is that you got, Ed?" inquired Mr. Crow, calmly ignoring the suggestion.

Mr. Higgins' new dog was enjoying a short nap in the middle of the sidewalk, after an apparently fatiguing effort to dislodge something in the neighbourhood of his left ear.

"Well," began Ed, eyeing the dog doubtfully, "all I know about him is that he's a black dog. My wife has been sizin' him up for a day or two, figgerin' on having him clipped here and there to see if he can't be made to look as respectable as that dog of Mrs. Smith. Hetty Adams has clipped that Newfoundland dog of hers. Changed him something terrible. When I come across them on the street today, I declare I only recognized half of him —an' I wouldn't have recognized that much if he hadn't wagged it at me. It beats all what women will do to keep up with the styles."

"I seen him today," said Mr. Spratt, "an' I never in all my life see a dog that looked so mortified. I says to Hetty, says I: 'In the name o' Heaven, Hetty,' says I, 'what you been doin' to Shep?' An' she says: 'I'd thank you, Newt Spratt, not to call my dog Shep. His name is Edgar.' So I says to Shep: 'Come here, Edgar—that's a good dog.' An' he never moved. Then I says: 'Hyah, Shep!' an' he almost jumped out of his hide, he was so happy to find somebody that knowed who he was. '*Edgar*, your granny!' says I to Hetty. 'What's the use of ruinin' a good dog by calling him Edgar?' An' Hetty says: 'Come here, Edgar! Come here, I say!' But Edgar, he never paid any attention to her. He just kep' on tryin' to lick my hand, an' so she hit him a clip with her parysol an' says: 'Edgar, must I speak to you again? Come here, I say! Behave like a gentleman!' 'There ain't no dog livin' that's goin' to behave like a gentleman if you call him names like that,' says I. 'It ain't human nature,' says I. An' just to prove it to her, I turned an' says to Shep: 'Ain't that so, Shep, old sport?'

An' what do you think that poor old dog done? He got right up on his hind legs and tried to kiss me."

"No wonder she wants to call him Edgar," said Harry Squires. "That's just the kind of thing an Edgar sort of dog would do."

"I was just going to say," said Mr. Crow, twisting his whiskers reflectively, "that maybe she does it because she's had smallpox, or been terribly scalded, or is cross-eyed, or something like that."

Mr. Squires inwardly rejoiced. He knew that the seed had been planted in the Marshal's fertile brain, that it would thrive in the night and sprout on the morrow. He saw delectable operations ahead; he was fond of the old man, but nothing afforded him greater entertainment than the futile but vainglorious efforts of Anderson Crow to achieve renown as a detective.

The reporter was a constant thorn in the side of Crow, who both loved and feared him. The *Banner* seldom appeared without some sarcastic advice to the Marshal of Tinkletown, but an adjoining column invariably contained something of a complimentary character, the one so adroitly offsetting the other that Mr. Crow never knew whether he was "afoot or horseback," to quote him in his perplexity.

Harry Squires had worked on a New York morning paper in his early days. His health failing him, he was compelled to abandon what might have become a really brilliant career as a journalist. Lean, sick and disheartened, he came to Bramble County to spend the winter with an old aunt, who lived among the pine-covered hills above the village of Tinkletown. That was twenty years ago. For nineteen years he had filled the high-sounding post of city editor on the *Banner*. He always maintained that the most excruciating thing he had ever written was the line at the top of the first column of the so-called editorial page, which said: "City Editor—Harry Sylvester Squires." Nothing, he claimed, could be more provocative of hilarity than that.

In his capacity as city editor, he wrote advertisements, personals, editorials, news-items, death-notices, locals and practically everything else in the paper except the poetry sent in by Miss Sue Becker. He even wrote the cable and telegraph matter, always ascribing it to a "Special Correspondent of the *Banner*." In addition to all this, he "made-up" the forms, corrected proof, wrote "heads," stood over the boy who ran the press and stood over him when he wasn't running the press, took all the blame and none of the credit for things that appeared in the paper, and once a week accepted currency to the amount of fifteen dollars as an honorarium.

Regarding himself as permanently buried in this out-of-the-way spot on the earth's surface, he had the grim humour to write his own "obituary" and publish it in the columns of the *Banner*. He began it by saying that he was going to tell the truth, the whole truth and nothing but the truth about the "deceased." He had written hundreds of obituaries during his career as city editor, he said, and not once before had he been at liberty to tell the truth. In view of the fact that he had no relations to stop their subscriptions to the paper, he felt that for once in his life he could take advantage of an opportunity to write exactly as he felt about the deceased.

He left out such phrases as "highly esteemed citizen," "nobility of character," "loss to the community," "soul of integrity" and other stock expressions. At the end he begged to inform his friends that flowers might be deposited at the *Banner* office or at his room in Mrs. Camp's boarding-house, as he was buried in both places. Buttonhole bouquets could be pinned upon him any day by simply stopping his customary funeral procession about town. Such attentions should always be accompanied by gentle words or exclamations of satisfaction, as for example: "How natural you look!" or "You owed me ten dollars, but I forgive you," or "It's a pity your friends allowed you to to be laid away in a suit of clothes like that," or "I don't believe half the things people said about you," or "It's a perfect shame you don't feel like resting in peace," or "Did you leave anything worth mentioning?" He also suggested that he would rest much easier in his grave if a slight increase in salary attended the obsequies.

From this it may be gathered that Harry Squires was a man who made the most out of a very ordinary situation.

Marshal Crow's suggestion met with instant response. "On the other hand, Anderson, the lady may be as beautiful as the fabulous houri and as devilish as Delilah. I don't want to take any steps in the matter without giving you your chance." He spoke darkly.

Mr. Crow pricked up his ears. "What do you mean by that?"

"As a newspaper man, I am determined to clear up the mystery of the Veiled Lady. If you persist in sitting around twiddling your thumbs and looking like a primeval goat, I shall send to New York and engage a detective to work on the case exclusively for the*Banner*. The *Banner* is enterprising. We intend

to give our subscribers the news, no matter what it costs. If you
—"

The Marshal swallowed the bait, hook and all. He arose from his chair and faced Mr. Squires. "I'll thank you, Harry Squires, to keep out of this. I didn't mean to say a word about it to you or anybody else until I had gone a little further with my investigations, but now I've got to let the cat out of the bag. I've been working day and night on her case ever since she came to town. Never mind, Newt—don't ask me. I'll announce the result of my investigations at the proper time an' not a minute sooner. Now I guess I'll be moseyin' along. It's gettin' purty late, an' I've got a lot of work to do before midnight."

He started down the steps. Harry Squires leaned back in his chair and scratched a match on the leg of his trousers. By the time he raised the lighted match to the bowl of his pipe, the smile had left his lips.

An uneventful week passed. The Veiled Lady made her daily excursions in the big high-powered car, pursued her now well-known domestic habits, retained her offensive aloofness, played games with the astounding Snooks, suffered no ill effects whatsoever from the inimical glares of the natives; and above all, she continued to set the fashions in Tinkletown.

Mr. Crow stalked the streets early and late. He lurked behind the corners of buildings; he peered sharply from the off-side of telephone poles as the big limousine swept haughtily by. He patrolled the Nixon neighbourhood by day and haunted it by night. On occasion he might have been observed in the act of scrutinizing the tracks of the automobile over recently sprinkled streets.

One evening, just after dusk,—after a sharp encounter with Harry Squires, who bluntly accused him of loafing on the job,—he sauntered past the Nixon cottage. His soul was full of bitterness. He was baffled. Harry Squires was right; he had accomplished nothing—and what was worse, he wasn't likely to accomplish anything. He sauntered back, casting furtive glances into the spacious front-yard, and concluded to ease his restless legs by leaning against a tree and crossing them in an attitude of profound nonchalance. The tree happened to be almost directly in front of the Nixon gate. Not to seem actually employed in shadowing the house, he decided to pose with his back to the premises, facing down the street, twisting his whiskers in a most pensive manner.

Suddenly a low, musical voice said:

"Good evening!"

Mr. Crow looked up into the thick foliage of the elm, then to the right and left, and finally in the direction of the cottage, out of the corner of his eye, after a sudden twist of the neck that caused him to wonder whether he had sprained it.

The Veiled Lady was standing at the gate. In the gathering darkness her figure seemed abnormally tall.

The Marshal hastily faced about and stared hard at the mystery.

"Evening," he said, somewhat uncertainly. Then he lifted his hat a couple of inches from his head and replaced it at an entirely new angle, pulling the rim down so far over the left eye that the right eye alone was visible. This shift of the hat instantly transformed him into a figure of speech; he became as "cunning as a fox." People in Tinkletown had come to recognize this as an unfailing symptom of shrewdness on his part. He always wore his hat like that when he was deep in the process of "ferreting something out."

"Have I the honour of addressing Mr. Anderson Crow?" inquired the lady.

"You have," said he succinctly.

"Field Marshal Crow?"

"Ma'am?"

"Or is it Town Marshal? I am quite ignorant about titles."

"That's the name I go by, ma'am."

"Your name is very familiar to me. Are you in any way related to the great detective?"

This was unexpected tribute. The only thing he could think up to say was, "I'm him," and then, apologetically: "—unless some one's been usin' my name without authority."

"Are you actually the great Anderson Crow? Do you know, I have always thought of you as a fictitious character—like *Sherlock Holmes*. Are you really *real*? Do I look upon you in the flesh?"

Mr. Crow was momentarily overwhelmed.

"Oh, I—I guess I'm not much different from other men, ma'am. I'm not half as important as folks make me out to be."

"How nice and modest you are! That is the true sign of greatness, Mr. Crow. I might have known that you would be simple."

"Simple?" murmured Anderson, to whom the word had but one meaning. He thought of Willie Jones, the village idiot.

"'Simplicity, thou art a jewel,'" observed the Veiled Lady. "Will you pardon a somewhat leading question, Mr. Crow?"

"Lead on," said he, still a trifle uncertain of himself.

"Who is that man standing against the tree beside you? Is

he a friend of yours?"

"Who is—is my what?"

"Your companion. Now he has moved over behind the tree."

Anderson shot a startled look over his shoulder.

"There ain't any man behind the tree. I'm all alone."

"Are you trying to make sport of me, Mr. Crow?"

"I should say not. I been standin' here fer some time, an' I guess I'd know if anybody was—"

"Do you think I am blind?" demanded the lady quite sharply.

"Not if you c'n see a man behind this tree," said he, with conviction. "You got the best eyesight of anybody I ever come across—that's all I got to say."

"I see him very distinctly."

Anderson obligingly circled the tree.

"Do you see him now?" he inquired in an amused tone.

"Certainly. He walked around the tree just ahead of you."

"What the—" began Anderson angrily, but checked the words in time. "You are mistaken. There ain't no one here, 'cept me."

"Is he one of your subordinates?" queried the woman, leaning forward in the attitude of one peering intently.

"Must be a shadow you're seein', ma'am," he suggested, and suddenly was conscious of the queer sensation that some one *was* on the opposite side of the tree.

"That's it!" she exclaimed eagerly. "A shadow! Aren't you detectives always shadowing some one?"

"Yes, but we don't turn into shadows to do it, ma'am. We just—"

"There he is! Standing directly behind you. What object can you possibly have, Mr. Crow, in lying to me about—"

"Lying?" gasped Anderson, after a swift, apprehensive glance over his shoulder. "I'm tellin' you the gospel truth. Maybe that confounded veil's botherin' your eyesight. Take it off, an' you'll see there ain't no one—"

"Ah! What a remarkable leap! He must be possessed of wings."

Mr. Crow himself moved with such celerity that one might have described the movement as a leap. He was within a yard of her when he next spoke; his back was toward her, his eyes searching the darkness from which he had sprung.

"Good Lord! You—you'd think there *was* some one there by the way you talk."

"He leaped from behind that tree to this one over here. It must be thirty feet. How perfectly amazing!"

By this time the good Marshal was noticeably impressed. There was no denying the fact that his voice shook.

"*Now* who's lying?" he cried out.

She took no offence. Instead she pointed down the dark sidewalk. It seemed to him that her arm was six feet long. He was fascinated by it.

"Now he is climbing up the tree—just like a squirrel. Look!"

Anderson felt the cold perspiration starting out all over his body.

"I—I swear I can't see anybody at all," the Marshal croaked weakly.

"Run over to that tree and look up, Mr. Crow," she whispered in great agitation. "He is sitting on that big limb, looking at us—his eyes are like little balls of fire. Send him away, please."

Haltingly the Marshal edged his way toward the tree. Coming to its base, he peered upward. He saw nothing that resembled a human figure.

"Be careful!" called out the Veiled Lady. "He is about to swing down upon your head. Hurry! There! Didn't you feel that?"

Anderson Crow made a flying leap for safety. He had the uncanny feeling that his hair was slowly lifting the hat from his head.

"Feel—feel what?" he gasped.

"He swung down by his hands and kicked at you. I was sure his foot struck your head. Ah! There he goes again. See him? He is climbing over my wall—no, he is running along the top of it. Like the wind! And he—"

"Good heavens! Am I—am I goin' blind?" groaned Mr. Crow, his eyes bulging.

"Now he has disappeared behind the rosebushes down in the corner of the lot. He must be the same man I have seen—always about this time in the evening. If he isn't one of your men, Mr. Crow, who in Heaven's name is he?"

"You—you have seen him before?" murmured the Marshal, reaching up to make sure that his hat was still in place.

"Four or five times. Last night he climbed up and stood beside that big chimney up there—silhouetted against the sky. He looked very tall—much taller than any ordinary man. The night before, he was out here on the lawn, jumping from bush to bush, for all the world like a harlequin. Once he actually leaped from the ground up to the roof of the porch, as easily as you would spring—Where are you going, Mr. Crow?"

"I—I thought I saw him runnin' down the street just now," said Anderson Crow, quickening his pace after a parting glance over his shoulder at the tall lady in the gateway. "Maybe I can overtake him if I—if I—But I guess I'd better hurry. He seems to be runnin' mighty fast."

He was twenty feet away when she called after him, a note of warning in her voice:

"You are mistaken! He is following you—he is right at your heels, Mr. Crow."

This was quite enough for Anderson Crow. He broke into a run. As he clattered past the lower end of the garden wall, a low, horrifying chuckle fell upon his ears. It was not the laugh of a human being. He afterwards described it as the chortle of a hyena—hoarse and wild and full of ghoulish glee.

Alf Reesling's house was two blocks down the street. Mr. Reesling was getting a bit of fresh air in his front yard. The picket gate was open, probably to let in the air, and he was leaning upon one of the posts. His attention was attracted by the sound of approaching footsteps. Almost before he knew what had happened, they were receding. Anderson swept past; his chin up, his legs working like piston-rods.

The astonished Alf recognized his friend and adviser.

"Hey!" he shouted.

It was a physical impossibility for Anderson to slacken his speed. At the same time, it was equally impossible for him to increase it. Alf, scenting excitement, set out at top speed behind him, shouting all the time.

Pursued and pursuer held their relative positions until

they rounded into Main Street. Reaching the zone of light—and safety—produced by show-windows and open doors, the Marshal put on the brakes and ventured a glance over his shoulder. Alf, lacking the incentive that spurred Anderson, lagged some distance behind. A second glance reassured the Marshal. Alf was lumbering heavily past Brubaker's drugstore, fully revealed.

Observing an empty chair on the sidewalk in front of Jackson's cigar-store, Mr. Crow directed his slowing footsteps toward it. He flopped down with an abruptness that almost dismembered it. He was fanning himself with his hat when Alf came up.

Alf leaned against the wooden Indian that guarded the portals. Presently he wheezed:

"Wha—what's—all—the—rumpus?"

Instead of replying, Mr. Crow pressed his hand to his heart and shook his head.

"Take your time," advised Alf sympathetically; whereupon Anderson nodded his head.

Sim Jackson ambled to the front door, and Mort Fryback hobbled across the street from his hardware store. Lum Gillespie dropped the hose with which he was sousing an automobile in front of his garage and approached the group.

In less than three minutes all of the nighthawks of Main Street were gathered about Anderson Crow, convinced that something unusual was in the air despite his protests.

Suddenly the Marshal's manner changed. He swept the considerable group with an appraising eye, and then in a tone of authority said:

"Now that I've got you all together, I hereby order you in

my capacity as an official of the State and county, to close up your stores an' consider yourselves organized into a posse. You will close up immejately an' report to me here, ready for active work."

Shortly after ten o'clock a group of fifteen or eighteen men moved silently away from Jackson's cigar-store, led by their commander-in-chief. He was flanked on one side by Bill Kepsal, the brawny blacksmith, and on the other by Sim Jackson, who happened to possess a revolver.

After the posse had turned into the unrelieved shades of Maple Street, Mr. Crow halted every few yards and said: "Sh!"

He had related a portion but not all of his experiences, winding up with the statement that poor Mrs. Smith had been terribly frightened by the mysterious prowler, and that it was their duty as citizens to put an end to his activities if possible.

"Her description of him don't fit anybody livin' in this town," he had said during the course of his narrative. "We ain't got anybody who c'n jump thirty foot, or who c'n shin up a chimbly like a squirrel. You never saw anybody as quick as he is, either. Supposin' you think you see him standin' right beside you. Zip! Before you could blink an eye, he's over there in front of Mort's store—just like that. Or up a tree! Spryest cuss I ever laid eyes on. Made me think of a ghost."

"Ghost?" said Newt Spratt, pausing in the act of rolling up his sleeves.

"You say you saw him, Anderson?" inquired Alf Reesling.

"Course I did. Tall feller with—"

"And the lady saw him too?"

"She saw him first, I been tellin' you. She seemed to be able to see quicker'n I could, 'cause she saw nearly every move he made. My eyesight ain't as good as it used to be, an' besides, she could see plainer from where she stood. Come on now—no time to waste. We got to post ourselves all around the place an'—an' nab him if he shows himself again. All you fellers have got to do is to obey orders."

At the corner of Maple and Sickle streets, a few hundred feet from the Nixon cottage, the cavalcade received a whispered order to halt. The Marshal, enjoining the utmost stealth, instructed his men where to place themselves about the grounds they were soon to invest from various approaches. After stealing over the stone wall, they were to crawl forward on hands and knees until each man found a hiding-place behind a bush or flower-bed. There he was to wait and watch. The first glimpse of the mysterious intruder was to be the signal for a shout of alarm; whereupon the whole posse was to close in upon him without an instant's delay.

In course of time, the posse successfully debouched upon the lawn and occupied crouching positions behind various objects of nature. The minutes slowly consolidated themselves into half an hour; they were pretty well started on the way toward the three-quarter mark, and still no sign of the sprightly stranger. Lights were gleaming behind the yellow shades of the downstairs window in the cottage; through the Japanese curtains enveloping the veranda a dull, restricted glow forced its way out upon the bordering flower-beds.

Suddenly out of what had become an almost sepulchral silence, came the sound of a woman's voice. The words she uttered were so startling that the listeners felt the flesh on their bones creep.

"But wouldn't poisoning be the surer and quicker way? Slip a few drops of prussic acid into his food, and death would be instantaneous."

Marshal Crow clutched Bill Kepsal's arm. "Did you hear that?" he whispered. She had spoken in hushed, quavering tones.

Then came a man's voice from the porch above, low and suppressed.

"Why not wait till he is asleep and let me sneak up to him and put the revolver to his head—"

"But—but suppose he should awake and—"

"He'll never open his eyes again, believe me. Poison isn't always sure to work quickly or thoroughly. We don't want a struggle."

"You may be right. I—I leave it to you."

"Good! The sooner the better, then. If we do it at once, François and Henry can bury him before morning. I think—"

"I cannot bear to talk about it. Creep in and see if he is asleep. Don't make the slightest noise. He—he must never know!"

Stealthy footsteps, as of one tiptoeing, were heard by the listeners below the porch. Then, a moment later, the sound of a woman sobbing.

The foregoing conversation was distinctly heard by at least half of Marshal Crow's posse. Three of the watchers, crouching not far from Anderson Crow and his two supporters, abruptly left their hiding-places and started swiftly toward the front gate. The Marshal intercepted them.

"Where are you going?" he whispered, grabbing the

foremost, who happened to be Elmer K. Pratt, the photographer.

"I was sure I saw that feller you were telling about skipping down toward the street," whispered Mr. Pratt, his voice shaking. "I'm going after him. I—"

"Keep still! Stay where you are. Alf, you round up the boys—collect 'em up here, quiet as possible. We got to prevent this terrible murder. You heard what they were plottin' to do. Surround the house. Close every avenue of escape. Three or four of us will bust in through the porch an'—You stay with me, Sim, an' you too, Bill. Get your pistol ready, Sim. When I give the word—foller me! Where's Alf? Is he surrounding the house? Sh! Don't speak!"

Shadowy figures began scuttling about the lawn, darting from bush to bush, advancing upon the house.

"Now—get ready, Sim," whispered Anderson.

The words were hardly out of his mouth when a dull, smothered report, as of one striking the side of a barrel, reached the ears of the assembling forces. Then a sharp, agonized cry from the lady in the veranda.

"Too late!" cried the Marshal, and dashed clumsily up the front steps, followed by four or five of his henchmen.

Yanking open the screen-door, he plunged headlong into the softly lighted veranda. Behind him came Sim Jackson, brandishing a revolver, and Bill Kepsal, clutching the hammer he had brought from his forge.

They stopped short. A woman in a filmy white gown, cut extremely low in the neck, confronted them, an expression of alarm in her wide dark eyes. She was very beautiful. They had never seen any one so beautiful, so striking, or so startlingly dressed. She had just arisen from the comfortable wicker chair beside the table, the surface of which was littered with magazines, papers and documents in all sorts of disorder.

"What is the meaning of this intrusion?" she demanded, recovering her composure after the first instant of alarm.

Mr. Crow found his voice. "Surrender peaceable," he said. "I've got you completely surrounded. Won't do any good to resist. My men are everywhere. Your partner will be shot down if he—"

"Why, you—you old goose!" cried out the lady, and forthwith burst into a merry peal of laughter.

The Marshal stiffened.

"That kind of talk won't—" he began, and then broke off to roar: "Quit your laughin'! You won't be gigglin' like that when you're settin' in the 'lectric chair. Hustle inside there, men! Take her paramour, dead or alive!"

"Oh, what a stupendous situation!" cried the beautiful lady, her eyes dancing. "You really are a darling, Mr. Crow—a perfect, old dear. You—"

"None o' that now—none o' that!" Mr. Crow warned, taking a step backward. "Won't do you any good to talk sweet to me. I've got the goods on you. A dozen witnesses have heard you plottin' to murder. Throw up your hands! Up with 'em! Now, keep 'em up! *An' stop laughin'!* You'll soon find out you can't murder a man in cold blood, even if he is a trespasser on your property. You can't go around killin'—Say, where is Mrs. Smith? Where's the lady of the house?"

"I am the lady of the house, Mr. Crow," said the lady, performing a graceful Delsartian movement with her long bare arms. Mr. Crow and his companions stared upward at her arms as if fascinated. "I am Mrs. Smith—Mrs. John Smith."

"I guess not," said Anderson sharply. "She wears a veil, asleep an' awake. Hold on! Put your hands down! She's signalin' somebody, sure as you're alive," he burst out, turning to the group of mouth-sagging, eye-roving gentlemen who followed every graceful curve and twist of those ivory arms. "What's the matter with you, Sim? Didn't I order you to go in there an' grab that bloody assassin? What—"

"Not on your life! He's got a gun," exclaimed Sim Jackson. "S'pose I'm goin' in there, an'—Oh, fer gosh sake!"

A man appeared in the door leading to the interior of the house.

"For the love o' Mike!" issued from the lips of the newcomer. "What in thunder—what's all this?"

It was Harry Squires.

He gazed open-mouthed, first at the beautiful, convulsed lady, and then at the huddled group of men.

"We are caught red-handed, Mr. Squires," said the beautiful lady. "Shall we go to the electric chair hand in hand?"

A slow grin began to reach out from the corners of Harry's mouth as if its intention was to connect with his ears.

"My God, Harry—you ain't mixed up in this murder?" bleated Anderson.

The old man's dismay was so genuine, his distress so pitiful, that the heart of Harry Squires was touched. His face sobered at once. Stepping forward, he held out his hand to the Marshal.

"Good old Anderson! It's all right. Buck up, old top! I'm sorry to say that blood has been shed here tonight. Come with me; I'll show you the corpse."

Mr. Crow was not to be caught napping. "Some of you fellers stay here an' guard this woman. Don't let her get away."

A few minutes later he stood beside Harry Squires in the cellar below the kitchen. There was a smell of gunpowder on the close, still air. They looked down upon the black, inanimate form of the French poodle.

"There, Mr. Hawkshaw," said Harry, "there lies all that is mortal of the finest little gentleman that ever wore a collar. Take off your hat, Sim—and you too, Bill—all of you. You are standing in the presence of death. Behold in me the assassin. I am the slayer of yon grisly corpse. Shackle me, Mr. Marshal. Lead me to the gallows. I am the guilty party."

Marshal Crow took off his hat with the rest—but he did it the better to mop his forehead.

"Do you mean to tell me there ain't been any man slew in this house?" he inquired slowly.

"Up to the hour of going to press," said the city editor of the *Banner*, "no human remains have been unearthed."

"Then, where in thunder is the feller who's been foolin' around Mrs. Smith's front yard, the—"

"Last I saw of him he was beating it down the street about two hours ago, and you were giving him the run of his life. I don't believe the rascal will ever dare come around here again. The chances are he's still running."

The Marshal muttered something under his breath, and shot a pleading look at Harry.

"Yes, sir," continued Harry solemnly, "I'll bet my head he'll never be seen in these parts again."

"If he hadn't got such a start of me," said Anderson,

regaining much of his aplomb, "I'd 'a nabbed him, sure as you're alive. He could run like a whitehead. I never seen such—"

"Shall we go upstairs, gentlemen, and relieve the pressure on Miss Hildebrand? She is, I may say, the principal mourner, poor lady."

"Miss Who?"

"Gentlemen, the lady up there is no other than the celebrated actress, Juliet Hildebrand. The Veiled Lady and she are one and the same. Before we retire from this spot, let me explain that Mr. Snooks, the deceased, was run over by her automobile an hour or so ago. His back was broken. I merely put an end to his suffering. Now come—"

"Mister Snooks?" inquired Anderson quickly. "Well, that solves one of the mysteries that's been botherin' me. An'—an' you say she's the big actress whose picture we see in the papers every now an' again?"

"The same, Mr. Crow. She has done me the honour to accept a play that I have been guilty of writing. She came up here to go over it with me before putting it into rehearsal, and incidentally to enjoy a month's vacation after a long and prosperous season in New York."

"Do you mean to say you've knowed all along who she was?" demanded Anderson. "Been comin' up here to see her every night or so, I suppose."

"More or less."

"That settles it!" said the Marshal sternly. "You are under arrest, sir. Have you got anybody to bail you out, er are you goin' to spend the night in the lock-up?"

"What's the charge, Mr. Hawkshaw?" inquired Harry, amiably.

"Practisin' without a dicense."

"Practising what?" asked Harry.

"Jokes!" roared Anderson gleefully, and slapped him on the back.

Again the Marshal slapped the culprit's back. "Yes, sir, the joke's on me. I admit it. I'll set up the seegars for everybody here. Sim, send a box of them 'Uncle Tom' specials round to my office first thing in the mornin'. Yes, sir, Harry, my boy, you certainly caught me nappin' good and plenty. Tain't often I git —"

"If you don't mind, Anderson," interrupted Elmer K. Pratt, "I'll take a nickel's worth of chewin'-tobacco. My wife don't like me to smoke around the house."

"Gentlemen," said Harry Squires, "there are a few bottles of beer in the icebox, and the cook will make all the cheese and ham sandwiches we can eat. I am sure Miss Hildebrand will be happy to have you partake of her—"

"Hold on a minute, Harry," broke in the Marshal hastily. His face was a study. The painfully created joviality came to a swift and uncomfortable end, and in its place flashed a look of embarrassment. He simply couldn't face the smiling Miss Hildebrand.

"If it's all the same to you," he went on, lowering his voice and glancing furtively over his shoulder at the departing members of his posse, "I guess I'll go out the back way." Seeing the surprised look on Harry's face, he floundered badly for a moment or two, and then concluded with the perfectly good excuse that it was his duty to lead Alf Reesling, the one-time town drunkard, away from temptation. In support of this resolve, he called out to Alf: "Come here, Alf. None o' that, now! You come along with me."

"I ain't goin' to touch anything but a ham sandwich," protested Alf with considerable asperity.

"Never mind! You do what I tell you, or I'll run you in. Remember, you got a wife an' daughter, an' — "

"Inasmuch as Alf has been on the water-wagon for twenty-seven years, Mr. Marshal, I think you can trust him — " began Harry, but Anderson checked him with a resolute gesture.

"Can't take any chances with him. He's got to come with me."

"Nonsense!" exclaimed Harry.

"An' besides," said Anderson, "a man in my position can't afford to be seen associatin' with actresses — an' you know it, Harry Squires. Come on, Alf!"

THE ASTONISHING ACTS OF ANNA

The case of Loop vs. Loop was docketed for the September term in the Bramble County Circuit Court at Boggs City. When it became officially known in Tinkletown, through the columns of the *Banner*, that Eliphalet Loop had brought suit for divorce against his wife Anna, the town experienced a convulsion that bore symptoms of continuing without abatement until snow fell, and perhaps—depending on the evidence introduced—throughout the entire winter. For Eliphalet, in accusing his wife, was obliged to state in his bill that the identity and whereabouts of "said co-respondent" were at present unknown to complainant. As Mrs. Loop emphatically— some said spitefully—declined to satisfy the curiosity of Mr. Loop, and the whole of Tinkletown as well, speculation took such an impatient attitude toward her that Eliphalet, had he been minded to do so, could have made use of any one of three hundred names in a village boasting an adult male population of three hundred and seventeen. Husbands who had been in the habit of loafing around the village stores for a couple of hours after supper, winter and summer, now felt constrained to remain later than usual for fear that evil-minded persons outstaying them might question the statement that they were going home; and many a wife who was seldom awake after nine stayed up until the man of the house was safely inside, where she could look at him with an intentness so strange that he began to develop a ferocious hatred for Mrs. Loop.

The town marshal, Anderson Crow, encountering the lugubrious Eliphalet in front of Dr. Brown's office early one morning several weeks after the filing of the complaint, put this question to him:

"See here, Liff, why in thunder don't you make that wife o' yourn tell who 'tis she's been carryin' on with?"

Mr. Loop was not offended. He was not even embarrassed.

"'Cause I ain't speakin' to her nowadays, that's why."

"But you got a right to speak to her, ain't you? She's livin' in the same house with you, ain't she? An' it's *your* house, ain't it? Stand up to her. Show her you got a little spunk."

"I been livin' out in the barn, Anderson, on the advice of my lawyer. He says as long as she won't git out, I've got to. Been sleepin' out there for the last three weeks."

"I'd like to see any woman drive me out of a comfortable bed!"

"I don't a bit mind sleepin' in the barn," said Eliphalet in apology. "It's kind of a relief to get away from them women. Hosses can't talk. I don't know as I've ever slept as well as I have —"

"The point is," broke in Anderson firmly, "this wife of yourn is causin' a great deal of misery in town, Liff. Somethin's got to be done about it."

"I ain't askin' anybody to share my misery with me," said Mr. Loop with some asperity.

"I bet I've heard fifty men's names mentioned in the last twenty-four hours," said Anderson, compressing his lips. "'Tain't fair, Liff, an' you know it."

"'Tain't my fault," said Mr. Loop stubbornly. "I won't ask her ag'in. You wouldn't either, if you'd got a wallop over the head with a stove-lid like I did when I asked her the first time."

He removed his weather-worn straw hat. "See that? Doc Brown had to take seven stitches in it, an' he says if old Hawkins the undertaker had seen it first, I wouldn't have had to send for a doctor at all. You ask her yourself, if you're so blamed anxious to know. I seen her out in the back yard just 'fore I left. She was lookin' kinder sad and down in the mouth; so I sez to her as gentle as I knowed how—an' as legally as possible, on the advice of my lawyer: 'Good mornin', Mrs. Loop.' An' then when I seen her lookin' around for somethin' to throw at me, I knowed it wasn't any use tryin' to be polite, so I sez: 'Git out o' my sight, you old cow!' And 'fore you could say scat, she was out o' my sight. I didn't know it was possible for me to be so spry at *my* age. Just as she was gettin' out o' my sight by me gettin' around the corner of the barn, I heard somethin' go ker-slam ag'inst the side of the barn, but I don't know what it was. Sounded like a milk-crock."

Anderson looked at him sorrowfully. "Well, you can't say I didn't warn you, Liff."

"Warn me about what?"

"'Bout advertisin' fer a wife. I told you no good could come of it. An' now I guess you'll agree that I was right."

"Oh, shucks! Anna was as good a woman as I ever had, Andy Crow, an' I don't know as I ever had a better worker around the place. Fer two years she—"

He choked up and began to sniffle.

"There ain't no denyin' the fact she lasted longer'n any of 'em," agreed Anderson. "I don't just exactly remember how many funerals you've had, Liff, but—say, just out o' curiosity, how many have you had? Me an' Mrs. Crow had a dispute about it last evenin'."

"It's cost me a lot o' money, Anderson, a turrible lot o' money," groaned Eliphalet, "what with doctors' bills an' coffins; an' nothin'—absolutely nothin'—to show fer it! No children, no —nothin' but mother-in-laws an' tombstones. By gosh, why is it mother-in-laws last so long? I've got five mother-in-laws livin' this minute, an' the good Lord knows I never done anything to encourage 'em. I've lost four wives an' not a single mother-in-law. It don't seem right—now, does it, Anderson?"

"Well, if you'd married somebody nearer your own age, Liff, you might stand some chance of out-livin' their mothers. But you been marryin' women anywheres from fifty to sixty years younger'n you are. You must be derned near eighty."

"If you git 'em too old, they're allus complainin' about doin' the work around the house and garden, an' then you got to git a hired girl. Specially the washin'!"

"Seems to me it'd be cheaper in the long run to work a hired girl to death rather than a wife," said Anderson tartly.

"Most generally it is," agreed Mr. Loop. "But I sorter got into the habit of marryin' hired girls, figgerin' they make the best kind of wives. I give 'em a good home, plenty to eat an'—" His eyes roamed aloft, as if searching for some other beneficence, and finally lighting on Dr. Brown's door-plate, found something to clinch his argument. "An' as fine a funeral as any woman could ask fer!" he concluded.

"Let's git back to the main question," said Anderson unfeelingly. He didn't have much use for Eliphalet. "What fer sort of lookin' feller is this man your wife's been carryin' on with?"

"Well," began Mr. Loop, squinting his bleary eyes reflectively, "I ain't never seen him 'cept when he was runnin', an' it was after dark besides. Twice I seen him jump out of one of our back winders when I got home earlier'n usual from lodge-meetin'. First time I made out he was a burglar an' hustled in to see if he had took anything. You see, I allus keep my pocketbook in a burey drawer in our bedroom; an' natcherly, as it was our bedroom winder he jumped out of, I—well, natcherly I'd be a little uneasy, wouldn't I?"

"Specially if you thought your wife might 'a' been rendered insensible by the robber," said Anderson.

"Natcherly," said Mr. Loop quickly. "Course, I thought of her first of all. Well, after I went to the burey an' found the pocketbook all safe, I asked Anna if she'd heard anybody tryin' to get in through the winder. She looked kinder funny-like fer a second er two an' then said no, she hadn't. I told her what I'd seen, and she said I must be drunk er somethin', 'cause she'd been in the room all the time havin' a bite of somethin' to eat 'fore goin' to bed. I never saw anybody that could eat more'n that woman, Anderson. She's allus eatin'. Course I believed her *that* time, 'cause there was a plate o' cold ham an' some salt-risin' biscuits an', oh, a lot of other victuals on the washstand, with only one knife an' fork. Her mother was sound asleep in her room upstairs; an' her sister Gertie,—who come to visit us six months ago an' is still visitin' us an' eatin' more'n any two hired men you ever saw,—Gertie, she was out in the kitchen readin' that Swede paper my wife takes. An' she said she didn't hear anybody either, an' up and told Anna she'd be afraid to live with a man that come home drunk every night in the week like I did. She's the meanest woman I ever see, Anderson. She—"

"I don't want to hear about that side of your wife's relations, Eliphalet Loop," interposed Anderson.

"Well," said Eliphalet patiently, "I kinder figered I might 'a' been mistaken about seein' him that first time, but when the same thing happened ag'in on the night I went over to set up with Jim Hooper's corpse, why, I jest natcherly begin to think it was kinder funny. What set me thinkin' harder'n ever was findin' a man's hat in my room, hangin' on the back of a chair. Thinks I, that's mighty funny—specially as the hat wasn't mine."

"What kind of a hat was it?" questioned Anderson, taking out his notebook and pencil. "Describe it carefully, Liff."

"It was a grey fewdory," said Mr. Loop.

"The one you been wearin' to church lately?"

"Yes. I thought I might as well be wearin' it, long as nobody claimed it," explained the ingenuous husband of Anna. "It was a couple of sizes too big fer me, so I stuffed some paper inside the sweat-band. I allus hate to have a hat comin' down on my ears, don't you? Kinder spreads 'em out."

"Well, the first thing we've got to do, Liff, is to find some one with a head two sizes bigger'n yours," said Anderson, giving his whiskers a slow, speculative twist.

"That oughtn't to be hard to do," said Eliphalet without hesitation. "I wear a five an' three-quarters. Most everybody I know wears a bigger hat than I do."

"That makes it more difficult," admitted Anderson. "Was it bought in Tinkletown or Boggs City?"

"It had a New York label stamped on the sweat-band."

"Bring it down to my office, Liff, so's I c'n examine it carefully. Now, when did you next see this man?"

"'Bout two weeks after the second time—up in our cow-pasture. He was settin' beside Anna on some rails back of the corn-crib, an' he had his arm around her—or part way round, anyhow; she's a turrible thick woman. Been fattenin' up somethin' awful in the last two years. I snook up an' looked at 'em through the blackberry bushes, layin' flat so's they couldn't see me."

"Was that all you did?"

"What else could I do?" demanded Mr. Loop in some surprise.

"Why, you could have tackled him right then an' there, couldn't you?"

"Didn't I tell you there was two of 'em?"

"Two men?"

"No. Him an' Anna. You don't suppose I could lick *both* of 'em, do you? I bet there ain't a man in town—'cept that blacksmith, Bill Kepsal—that c'n lick Anna single-handed. Besides, I ain't half the man I used to be. I'm purty nigh eighty, Anderson. If I'd been four or five years younger, I'd ha' showed him, you bet."

"Umph!" was Mr. Crow's comment. "How long did they set there?"

"I can't just perzactly say. They was gone when I woke up!"

"When you what?"

"Woke up. It was gittin' purty late, long past my bedtime, an' I'd had a hard day's work. I guess I muster fell asleep."

"Was Mrs. Loop up when you got back home?"

"Yes, she was up."

"What did you say to her?"

"I—I didn't git a chance to say anything," said Eliphalet mournfully. "All three of 'em was eatin' breakfast, an' I got the most awful tongue-lashin' you ever heard. 'Cused me of everything under the sun. I couldn't eat a mouthful."

"Served you right," said Anderson sternly. "Well, did you ever see him ag'in?"

"I ain't sayin' as it was the same feller," qualified Mr. Loop, "but last night I seen a man streakin' through the potato-patch lickety-split some'eres round nine o'clock. He was carryin' a bundle an' was all stooped over. I yelled at him to stop er I'd fire. That seemed to make him run a little faster, so I took after him, an' run smack into Anna comin' round the corner of the hen-roost. Soon as I got my breath, I asked her what in tarnation she was doin' out at that time o' night."

"Well, go on. What did she say?" demanded Anderson as Mr. Loop paused to wipe his forehead.

"She—she insulted me," said Mr. Loop.

"How?" inquired Marshal Crow sceptically.

"She called me a skunk."

Mr. Crow was silent for some time, tugging at his whiskers. He stared intently at the upper corner of Dr. Brown's cottage. His lip twitched slightly. Presently, feeling that he could trust his voice, he asked:

"Why don't you offer a reward, Liff?"

"I thought of doin' that," said Mr. Loop, but a trifle half-heartedly.

"If you offer a big enough reward, I'll find out who the feller is," said Anderson. "Course, you understand it ain't my duty as marshal to ferret out matrimonial mysteries. I'd have to tackle it in my capacity as a private detective. An' you couldn't hardly expect me to do all this extry work without bein' paid fer it."

Mr. Loop scratched his head. Then he scratched a small

furrow in the gravel roadway with the toe of one of his boots.

"Well, you see, I got to pay a lawyer right smart of a fee; an' besides—"

Anderson interrupted him sternly. "You owe it to your feller-citizens to clear up this mystery. You surely don't think it is fair to your friends, do you, 'Liphalet Loop? Purty nigh every man in town is bein' suspicioned, an'—"

"That ain't any business o' mine," snapped Eliphalet, showing some ire. "If they feel as though the thing ought to be cleared up jest fer*their* sakes, why don't they git together an' offer a reward? I don't see why I ought to pay out money to 'stablish the innocence of all the men in Tinkletown. Let them do it if they feel that way about it. I got no objection to the taxpayers of Tinkletown oppropriatin' a sum out of the town treasury to prove they're innocent. Why don't you take it up with the selectmen, Anderson. I'm satisfied to leave my complaint as it is. I've been thinkin' it over, an' I believe I'd ruther git my divorce without knowin' who's the cause of it. The way it is now, I'm on friendly terms with every man in town, an' I'd like to stay that way. It would be mighty onpleasant to meet one of your friends on the street an' not be able to speak to him. Long as I *don't* know, why—"

"Wait a minute, Liff Loop," broke in Anderson sternly. "Don't say anything more. All I got to say is that it wasn't *you* your wife insulted when she called you a skunk. Good mornin', sir."

He turned and strode away, leaving the amazed Mr. Loop standing with his mouth open. Some time later that same afternoon Eliphalet succeeded in solving the problem that had been tantalizing him all day. "By gum," he bleated, addressing the high heavens, "what a blamed old fool he is! Anybody with any sense at all knows that you *can't* insult a skunk."

Briefly, Mr. Loop's fifth matrimonial experience had been, in the strictest sense, a venture. After four discouraging failures in the effort to obtain a durable wife from among the young women of Tinkletown and vicinity, he had resolved to go farther afield for his fifth. So he advertised through a New York matrimonial bureau for the sort of wife he might reasonably depend upon to survive the rigours of climate, industry and thrift. He made it quite plain that the lucky applicant would have to be a robust creature, white, sound of lung and limb, not more than thirty, and experienced in domestic economy. Nationality no object. Mr. Loop's idea of the meaning of domestic economy was intensely literal. Also she would have to pay her own railroad fare to Boggs City, no matter whence she came, the same to be refunded in case she proved acceptable. He described himself as a widower of means, young in spirit though somewhat past middle age, of attractive personality and an experienced husband.

The present Mrs. Loop was the result of this spirit of enterprise on his part. She came from Hoboken, New Jersey, and her name was Anna Petersen before it was altered to Loop. She more than fulfilled the requirements. As Mr. Loop himself proclaimed, there wasn't "a robuster woman in Bramble County;" she was exceedingly sound of lung, and equally sound of limb. What pleased him more than anything else, she was a Swede. He had always heard that the Swedish women were the most frugal, the most industrious, and a shade more amenable to male authority than any others.

Anna was a towering, rather overdeveloped female. She revealed such astonishing propensities for work that she had been a bride but little more than a week when Eliphalet decided that he could dispense with the services of a hired man. A little later he discovered, much to his surprise, that there really wasn't quite enough work about the house to keep her occupied all the time, and so he allowed her to take over some of the chores he had been in the habit of performing, such as feeding the horses and pigs, and ultimately to chop and carry in the firewood, wash the buckboard, milk the cows, and—in spare moments—to weed the garden. He began to regard himself as the most fortunate man alive. Anna appeared to thrive where her predecessors had withered and wasted away. True, she ate considerably more than any of them, but he was willing to put up with that, provided she didn't go so far to eat as much as *all* of them. There were times, however, when he experienced a great deal of uneasiness on that score.

The fly avoided his ointment for something like three months. Then it came and settled and bade fair to remain and thrive upon the fat of his land. Anna's mother came to live with them. He now realized that he had been extremely shortsighted. He should have stipulated in his advertisement that none except motherless young women need apply.

Mrs. Petersen was his fifth mother-in-law, and he dolefully found himself contending with the paraphrase: like mother, like daughter. His latest mother-in-law proved to be a voracious as well as a vociferous eater. She fell little short of Anna in physical proportions, but his wife assured him that it would be no time at all before she'd have her as plump as a partridge! Mr. Loop undertook the experiment of a joke. He asked her if *partridge* was the Swede word for *hippopotamus*. After that he kept his jokes to himself.

A year and a half went by. Then Miss Gertie Petersen came up from Hoboken for a flying visit. She was a very tall and lean young woman. Mr. Loop shuddered. The process of developing her into a partridge was something horrible to contemplate. But Anna was not dismayed. She insisted that the country air would do her sister a world of good. Mr. Loop was a pained witness to the filling out of Gertrude, but something told him that it wasn't the country air that was doing it. She weighed in the neighbourhood of one hundred and fifty pounds when she flew in for the visit. At the end of six months she strained the scales at two hundred and twenty. There was a good deal of horse-sense in his contention that if all this additional weight was country air, she'd have to be pretty securely anchored or she'd float away like a balloon.

But he did not openly complain. He had acquired the wisdom of the vanquished. He was surrounded by conquerors. Moreover, at butchering-time, he had seen his wife pick up a squealing shoat with one hand and slit its throat with the other in such a skilful and efficient manner that gooseflesh crept out all over his body when he thought of it.

And during those long, solitary nights in the barn he thought of it so constantly that everything else, including the encroachment of the home-wrecker, slipped his mind completely. He never ceased wondering how he screwed up the courage to institute proceedings against Anna, notwithstanding the fact that the matter had been vicariously attended to by his lawyer and a deputy from the county sheriff's office.

Marshal Crow fell into a state of profound cogitation after leaving Mr. Loop. The old man had put a new idea into his head. Late in the afternoon he decided to call a meeting of citizens at the town hall for that night. He drafted the assistance of such able idlers as Alf Reesling, Newt Spratt, Rush Applegate, Henry Plumb and Situate M. Jones, and ordered them to impress upon all male citizens of Tinkletown between the ages of twenty-one and seventy-five the importance of attending this meeting. Ebenezer January, the barber, and George Washington Smith, the garbage-wagon driver, were the only two men in town whose presence was not considered necessary. They, with their somewhat extensive families, represented the total coloured population of Tinkletown.

When the impromptu gathering was called to order that night by Ezra Pounder, the town clerk (acting in an unofficial capacity), there were nearly two hundred and fifty men present, including Messrs. January and Smith. Uncle Dad Simms, aged eighty-four, was present, occupying a front seat. He confessed for the first time in his life that he was a little "hard o' hearin'." This was a most gratifying triumph for his fellow-citizens, who for a matter of twenty years had almost yelled their lungs out advising him to get an ear-trumpet, only to have him say: "What in thunder are you whisperin' about?"

The three clergymen of the town put in an appearance, and Elmer K. Pratt, the photographer, brought his seven-months-old baby, explaining that it was *his* night to take care of her. He assured the gentlemen present that they were at liberty to speak as freely and as loudly as they pleased, so far as his daughter was concerned; if she got awake and started to "yap," he'd spank the daylights out of her, and if that didn't shut her up he'd take her home.

Anderson Crow, wearing all his decorations, occupied a chair between Mr. Pounder and Harry Squires, the *Banner* reporter. By actual count there were seven badges ranging across his chest. Prominent among them were the familiar emblems of the two detective associations to which he paid annual dues. Besides these, one could have made out the star of the town marshal, the shield of the fire chief, badges of the Grand Army of the Republic, Sons of Veterans, Sons of the Revolution, and the Tinkletown Battlefield Association.

Harry Squires, at the request of Mr. Crow, arose and stated the object of the meeting.

"Gentlemen," he began, "the time has come for action. We have been patient long enough. A small committee of citizens got together today, and acting upon the suggestion of our distinguished Marshal, decided to make a determined effort to restore peace and confidence into the home of practically every gentleman in this community. It is a moral certainty that all of us can't be the individual in Mr. Loop's woodpile, but it is also more or less an immoral certainty that Mrs. Loop obstinately refuses to vindicate an overwhelming majority of the citizens of this town.

"The situation is intolerable. We are in a painful state of perplexity. One of us, gentlemen, appears to be a *Lothario*. The question naturally arises: which one of us is it? Nobody answers. As a matter of fact, up to date, nobody has actually *denied* the charge. Can it be a matter of false pride with us? Ahem! However, not only does Mrs. Loop decline to lift the shadow of doubt, but Mr. Loop has assumed a most determined and uncharitable attitude toward his friends and neighbours. He positively refuses to come to our rescue. We have put up with Mr. Loop for a great many years, gentlemen, and what do we get for our pains? Nothing, gentlemen, nothing except Mr. Loop's cheerful wink when he passes us on the street. Our esteemed Marshal today proposed to Mr. Loop that he offer a suitable reward for the apprehension of the man in the case. He gave him the opportunity to do something for his friends and acquaintances. What does Mr. Loop say to the proposition? He was more than magnanimous. He as much as said that he couldn't bear the idea that any one of his numerous friends was innocent.

"Now, while Mr. Loop may feel that he is being extremely generous, we must feel otherwise. Gentlemen, we have arrived at the point where we must take our reputations out of Eliphalet Loop's hands. We cannot afford to let him trifle with them any longer. Mr. Loop refuses to employ a detective. Therefore it is up to us to secure the services of a competent, experienced sleuth who can and will establish our innocence. It will cost us a little money, possibly fifty cents apiece; but what is that compared to a fair name? I am confident that there isn't a man here who wouldn't give as much as ten dollars, even if he had to steal it, in order to protect his honour. Now, gentlemen, you know what we are here for. The meeting is open for suggestions and discussion."

He sat down, but almost instantly arose, his gaze fixed on an object in the rear of the hall.

"I see that Mr. Loop has just come in. Perhaps he has some news for us. Have you anything to say, Mr. Loop?"

Mr. Loop got up and cleared his throat.

"Nothin'," said he "except that I'm as willin' as anybody

to subscribe fifty cents."

Harry Squires suddenly put his hand over his mouth and turned to Marshal Crow. The Marshal arose.

"This ain't no affair of yours, Liff Loop. Nobody invited you to be present. You go on home, now. Go on! You've contributed all that's necessary to this here meetin'. Next thing we know, you'll be contributin' your mother-in-law too. Get out, I say. Open the door, Jake, an' head him that way. Easy, now! I didn't say to *stand* him on his head. He might accidently squash that new fewdory hat he's wearin'."

After Mr. Loop's unceremonious departure, the Marshal resumed his seat and fell to twisting his sparse whiskers.

"What is your opinion, Mr. Crow," inquired Harry Squires, "as to the amount we would have to pay a good detective to tackle the job?"

Mr. Crow ran a calculating eye over the crowd. He did not at once reply. Finally he spoke.

"Between a hundred and five an' a hundred an' seven dollars," he said. "It might run as high as hundred and ten," he added, as two or three belated citizens entered the hall.

"Can we get a goot man for dot amoundt?" inquired Henry Wimpelmeyer, the tanyard man.

"Well, we can get one that c'n tell whether it's daylight or dark without lightin' a lantern to find out," said Mr. Crow in a slightly bellicose tone.

"I ain't so sure aboudt dot," said Henry, eying the Marshal skeptically. He had had it in for Marshal Crow ever since that official compelled him to hang an American flag in front of his tanyard.

Luckily Uncle Dad Simms, who had not heard a word of

the foregoing remarks, piped up.

"This ain't no time to be thinkin' of unnecessary improvements, what with peace not signed yet, an' labor an' material so high. I don't see that there's any call for a new roof, anyway. S'posin' it does leak a little once in a while. We've all got umbrellas, I guess, an'—"

"Wake up, wake up!" bawled Alf Reesling, close to the old man's ear. "We ain't talkin' about a roof. Loop! That's what we're talkin' about!"

"What say?" squealed Uncle Dad, putting his hand to his ear. "My hearin' is a little bad lately."

"I said you was the derndest old nuisance in town; that's what I said—an' I don't care whether you hear me or not," roared Alf in exasperation.

"That's better," said Uncle Dad, nodding his head approvingly. "But I wish you wouldn't chaw tobacker, Alf," he added rather plaintively.

"Order!" commanded Marshal Crow, pounding on the table with his cane. "Now, feller-citizens, let us git down to business. Most of us have got to be home before nine o'clock, or the dickens will be to pay. All those in favour of employin' a detective to unearth this dark mystery raise their right hands."

"Just a moment, please," called out the Reverend Mr. Maltby, of the Congregationalist church. "I presume I am safe in saying that Father Maloney, the Reverend Mr. Downs and myself are hardly to be regarded as interested parties—"

He was interrupted by Father Maloney, who sprang to his feet and shouted in his most jovial voice:

"Nonsense, my dear Maltby! I consider it a great honour to be considered in the list of suspects. Nothing could give me more pleasure than the feeling that my parishioners trusted me sufficiently to take me to their hearts and say: 'He is one of us.' I should consider myself very badly treated if they were to leave me out of the case. Come—join me. Let us get all we can out of a most delicate situation. What do you say, friend Downs?"

The Methodist minister, an elderly person, looked a trifle dashed for a moment or two, and then heartily declared himself as with Father Maloney. Whereupon Mr. Maltby said he guessed it would be all right, provided Mr. Squires promised not to publish the names.

Harry Squires promptly announced that he intended to save labour and space by stating briefly and concisely that if any of his feminine readers cared to have a list of "those present," she could get it very easily and alphabetically by consulting the telephone-book.

The outcome of the meeting may be recorded in a very few words, although a great many were required in its achievement. Virtually everybody, including the coloured gentry, had something to say on the subject, and most of them said it without reservations. After Mr. Squires had announced that any man who voted in the negative would automatically convict himself, there wasn't a man present who failed to subscribe fifty cents toward the civic honour fund. It was found, on computation, that the total amount was one hundred nine dollars and fifty cents. Marshal Crow at once increased his contribution to one dollar, declaring it would be mortifying to offer a reward of less than one hundred and ten dollars to any decent, self-respecting detective.

Messrs. January and Smith insisted on their rights as citizens to join in the movement. Mr. January took the floor and vociferously harangued the assemblage at some length on certain provisions of the Proclamation of Emancipation, and Mr. Smith said that "this wasn't no time to draw the colour-line."

Mr. Crow consented to undertake the baffling case, and it was "so ordered."

"Have you got a clue?" whispered Alf Reesling as he started homeward in the wake of the preoccupied sleuth.

"No, but I will have 'fore mornin'," replied Anderson.

And he never uttered truer words in all his life.

Being a man of action, Mr. Crow began operations at once. He went home and for nearly an hour worked over the list of subscribers to the fund, aided by his wife and daughters. Among them they separated the wheat from the chaff. At least twenty per cent. of the contributors were set aside in a separate group and labelled "no good." Ten per cent. were designated as "fairly good," and the remainder as "good." It must not be assumed that the division had anything to do with the Loop mystery. Mr. Crow was merely figuring out who would pay and who would not.

It was shortly after ten o'clock when he started, in a roundabout way, for the home of Eliphalet Loop. The more direct route would have been down the street from his own house to the Boggs City pike, first turn to the left, fifty paces straight ahead, and he would have found himself at Eliphalet's front gate—in all, a matter of half a mile. But he preferred to descend upon the premises from an unexpected angle. So he approached by a far, circuitous way and arrived at the gate after traversing something like three miles of wood and pasture-land, stealthily following the stake-and-rider fences in order to screen his movements. He was well aware that Mr. Loop did not own a dog, on account of the expense.

The house was dark. Mr. Crow leaned against the hitching-post and mopped his brow. Then he blew his nose. It was his custom when he blew his nose, to blow it with tremendous force. Having performed these highly interesting feats he restored his handkerchief to his hip pocket. He remembered quite clearly doing all these things. Afterwards he claimed that he blew his nose as a signal. In any case, it *proved* to be a signal. A thinly pleated light appeared in one of the front windows of the house, narrow little streaks one above the other, shining through the window-slats.

The Marshal of Tinkletown stared. He craned his neck. A chill of excitement swept over him. Was he about to witness the surreptitious departure of the unwelcome guest? Had he arrived in the nick of time? And what in the world was he to do if the fellow had a revolver? Fascinated, he watched one of the blinds slowly swing outward. He held his breath.

Suddenly it dawned on him that the visitor was still *expected*, and not on the point of departing. In that case it behooved him to retire to a less exposed spot, where he could observe the fellow without being observed.

Stooping low, he stole across the road and wound his way through the scraggly hedgerow and into the brambles beyond. Just as he was settling himself down for his vigil, a most astonishing thing occurred.

A hand fell heavily upon his shoulder, and something cold punched him in the back of the neck—and remained fixed in that spot.

"Don't move or I'll blow your brains out," whispered a

voice in his ear. The grip on his shoulder tightened.

"Who—who—" he started to gasp.

"Shut up!" hissed the voice of the invisible one. "I've got you dead to rights. Get up! Put your hands up!"

"I—I got 'em up," gulped Mr. Crow, in a strangled voice. "Don't shoot, Mister! I—I promise to let you go, I swear I will. It's—"

"By thunder!" fell from the lips of the captor. It was an exclamation of surprise, even dismay.

"Take it away, if it's a revolver," pleaded Anderson. "I withdraw from the case. You c'n go as fer as you like. Eliphalet —"

"Stand still. I can't take a chance with you. You may be trying to fool me with this rube talk. Keep 'em up!"

Swiftly the stranger ran a hand over Mr. Crow's person.

"You *ought* to have a gun," he said in a puzzled voice.

"I loaned it last winter to Milt Cupples, an' he—"

"Who the devil are you?"

"I'm the marshal of Tinkletown, an' my name is Crow— A. Crow. I made a mistake, takin' up this case. Go on in and see Mrs. Loop if you feel like it. I won't say a word to anybody—"

"Get down on your knees, Mr. Crow, here beside me, an'—"

"Oh, Lordy, Lordy! You shorely ain't going to shoot, Mister!"

"I don't want you to pray. I want you to keep still. Don't make a sound—do you hear?"

"I've got a wife an' children—"

"Shut up! Look! She's put out the light. Keep your eyes skinned, old man! He must be near. Don't make a sound. My partner's in that rain-barrel at the corner of the house. If we can get him between us, he won't have any more chance than a snowball in—Look! There he is, sneaking across the yard! By golly, we've got him at last."

What happened in the next fifteen seconds was a revelation to the most recent addition to the forces of the International Society of Sleuths. He witnessed the quick, businesslike methods of two of the craftiest men in the craftiest organization in the world—the United States Secret Service.

Two words were spoken. They came, loud and imperative, from a point near the house.

"Hands up!"

The skulking figure in the yard stopped short, but only for a fraction of a second. Then he made a wild spring toward the front gate.

A shot rang out.

The man at Anderson's side leaped forward through the hedge. Mr. Crow was dimly conscious of a mishap to his erstwhile captor. He heard him curse as he went sprawling over a treacherous vine.

Mr. Crow did not waste a second's time. He leaped to his feet and started pellmell for home. With rare sagacity he avoided the highway and laid his course well inside the hedgerow. He knew where he could strike an open stretch of meadowland, and he headed for it through the brambles.

He heard shouts behind him, and the rush of feet. If he could only get clear of the cussed bushes! That was his thought as he plunged along.

Down he went with a crash!

As the marshal tried to rise, a huge object ploughed through the hedge beside him, and the next instant he was knocked flat and breathless by the impact of this hurtling body.

The next instant two swift, ruthless figures came plunging through the hedge, and he found himself embroiled in a seething mix-up of panting, struggling men.

Presently Crow sat up. The steady glare of a "dark-lantern" revealed a picture he was never to forget.

A single figure in a kneeling position, hands on high, was crying:

"Don't shoot! Don't shoot!"

Over him stood two men with pistols levelled at the white, terrified face.

Anderson, to his dying day, was to remember those bulging eyes, the flabby and unshaven face, the mouth that appeared to be grinning—but never had he seen such an unnatural grin!

"Stand up!" commanded one of the men, and the victim struggled to his feet. In less time than it takes to tell it, the fellow was searched and hand-cuffed. "Run back there, Pyke, and see that the woman don't take a crack at us with a shotgun. She'd do it in a minute." As his companion darted back into the roadway, the speaker turned to his captive. "Where's your gun?"

By this time Anderson Crow was on his feet. He was clutching something in his hand. He looked at it in stark astonishment. It was an automatic pistol. In raising himself from the ground his hand had fallen upon it.

"I don't know," said the captive sullenly. Then his gaze fell upon the gaunt figure of Anderson Crow. A frightful scowl transfigured his face. Mr. Crow involuntarily drew back a step and reversed the pistol in his hand, so that its muzzle was pointing at the enemy instead of at himself. Between imprecations the prisoner managed to convey the fact that he realized for the first time that it was a human being and not a log that had brought him to earth.

Mr. Crow found his voice and some of his wits at the same time.

"I'll learn you not to go rampagin' around these parts carryin' concealed weapons, you good-fer-nothin' scamp! I've got your gun, blast ye!" He turned triumphantly to the surprised secret-service man. "I took it away from him soon as I had him down, an'—"

"Holy mackerel!" gasped the operative. "Did—did you head him off and—and down him? You? Well, I'll be hanged!"

"I sorter knowed he'd strike about here, tryin' to make the woods up yonder, so I hustled down here to head him off while you fellers—"

"Never mind now," broke in the other. "Tell it to me later. Come on, both of you. We're not through yet." He urged the burly captive through the hedge. Marshal Crow followed very close behind.

They found a terrified, excited group on the front porch —three sturdy females in nightgowns, all with their hands up! Below, revealed by the light streaming through the open door, stood a man covering them with a revolver. Fifteen or twenty minutes later Mr. Crow dug the shivering Eliphalet Loop out of the hay-mow and ordered him forthwith to join his family in the kitchen, where he would hear something to his advantage.

The happiest man in Bramble County was Eliphalet Loop

when he finally grasped the truth. The prisoner turned out to be his wife's first husband—he grasped that fact some little time before he realized that *he* wasn't even her second husband, owing to certain fundamental principles in law—and a fugitive from justice. The man was an escaped convict, the leader of a gang of counterfeiters, and he was serving a term in one of the federal prisons when he succeeded in his break for liberty. For many months the United States Secret Service operatives had been combing the country for him, hot and cold on his trail, but always, until now, finding themselves baffled by the crafty rogue, who, according to the records, was one of the most dangerous, desperate criminals alive. Finally they got track of his wife, who had lived for a time in Hoboken, but it was only within the week that they succeeded in locating her as the wife of Eliphalet Loop. The remainder of the story is too simple to bother about.

"Of course, Mr. Loop," said one of the secret-service men, "you can prosecute this woman for bigamy."

Mr. Loop shook his head. "Not much! I won't take no chance. She might prove that she wasn't ever married to *this* feller, an' then where would I be? No, sirree! You take her along an' lock her up. She's a dangerous character. An' say, don't make any mistake an' fergit to take her mother an' sister, too."

The next evening Mr. Crow sat on the porch in front of Lamson's store. His fellow-townsmen were paying up more promptly than he had expected. Practically three-fourths of the reward was in his coat pockets—all silver, but as heavy as lead.

"Yes, sir," he was saying in a rather far-reaching voice, for the outer rim of the crowd was some distance away, "as I said before several times, I figgered he would do just what he did. I figgered that I'd have to outfigger him. He is one of the slickest individuals I have ever had anything to do with—an' one of the most desperit. I—er—where was I at, Alf?... Oh, yes, I recollect. He was a powerful feller. Fer a second or two I thought maybe he'd get the best of me, being so much younger an' havin' a revolver besides. But I hung on like grim death, an' finally— Thanks, Jim; I wasn't expectin' you to pay 'fore the end of the month. Finally I got my favourite holt on him, an' down he went. All this time I was tryin' to git his revolver away from him. Just as I got it, the secret-service men came dashin' up an'—What say, Deacon? Well, if the rest of the crowd ain't tired o' hearin' the story, I don't mind tellin' it all over."

Harry Squires, perched on the railing, assured him that the crowd wouldn't mind in the least.

"The real beauty of the story Anderson," he added dryly, "is that it has so much of the spice of life in it."

"What's that?"

"I mean variety."

NO QUESTIONS ANSWERED

REWARD!!! $25.00 For the Apprehension or Capture of Person or Persons Who Successfully Stole the Fashionable Bulldog Belonging to Mrs. M. Fryback on or About Friday of Last Week! P/

N. B.—Said dog occasionally answers to the name of Marmaduke, but mostly to Mike.

An Additional Reward of Three Dollars Cash will be paid for the return of said dog, with or without said Criminals. No Questions asked.

A. Crow, Marshal of Tinkletown.

The foregoing poster, fresh from the press of the *Banner* printing office, made itself conspicuous at no less than a dozen points in the village of Tinkletown on a blustery February morning. Early visitors to the post office in Lamson's store were the first to discover it, tacked neatly on the bulletin board. Others saw it in front of the Town Hall, while others, who rarely took the trouble to look at a telephone pole before leaning against it, found themselves gazing with interest at the notice that covered the customary admonition:

"Post No Bills."

Of course every one in Tinkletown knew, and had known for the matter of a week or more, that Mort Fryback's bulldog was "lost, strayed or stolen," but this was the first glaring intimation that Mort had also lost his mind. In the first place, Mike—as he was familiarly known to every inhabitant—wasn't worth more than a dollar and a half when he was in his prime, and that, according to recollection, must have been at least twelve or fifteen years prior to his unexplained disappearance. In the second place, it was pretty generally understood that Mike—recently Marmaduke—had surreptitiously taken a dose of prussic acid in a shed back of Kepsal's blacksmith shop and was now enjoying a state of perfect rejuvenation in the happy hunting ground.

Mr. Alf Reesling, the town drunkard, after having scanned four of the notices on his way to the post office, informed a group of citizens in front of Brubaker's drugstore that Anderson Crow would do almost anything to get his name into print. Alf and the town marshal had had one of their periodical "fallings out," and, for the moment at least, the former was inclined to bitterness.

"To begin with," explained Alf, "there ain't a dog in this town that's worth stealin', to say nothin' of three dollars. You can't tell me that Mort Fryback would give three dollars to get that dog back, not even if he was alive—which he ain't, if you c'n believe Bill Kepsal. No, sir; it's just because Anderson wants to see his name in print, that's what it is. I bet if you was to ask Mort if he has agreed to pay—how much is it all told?—twenty-eight dollars—if he has agreed to pay all that money for *nothin'*, he'd order you out of his store."

"Mrs. Fryback told my wife a couple of weeks ago that Marmaduke was a prize bull, and she wouldn't take a hundred dollars for him," said Newt Spratt. "Seems that she had somebody look up his pedigree, and he turns out to be a stepson or something like that of a dog that won first prize at a bench show—whatever that is—in New York City."

"Ever since that actress woman was here last fall,—that friend of Harry Squires, I mean,—every derned dog in town has turned out to be related some way or other to a thoroughbred animal in some other city," said Alf. "Why, even that mangy shepherd dog of Deacon Rank's—accordin' to Mrs. Rank—is a direct descendant of two of the finest Boston terriers that ever came out of Boston. She told me so herself, but, of course, I couldn't ask how he happened to look so much like a shepherd dog and so little like his parents, 'cause there's no use makin' poor Mrs. Rank any more miserable than she already is—she certainly don't get any fun out of life, livin' with the deacon from one year's end to the other. Yes, sir; just because that actress woman paraded around here for a month or so last fall with a French poodle, is no reason, far as I can see, why all the women in town should begin puttin' leashes on their dogs and washin' 'em and trimmin' 'em and tying red ribbons around their necks —yes, and around some of their tails, too. I'll never forget that stub-tail dog of Angie Nixon's going around with a blue bow stickin' straight up behind him, and lookin' as though he'd lost something and got dizzy looking for it. And Mort's dog, Mike— poor old Mike,—why, he got so he'd go down to Hawkins' undertakin' shop every time he could get a minute off and bark till Lem would let him in, and then he'd lay down in a corner and go to sleep, and Lem always swore the poor dog was as mad as a hornet when he woke up and found he was still alive."

"What puzzles me is why Mort Fryback's offerin' this reward, and all that, if he knows the dog is dead. It costs money to have bills like this printed at the *Banner* office." So spoke Elmer Pratt, the photographer. "Wasn't he present at the obsequies?"

"No, he wasn't," said Alf. "He claims now that he don't know anything about it, and, besides, Bill Kepsal says he'll beat the head off of anybody that says Mike passed away on his premises—including Mort. So naturally Mort denies it. He told me yesterday he would deny it even if he had both of his legs; but what chance, says he, has a one-legged man got with big Bill Kepsal?"

"Here comes Anderson now," said Mr. Spratt, his gaze fixed on an approaching figure.

It was zero weather in northern New York State, and the ancient Marshal of Tinkletown was garbed accordingly. The expansive collar of his brass-buttoned ulster was turned up, completely obscuring the ear-flaps and part of the coonskin cap he was wearing. An enormous pair of arctics covered his feet; his grey and red mittens were of the homemade variety; a muffler of the same material enveloped his gaunt neck, knotted loosely under his chin in such a way as to leave his whiskers free not only to the wind but to the vicissitudes of conversation as well. The emblem of authority, a bright silver star, gleamed on the breast of his ulster.

He stopped when he reached the group huddled in front of the drugstore, and glared accusingly at Alf Reesling.

"I thought I told you to keep off the streets," he said ominously. "Didn't I tell you yesterday I'd run you in if I caught you drunk in the streets again?"

"Yes, you did," replied Alf, in a justifiably bellicose manner; "but I still stick to what I said to you at first when you said that to me."

"What was that?"

"I said you couldn't ketch me even if I was dead drunk and unconscious in the gutter, that's what I said."

"For two cents, I'd show you," said Anderson.

"Well, go ahead. Just add two cents to what you claim I already owe you, and go ahead with your runnin' me in. But before you do it, lemme warn you I'll sue you for false arrest, and then where'll you be? I got five witnesses right here that'll swear I ain't drunk now and haven't been in twenty-three years."

"That shows just how drunk you are," said Anderson triumphantly. "Far as I can see, there are only four men here."

"Don't you call yourself a man?"

"What say?"

"I mean I got five witnesses includin' you, that's what I mean. I'm gettin' sick of you all the time tellin' me I been drinkin' again, when you know I ain't touched a drop since 1896. Why, dog-gone you, Andy Crow, if it wasn't for me an' the way you keep on talkin' about juggin' me, you wouldn't have any excuse at all fer bein' town marshal. You—"

"That'll do now," interrupted Anderson severely. "You have said them very words to me a thousand times, Alf Reesling, and—Who's that coming out of the post office?"

The group gradually turned to look up the street. Tinkletown is a slow place. Its inhabitants do everything with a deliberation that suggests the profoundest ennui. For example, a gentleman of Tinkletown rarely raised his hat on meeting a lady. He invariably started to do so, but as the ladies of the place were in the habit of moving with more celerity than the gentlemen, he failed on most occasions to complete the undertaking. What's the sense of takin' your hat off to a woman, he would argue, if she's already got past you? So far as anybody knew, there wasn't a woman in town with an eye in the back of her head.

"Looks like a stranger," said Newt Spratt.

"It certainly does," agreed Anderson. "Yes, I'm right," he added an instant later.

The object of interest was crossing the street in the direction of the Grand View Hotel. The group watched him with mild interest. In front of the two-story frame building that seemed to stagger, or at least to shrink, under the weight of its own importance, the stranger—a man—paused to glance at one of the placards heralding the misfortune and at the same time the far from parsimonious regard of the lady who had been despoiled of a fashionable bulldog. Having perused the singularly comprehensive notice, he deliberately tore it down, folded it with some care, and stuck it into his overcoat pocket. Then he entered the Grand View Hotel.

"Well, I'll be ding-blasted!" exclaimed Marshal Crow.

Mr. Reesling's animosity gave way to civic pride. "By jingo, Anderson," he cried, "if you want any help arrestin' that scoundrel, call on me! Comin' around here defacin' things like that—he ought to go to jail."

Elmer K. Pratt, the photographer, voiced a time-tried but fruitless criticism. "If you'd paste 'em up instead of tackin' 'em up, people couldn't take 'em down like that. I've told you—"

"If you got any complaints to make about me, Elmer, you'd better make 'em to the town board and not to Alf Reesling and Newt Spratt," interrupted Marshal Crow testily. "Besides I do paste 'em up when I run out of tacks."

He started off toward the Grand View, his head erect, his

whiskers bristling with indignation.

"Shall we go with you, Anderson?" inquired Alf.

"'Tain't necessary," replied the Marshal, "but you might go over and wait for me in front of the hotel."

"If you need any help, just holler," said Alf.

Entering the office of the Grand View Hotel, Marshal Crow looked around for the despoiler. Save for the presence of the proprietress, Mrs. Bloomer, relict of the founder of the hostelry, the room was quite empty. Mrs. Bloomer, however, filled it rather snugly. She was a large person, and she had a cold in the head which made her feel even larger. She was now engaged in sweeping the floor.

"Mornin', Jennie," was Anderson's greeting. "Where's the feller that's stoppin' here?"

Mrs. Bloomer had the sniffles. "He's gone up to his room," she said. Then after another sniffle: "Why?"

"I want to see him."

"Well his room's at the head of the stairs, to your right."

Anderson twisted his whiskers in momentary perplexity.

"Might be better if you asked him to come down."

"Ask him yourself," she said. "I don't want to see him."

Marshal Crow made a mental reservation to yank Mrs. Bloomer up before Justice Robb the next time she left the garbage can standing on the sidewalk overnight.

He hesitated about going up to the guest's bedroom. It wasn't quite the legal thing to do. The more he thought of it, the longer he hesitated. In fact, while he was about it, he thought he would draw a chair up to the big sheet-iron stove and sit down.

"Won't you take off your overcoat and goloshes?" inquired the landlady, but in a far from hospitable manner.

"How long has this feller been here?" demanded Anderson, moving his left foot a little, but not quite far enough to avoid the broom.

"Last night."

"Um-m! What's his name and where's he from?"

"Go and look at the register, and then you'll know as much as I do. It's a public register. Nothing secret about it."

Anderson got up suddenly. "I guess I'll go look while you're sweepin' around here."

The register on the little counter in the corner revealed the name of a single arrival below the flowing Spencerian hand of Willie Spence, the clerk, head waiter, porter and bell-boy of the Grand View Hotel. Willie, because of his proficiency as a chirographer, always wrote the date line in the register. He was strong on flourishes, but somewhat feeble in spelling. Any one with half an eye could see that there was something wrong with a date line that read: "Febury 25nd 1919." The lone guest's name, written in a tight "running" hand with total disregard for the elementary formation of letters, might have been almost anything that occupied less than two inches of space. Even his place of residence was a matter of doubt.

The Marshal put on his spectacles and studied the signature. As far as he could make out, the man's name was something like "Winnumnn Millmmmln." It was a name that baffled him. The longer he studied it, the worse it became.

"Seems to me, Jennie, if I was runnin' this hotel, I'd have Willie Spence register for the guests, and save 'em the trouble."

"Can't you make it out?"

"Course I can," he replied promptly. "It's as plain as day to me, but I'll bet you a good cigar you can't make it out."

She fell into the trap. "All right, I take you up. It's Mr. & Mrs. George F. Fox."

Mr. Crow stared at her for a second or two. Then he recovered himself. "You're right," he said. "What kind of a cigar do you smoke, Jennie?"

As he had feared, she promptly named the highest-priced cigar she had in stock, a three-for-a-quarter brand, and then coolly announced that if he'd leave a dime on the show case, she'd get it.

"Got his wife with him, I see," remarked Anderson.

"Yep," said Mrs. Bloomer.

"What's his business?"

"I asked him last night," said she, pausing in her work to fix Anderson with a rather penetrating look. "He said he was a trained elephant."

"A—a what?"

"A trained elephant."

"You don't say so!"

"And his wife is a snake-charmer," she added uneasily.

Anderson blinked rapidly. "Well, of all the—But what on earth's he doing here in Tinkletown?"

"I didn't ask any more questions after that," said she, with a furtive glance up the stairway. "I'd give a good deal to know what they've got in them big black valises they brought with 'em. Three times as big as regular valises, with brass trimmin's. I hope she aint got any reptiles in 'em."

Marshal Crow took that instant to consult the office clock. "By ginger!" he exclaimed, with some sprightliness. "I got to be movin' along. I'm follerin' up a clue in that dog case."

Mrs. Bloomer's anxious gaze was bent on a dark corner

back of the stairway.

"I do hope, if she *has* got any snakes in them valises, she won't let 'em get loose and go crawlin' all over the place. I——"

Mr. Crow sent a quick, searching look about the office as he strode toward the door.

"Ain't you going up to his room?" inquired Mrs. Bloomer.

"Not just now," replied Anderson, and closed the door quickly behind him.

Alf Reesling and his companions were waiting impatiently on the sidewalk. They were actively disappointed when the Marshal emerged empty-handed.

"Was he too much fer you?" was Alf's scathing inquiry.

"How many times have I got to tell you, Alf, that I'm able to deduce these cases without your assistance? Now, this is a big case, and you leave it to me to handle. When I get ready to act, you'll hear something that will make your hair stand on end. Hold on, Newt! Don't ask any questions. Don't——"

"I wasn't going to ask any questions," snapped Newt. "I was going to tell you something."

"You was, eh? Well, what was you going to tell me?"

"Mort Fryback went by here a couple of minutes ago an' he says for you to come into his store right away."

Anderson frowned. "I bet he's confessed."

"Who? Him? What's he got to confess?" demanded Alf.

"Never mind, never mind," said the Marshal quickly. "I'll step in and see him now."

Leaving his "reserves" standing in front of the Grand View, Mr. Crow hurried into Fryback's hardware store.

Mort was pacing—or, strictly speaking, stumping—back

and forth behind the cutlery counter. His brow was corrugated with anxiety. The instant he saw the Marshal he uttered an exclamation that might have been construed as either relief, dismay or wrath. It was, as a matter of fact, inarticulate and therefore extremely difficult to classify. Anderson, however, deduced it as dismay. Mr. Fryback came out from behind the counter, stumped over to the stove, in which there was a crackling fire and, after opening the isinglass door, squirted a mouthful of tobacco juice upon the coals. Whereupon it became possible for him to articulate.

"I been lookin' everywhere fer you," said he, somewhat breathlessly. "Where you been?"

"'Tendin' to business," retorted Anderson. "What's the matter?"

Mr. Fryback took the precaution to ascertain that there were no listeners in the store. "Somebody—some woman, you c'n bet on that—told my wife last night that I poisoned old Mike."

"Well, you did, didn't you?"

"Of course I did. That is, I hired Charlie Brubaker to do it. But she says I did it with my own hands, and—my gosh, Anderson, I never went through such a night in my life as last night." He mopped his brow. "You'd think I was a murderer. Course, I denied it. I swore he wasn't dead, and that I'd increase the reward to a hundred dollars just to show her. What I want you to do, right away, is to have a new set of bills printed, offerin' a hundred dollars reward for that dog, instead of three. It's the only chance I've got of ever being able to live in my own house again."

The Marshal eyed him reflectively. "If you could get her

to agree to let you offer the reward for Mike, dead or alive—"

"She wants him alive, and no other way."

"Can't you buy her off?"

Mr. Fryback groaned. "I could—" he began dismally, and then fell to chewing with great vigour.

"What would it cost?" inquired Anderson, feelingly.

"An automobile," replied Mr. Fryback, after opening and closing the stove-door once more. "It would be cheaper, you see, to offer a hundred dollars for Mike," he explained, ingenuously.

"It certainly would," agreed the Marshal, "seein' as you wouldn't have to pay fer anything except the printin' of the notices. If you wanted to show how much you think of your wife, and how anxious you are to please her, you could go as high as a thousand dollars, Mort."

"Would you, reely, Anderson?"

"Sure. She could lord it over all these women—includin' my wife—who've been sayin' Mike wasn't worth fifty cents and didn't have a pedigree any longer than his tail. Why, if she wanted to go on lyin' about the value of that old dog, she could tell people she had been offered a thousand dollars for Marmyduke by a well-known dog collector in New York."

"That *might* please her," reflected Mort. "Course, this thing has already cost me quite a lot of money, outside the printin'. I've had to give Bill Kepsal a receipt in full fer what he owes me, and that young Brubaker's been in twice to price base-burner stoves. He says if he c'n get a good one fer ten dollars he'll take it, and his heart seems to be set on that seventy-dollar Regal over yonder. I'm in an awful fix, Anderson."

"Well, you can't say I didn't advise you to let Mike die a natural death."

"I wish to goodness I had," lamented Mort.

The door opened at that juncture, and in walked a man and a woman. The former was carrying a square black "valise," inadequately described by Mrs. Bloomer as twice the natural size. As a matter of fact, it was more like a half-grown trunk, to quote no less an authority than the town marshal.

The proprietor of the hardware store was, at a glance, qualified to pass an opinion on the personal appearance of the two strangers. His companion's attention, however, was devoted so earnestly to the big black "valise," that he couldn't have told, for the life of him, whether the customers were young or old, black or white. His fascinated gaze was riveted upon the object the man deposited carefully on the floor near the door.

"You are a locksmith, I perceive," remarked the strange man, addressing Mort. "I'd like to have you see if you can open this box for me. We've lost or mislaid the key."

"What fer sort of a lock is it?" asked Mort, approaching.

"Hold on, Mort!" called out Mr. Crow. "Don't monkey with that trunk."

The two strangers turned on him.

"Well, who the deuce have we here?" said the man, with some acerbity.

"Oh, what a nice old policeman!" cried the lady, fixing the Marshal with a pair of intensely blue eyes. Mr. Crow looked at her in amazement. Could any one as pretty, as dainty and as refined-looking as she be engaged in the awful business of charming snakes?

"Before we go any further, mister, I've got to know what's inside that box," said Anderson firmly.

"What's the matter with you?" demanded the other.

"There's nothing in it that need excite the law, my good man."

"This is our town marshal, Anderson Crow," explained Mort Fryback.

"I might have known it," said the stranger. "I've heard a good deal about Mr. Crow. Well, what's the answer?"

"That's what I want to know," snapped Anderson. "What is the answer? What kind are they? And how many have you got?"

The stranger was on the point of exploding with indignation when his fair companion intervened.

"Leave it to me, George dear. You always fly into such a temper. If you'd only let me attend to the small things, while you look out for the big ones, we'd get along so much better. Wouldn't we, Mr. Crow?"

She appealed to Mr. Crow so abruptly and so sweetly that he said he guessed so before he could check himself.

"If you will stay here until we find a key that will fit, Mr. Crow, you will see with your own eyes what will make them pop out of your head."

"Mort, you keep away from that box, I say!" commanded Anderson, now sure of his ground. "Do you want to get bit?"

"Oh, dear me, they won't bite you!" cried the young lady. "I promise you they are most amiable. I have been handling them for several weeks and—"

Her husband interrupted her. He revealed symptoms of increasing annoyance.

"See here, let's get busy and open this thing. They've got to be fed, you know,—and it's all damned poppycock discussing the matter any longer."

Marshal Crow held up his hand as if stopping traffic in

Main Street.

"You are in the presence of the law, Mr. Wolf," he began. The young woman giggled. He glared at her.

"My name is Fox," said the young man, curtly.

"That don't make any difference," retorted the Marshal. "Mine's Crow, and I represent the law. You—"

"How delicious!" said Mrs. Fox. "So like that cunning poem of Guy Wetmore Carryl's. You know it, of course, Mr. Crow?"

She declaimed:

"'I blush to add that when the bird
  Took in the situation
He said one brief, emphatic word,
  Unfit for publication.
The fox was greatly startled, but
He only sighed and answered "tut"'"

"Don't be silly, Bess," said her husband. "This is no time to recite poetry."

"I don't see any sense in it, anyhow," said Marshal Crow.

Mr. Fryback emerged from behind the cutlery counter, whither he had repaired in some haste when it became evident that Mrs. Fox was likely to remain for some time. He was wiping his lips with the back of his hand, and what very recently might have been mistaken for a prodigious swelling in his cheek had strangely subsided.

"Why shouldn't I fit a key to that lock, Andy?" he demanded, rather hotly. "What right have you got to interfere with my business?"

The Marshal's lips parted to utter a sharp retort, but the

words failed to issue. Young Mrs. Fox suddenly stooped over and peered intently at several heretofore unnoticed holes at one end of the black box. These holes, about an inch in diameter, formed a horizontal row. Much to Mr. Crow's alarm, the young lady pulled off her glove and stuck a finger into one of the little apertures and apparently wriggled it without fear or trepidation. Almost instantly there was an ominous rustling inside the box. Withdrawing her finger, she called out:

"Please look!"

The invitation was unnecessary. Mr. Crow was looking for all he was worth.

"Good gracious, ma'am!" he gasped. "Don't stir 'em up like that. Next thing they'll crawl out of them holes and—"

"Why, you poor old goose!" she said, but not disrespectfully. "They're much too large to crawl through these holes. I wish I could catch hold of one of their tails and—Look!" She held her finger close to the hole and a long, thin black tongue darted through and began to writhe about in a most malevolent manner.

"For gosh sake!" exclaimed the Marshal, retreating a couple of steps. This sudden action on his part brought a venomous oath from Mr. Fryback, and an instant apology as well.

"You'd cuss, too," explained the blasphemer to the lady, "if a clumsy elephant, stepped on the only good foot you've got."

"If you think I'm the one that claims to be an elephant—" began Anderson.

"Cootchy, cootchy, cootchy," cooed the lady, addressing the row of holes. Whereupon the rustling in the interior of the devilish box increased to a turmoil. The two citizens of Tinkletown stared wide-eyed at the three little circles, and their eyes grew wider as they saw that one of them was now completely stopped up by a dark, ugly object that bore resemblance to nothing they had ever seen before—a wet, shiny thing that was alive and quivering.

The unnatural Mrs. Fox promptly poked her finger through the hole and rubbed the snout of what must have been a full-sized boa-constrictor. Instantly to their horror, the black obstruction, went through a process of splitting, and several deadly fangs were revealed. Once more the wriggling black tongue darted out to caress the lady's unprotected finger.

"Oh, you darling!" cried the lady. "Please, Mr. Locksmith, see if you can't find a key that will fit the lock."

Marshal Crow dragged his friend toward the door.

"Did you see it?" he whispered hoarsely.

Before Mort could answer, the door flew open and in rushed Mrs. Bloomer, bareheaded and in a great state of agitation.

"For heaven's sake, Anderson, hurry up and come with me," she cried. "Bring a pistol—and, Mort, you get a couple of axes and a pitchfork or two. My God, something awful is loose in one of them rooms upstairs! The most terrible racket is going on in there. I—Oh, there you are!" She caught sight of her lodgers. "Arrest them, Anderson! Lock them up at once. They're dangerous people. They oughtn't to be running at large. Oh, that awful thing! It sounds like it was twenty feet long, and it's thrashing all over the room. Oh, my God! What a scare I've had! Oh, you needn't look at me innocent like that, you two. You're in for it, or my name ain't Jennie Bloomer. Call a posse,

Anderson, and surround the hotel. Thank Heaven, the door of that room is locked, but goodness knows how soon it will be crawlin' through the transom."

At that instant she discovered that her skirt was almost touching the big black box on the floor. Emitting a sharp squeal, she gave an elephantine leap to the shelter of Anderson's arms, almost bowling him over.

"God knows what she's got in that valise," she whimpered.

Mr. Fox put on an exceedingly bold front. Realizing that he was cornered, he adopted a lightly boastful air.

"What we've got in this valise, as you call it, madam, is worth more than your whole blamed hotel."

"Keep away from that valise," warned Anderson Crow, addressing Mr. Fox. "Give me time to think. Somethin's got to be done, and right away. I can't take any chances of these terrible things gettin' loose an' drivin' our citizens out of town."

"The first thing you got to do, Anderson Crow," shouted Mrs. Bloomer, "is to capture the reptile that's loose in my hotel. That's what you got to do." She turned upon the pretty Mrs. Fox. "Snake charmer! That's a nice business for a woman to be in. Don't come near me."

"I am not thinking of coming near you, you old rip!" said Mrs. Fox, losing her temper in a very womanly fashion.

"None o' that, now—none o' that," warned the town marshal. "Keep a civil tongue in your head, young woman."

"Why, you long-whiskered old—" began the lady, but her husband spared the Marshal a whirlwind of revelations by taking her arm and leading her to the rear of the store, where for some minutes they were in close and earnest conference.

"The thing to do," said Mort Fryback, "is to take this box down to the crick an' drop it in, all locked and everything. That will put an end to the cussed things, better'n any other way I know."

A furious commotion took place inside the box, preventing further discussion on the part of the retreating observers. It was as if a dozen huge and powerful serpents were exerting every effort to escape.

The voice of Mrs. Fox, clear as a bell, assailed them from behind.

"They're hungry, poor things," she cried. "Perfectly ravenous."

"That settles it," said Marshal Crow. "We've got to git rid of 'em if we have to set fire to your store, Mort. They're terrible when they haven't been fed fer a long time. Swaller pigs an' sheep—*and* children whole, they say."

Mr. Fox approached. He was now very polite and ingratiating.

"Permit me," he observed, "to offer a solution. If you will give me a bunch of keys, my friend, I will remove the case to my room and open it—if possible. No harm will come to anybody, and in one hour or so, my wife and I will be on our way. My automobile is in your local garage, Mr. Hawk, and we can be ready to start as soon as we have fed and aired the—er—shall we say contents?"

"You arrest him, Anderson," cried Mrs. Bloomer. "Hold him till I estimate the damage that's been done to my property. He's got to pay fer that before he can get out of this town."

"I guess you'd better step over to the calaboose with me, mister," said Anderson firmly. "And you too, ma'am. This here lady prefers charges against you, an' it's my duty to—"

"What is the charge, madam?" demanded Mr. Fox, lighting a cigarette.

"Never mind," said the Marshal; "we'll attend to that later."

Mr. Fryback put in a word at this point. "Yes, but who's going to take charge of this here box? It can't stay here in my place. First thing you know the derned things will gnaw a hole in the side and git out."

"If it is not too far, Mr. Officer, I should be happy to carry the box over to the lock-up—unless, of course, some one else will volunteer. I see quite a number of citizens looking in through the window. Doubtless some of them might—"

"How long after a man's been on a bad spree is he likely to think he sees snakes?" demanded Anderson, struck with an idea.

"The time varies," replied Mr. Fox, rather startled.

"Alf ain't been tight in a good many years," mused the Marshal. "I guess it would be safe to let him carry 'em. Don't you think so, Mort?"

"Him and Newt Spratt," said Mort. "Newt's always braggin' about not being afraid of anything."

"Well, perhaps it would be just as well not to tell 'em what's in this here box," said Anderson. He turned to the pair of strangers. "Only they ain't going to carry it to the calaboose. They're going to carry it to the crick, an' throw it in."

The young woman uttered a cry of dismay, and her husband uttered something distinctly out of place, for Mrs. Bloomer again told him he ought to be ashamed of himself.

After a few whispered words in the ear of the distracted

young woman, Mr. Fox turned to the others.

"I'll tell you what we'll do, gentlemen," said he, and then added, with a polite bow to the corpulent Mrs. Bloomer, "and ladies. Mrs. Fox and I had planned giving a little exhibition at the hotel, but that now seems to be out of the question. Kindly bear in mind that we are not visiting your little city on pleasure bent. We are here strictly for business. As a rule we do not make one-night stands. But we have been attracted to your charming city almost against our will—although, I may add, it was at the earnest invitation of one of your most important denizens—I should say citizens. You will agree, I am sure, that it would hardly pay us to visit a place like this unless we were reasonably assured of something in the way of pecuniary benefits. You may not know it, gentlemen, but we have had a bona-fide offer of one hundred dollars—and that isn't to be sneezed at, is it? We— Please bear with me, Mr. Hawk. I shall not detain you—"

"My name is Mr. Crow," snapped Anderson.

"Sorry," apologized Fox. "I fear I confused you with the celebrated Hawkshaw, the detective."

Mr. Crow turned purple.

"That's what Harry Squires, the reporter on the *Banner*, calls him most of the time," volunteered Mort Fryback. "That, an' Shellback Holmes."

"Such is fame," said Mr. Fox agreeably. "Well, to get right down to cases, Mrs. Fox and I propose that you allow us to give our little exhibition in the Town Hall,—if you have one—and—"

"Not much!" roared Anderson. "I've had enough of this talk. I'm going to take action at once." He flung open the front door and addressed the group in front of the store, now increased to nearly a score, including several scattered women and children—and Ed Higgins' dog. "I call on all you men to assist me in surrounding the Grand View Hotel. There is dangerous work ahead, and I want only the bravest,—wait a second, Newt, don't go away,—and most determined men in town to volunteer. Here, Mort, you hand out some axes, an' pitchforks, an' crowbars, an'—"

"Oh, for heaven's sake, George," cried Mrs. Fox frantically, "don't let them do it. Stop them!"

But the stranger motioned for her to be silent.

Some time was spent in explaining the situation to the posse, and in stationing a group of the hardiest men beneath certain windows of the second floor back. During this arrangement of forces, three of the bravest men in Tinkletown had to go to the post office for some very important letters, and two more rushed over to see that they came back.

Anderson Crow marshalled a dozen or more able-bodied conscripts in Main Street, preparatory to a frontal attack on the suite at the head of the stairway. He had commandeered a double-barreled shotgun belonging to Bill Kepsal, and with this he proposed to "shoot the daylights" out of the serpent through the transom if it hadn't crawled under the bed where he couldn't "get a bead on it."

In the meantime, Mr. Fox had carried the big black box out of Fryback's store, and his wife was now standing guard over it on the porch of the Grand View Hotel.

Marshal Crow was issuing commands right and left, and the squad, augmented by a step-ladder from the hardware shop, was about to enter the hotel, when Mrs. Fox uttered an excited little shriek, and then these desolating words:

"Oh, George, I've found it! I've got the key. It was away down in my muff."

Before any action could be taken to restrain the impetuous young woman, she was inserting the key in the lock!

Those nearest her collided violently with those farther away, and in less time than it takes to mention it, there was no one within a radius of fifty feet—except a new arrival on the scene.

To the intense horror of Mort Fryback, his wife emerged from the Grand View Hotel and entered the danger zone.

"Hey, Maude!" he bellowed. "Keep away from that! For the love of—" He clapped his hand over his eyes. Mrs. Fryback had reached the side of the eager Mrs. Fox just as that lady lifted the lid of the box.

Now, Mrs. Fryback was Mort's third wife; according to longevity statistics, she was much too young to die. As a matter of fact, she was little more than a bride. That probably accounts for the brand-new mink coat and muff she was sporting. Moreover, it accounts for Mort's surprising mendacity and even more amazing humility in relation to the taking-off of Mike. No doubt in similar circumstances, he would have told his second wife, who died when she was pretty well along in years, that he'd show her who was boss in his home, and if she didn't like what he did to Mike, she could lump it. But, alas, between a vacillating young wife who has you under her thumb and a constant old one who has been thoroughly squashed under yours for a great many years, there is a world of difference.

Others who stared in horror at the picture on the porch, groaned audibly as young Mrs. Fox looked up into the face of the unsuspecting victim and smiled. Thus encouraged, young Mrs. Fryback, disdaining death, smiled in return and stooped over to look into the depths of that unspeakable box. Instead of starting back in alarm, she uttered a shrill little cry of delight, and dropping to her knees plunged both hands into the nest of wriggling horrors!

Lucius Fry, who had hastily set up the step-ladder, and was now balancing himself somewhat precariously at the top of it, let out a lugubrious howl.

"She's a goner!" he announced.

The two young women had their heads close together and were conversing. Marshal Crow, armed with the double barreled shotgun, began a cautious circuitous advance, his finger on the trigger.

He stopped short when about twenty feet from the women, and spasmodically pulled the trigger. There is no telling what might have happened if the gun had been loaded.

Mr. Fox had deliberately overturned the box and—out scampered three sprightly Boston terrier puppies!

Ten minutes later all but one of Mort Fryback's farming utensils were back in stock. The missing implement, a hatchet, was furtively on its way to the barber-shop of one Ebenezer January, coloured.

Mr. and Mrs. Fryback, Marshal Crow and the amiable Foxes discussed the "points" of the frolicsome puppies in the rear of the hardware store.

"I just adore this one, Mrs. Fox," said Mrs. Fryback, pointing to a rugged little rascal who was patiently gnawing at Mr. Fryback's peg-leg. "Do you really recommend him as the best of the lot, Mr. Fox?" she inquired, turning her shining eyes upon the gentleman.

"Absolutely," said Mr. Fox. "Wouldn't you say so, Mr. Crow?"

"Ab-so-lutely," said Anderson.

"Then I'll take him," said Mort's wife, and Mort not only sighed but wiped a fine coat of moisture from his brow. "One hundred dollars is the very least you will take?"

"The very least, Mrs. Fryback. He is a thoroughbred, you know. My kennels are famous, as you doubtless noted in my advertisement in *Town and Country*—and I can personally guarantee every pup that comes out of them. In your letter to me, Mrs. Fryback, you stated that only the best I had on hand would be considered. The mother of these puppies has a pedigree a yard long, and the father, as I mentioned before, is Stubbs the Twelfth. Nothing more need be said. The mother, Bonnie Bridget, you have just seen. Stubbs the Twelfth belongs to a millionaire in Albany. Allow me to congratulate you, madam,"— extending his hand,—"on having secured one of the finest dogs in America. And you also, Mr. Fryback, on having a wife who is such a discriminating judge of thoroughbreds."

Mr. Fryback looked a trifle startled, but said nothing.

"If you ever come to our town, Mr. Crow, I hope you will look us up," broke in Mr. Fox. "Our place is about two miles out in the country. By the way, has Mrs. Crow a good dog —I mean one that she can be proud of?"

"She has a thoroughbred setter," said Marshal Crow, compressing his lips.

"A hundred dollars is a lot of money fer a dog," murmured Mr. Fryback. He met his wife's eye for a second and then added: "But, of course, my wife has just lost one that was worth a thousand dollars, so—I guess it ain't so much, after all."

"Marmaduke was a really wonderful dog, Mrs. Fox," vouchsafed Mort's wife, assuming a sad and pensive expression.

"I am sure he must have been," said Mrs. Fox.

"One hundred dollars is very cheap, sir, for a thoroughbred Boston terrier in these days," said Mr. Fox. "Isn't that so, Mr. Crow?"

"Cheap as dirt," said Anderson.

"Mortimer, will you please give Mr. Fox the money?" said Mrs. Fryback. "And, by the way, Mr. Crow, I hope you take down all those reward notices at once. I wouldn't know what to do with Marmaduke now, even if some one did bring him back to me."

"I know what I'd order you to do with him," said Anderson, meeting Mort's melancholy gaze at last.

"What, may I inquire?"

"I'd order you to bury him," said the town marshal, speaking in his capacity as chairman of the Board of Health.

Mrs. Fryback looked at him steadily for a second or two, and then slowly closed an eye.

SHADES OF THE GARDEN OF EDEN!

It wasn't often that Marshal Crow acknowledged that he was in a quandary. When he *did* find himself in that rare state of mind, he invariably went to Harry Squires, the editor of the *Banner*, for counsel—but never for advice. He had in the course of a protracted career as preserver of the peace and dignity of Tinkletown, found himself confronted by seemingly unsolvable mysteries, but he always had succeeded in unravelling them, one way or another, to his own complete satisfaction. Only the grossest impudence on the part of the present chronicler would permit the tiniest implication to creep into this or any other chapter of his remarkable history that might lead the reader to suspect that he did not solve them to the complete satisfaction of any one else. So, quite obviously, the point is not one to be debated.

Now, as nearly every one knows, Tinkletown is a temperance place. There is no saloon there,—unless, of course, one chooses to be rather nasty about Brubaker's Drugstore. Away back in the Seventies,—soon after the Civil War, in fact,—an enterprising but misguided individual attempted to establish a bar-room at the corner of Main and Sickle Streets. He opened the Sunlight Bar and for one whole day and night revelled in the conviction that he had found a silver mine. The male population of Tinkletown, augmented by a swarm of would-be inebriates from all the farms within a radius of ten miles, flocked to the Sunlight Bar and proceeded to get gloriously and collectively drunk on the contents of the two kegs of lager beer that constituted an experimental stock in trade.

The next morning the women of Tinkletown started in to put the Sunlight Bar out of business. They did not, as you may suspect, hurl stones at the place, neither did they feloniously enter and wreak destruction with axes, hatchets and hoe-handles. Not a bit of it. They were peaceful, law-abiding women, not sanguinary amazons. What they did was perfectly simple.

It is possible, even probable, that they were the pioneer "pickets" of our benighted land. At any rate, bright and early on the second day of the Sunlight Bar, the ladies of Tinkletown brought their knitting and their sewing down to the corner of Main and Sickle streets and sat themselves down in front of the shrinking "silver mine." They came with rocking-chairs, and camp-chairs, and milk-stools, and benches, too, and instead of chanting a doleful lay, they chattered in a blithe and merry fashion. There was no going behind the fact, however, that these smiling, complacent women formed the Death Watch that was to witness the swift, inevitable finish of the Sunlight Bar.

They came in relays, and they stayed until the lights went out in the desolate house of cheer. The next day they were on hand again, and the next, and still the next. Fortunately for them, but most unluckily for the proprietor of the Sunlight Bar, the month was August: they could freeze him out, but he couldn't freeze them out.

Sheepish husbands and sons passed them by, usually on the opposite sidewalk, but not one of them had the hardihood to extend a helping hand to the expiring saloon. At the end of a week, the Sunlight Bar drew its last breath. It died of starvation. The only mourner at its bier was the bewildered saloon-keeper, who engaged a dray to haul the remains to Boggs City, the County seat, and it was he who said, as far back as 1870, that he was in favour of taking the vote away from the men and giving it exclusively to the women.

Tinkletown, according to the sage observations of Uncle Dad Simms, was rarely affected by the unsettling problems of the present day. This talk about "labour unrest" was ridiculous, he said. If the remainder of the world was anything like Tinkletown, labour didn't do much except rest. It was getting so that if a workin'-man had very far to walk to "git" to his job, he had to step along purty lively if he wanted to arrive there in plenty of time to eat his lunch and start back home again. And as for "this here prohibition question," he didn't take any stock in it at all. Tinkletown had got along without liquor for more than a hundred years and he guessed it could get along for another century or two without much trouble, especially as it was only ten miles to Boggs City where you could get all you wanted to drink any day in the week. Besides, he argued, loudly and most violently, being so deaf that he had to strain his own throat in order to hear himself, there wasn't anybody in Tinkletown except Alf Reesling that ever wanted a drink, and even Alf wouldn't take it when you offered it to him.

But in spite of Uncle Dad's sage conclusions, it was this very prohibition question that was disturbing Anderson Crow. He sauntered into the *Banner* office late one afternoon in May and planked himself down in a chair beside the editor's desk. There was a troubled look in his eyes, which gave way to vexation after he had made three or four fruitless efforts to divert the writer's attention from the sheet of "copy paper" on which he was scribbling furiously.

"How do you spell beverage, Anderson?" inquired Mr. Squires abruptly.

"What kind of beverage?" demanded Mr. Crow.

"Any kind, just so it's intoxicating. Never mind, I'll take a chance and spell it the easiest way. That's the way the dictionary spells it, so I guess it's all right. Well, sir, what's on your mind?— besides your hat, I mean. You look worried."

"I am worried. Have you any idee as to the size of the apple crop in this neighbourhood last summer and fall, Harry?"

"Not the least."

"Well, sir, it was the biggest we've had since 1902, 'specially the fall pickin.'"

"What's the idea? Do you want me to put something in the *Banner* about Bramble County's bumper crop of pippins?"

"No. I just want to ask you if there's anything in this new prohibition amendment against apple cider?"

"Not that I'm aware of."

"Well, do you know it's impossible to buy a good eatin' or cookin' apple in this town today, Harry Squires?"

"You don't say so! In spite of the big crop last fall?"

"You could buy all you wanted last week, by the bushel or peck or barrel,—finest, juiciest apples you ever laid your eyes on."

"Well, I don't like apples anyway, so it doesn't mean much in my life."

Anderson was silent for a moment or two, contemplating his foot with singular intentness.

"Was you ever drunk on hard cider?" he inquired at last, —transferring his gaze to the rapidly moving hand that held the pencil.

The reporter jabbed a period,—or "full stop," as they call it in a certain form of literature,—in the middle of a sentence, and looked up with sudden interest.

"Yes," he said, with considerable force. "I'll never forget it. You can get tighter on hard cider than anything else I know of."

"Well, there you are," exclaimed the Marshal, banging his gnarled fist on the arm of the chair. "And as far as I c'n make out, there ain't no law ag'inst cider stayin' in the barrel long enough to get good and hard, an' what's more, there ain't no law ag'ainst sellin' cider, hard or sweet, is there?"

"I get your point, Anderson. And I also get your deductions concerning the mysterious disappearance of all the apples in Tinkletown. Apparently we are to have a shortage of dried apples this year, with an overflow of hard cider instead. By George, it's interesting, to say the least. Looks as though an apple orchard is likely to prove more valuable than a gold mine, doesn't it?"

"Yes, sir! 'Specially if you've got trees that bear in the fall. Fall apples make the best cider. They ain't so mushy. And as fer the feller that owns a cider-press, why, dog-gone it, he ought to be as rich as Crowsis."

"I seem to recall that you have a cider-press on your farm on Crow's Mountain,—and a whacking good orchard, too. Are you thinking of resigning as Marshal of Tinkletown?"

"What say?"

"I see you're not," went on Harry. "Of course you understand you can't very well manufacture hard cider and sell it and still retain your untarnished reputation as a defender of the law."

"I'm not figurin' on makin' hard cider," said Anderson, with some irritation. "You don't *make* hard cider, Harry. It makes itself. All you do is to rack the apple juice off into a barrel, or something, with a little yeast added, and then leave it to do the work. It ferments an' then, if you want to, you rack it off again an' bottle it an'—well, gee whiz, how tight you c'n get on it if you ain't got sense enough to let it alone. But I ain't thinkin' about what I'm goin' to do, 'cause I ain't to do anything but make applebutter out of my orchard,—an' maybe a little cider-vinegar fer home consumption. What's worryin' me is what to do about all these other people around here. If they all take to makin' cider this fall,—or even sooner,—an' if they bottle or cask it proper,—we'll have enough hard cider in this township to give the whole state of New York the delirium trimmins."

"I don't see that you can do anything, Anderson," said Squires, leaning back in his chair and puffing at his pipe. "You can't keep people from making cider, you know. And you can't keep 'em from drinking it. Besides, who's going to take the trouble to ascertain whether it contains one-half of one percent alcohol? What interests me more than anything else is the possibility of this township becoming 'wet' in spite of itself,—an' to my certain knowledge, it has been up to now the barrenest desert on God's green earth."

"People are so all-fired contrary," Anderson complained. "For the last fifty years the citizens of this town and its suburbs have been so dead set ag'inst liquor that if a man went up to Boggs City an' got a little tipsy he had to run all the way home so's he'd be out of breath when he got there. Nobody ever kept a bottle of whiskey in his house, 'cause nobody wanted it an' it would only be in the way. But now look at 'em! The minute the Government says they can't have it, they begin movin' things around in their cellars so's to make room fer the barrels they're going to put in. An' any day you want to drive out in the country you c'n see farmers an' hired men treatin' the apple-trees as if they was the tenderest plants a-growin'. I heard this mornin' that Henry Wimpelmeyer is to put in a cider-press at his tanyard, an' old man Smock's turnin' his grist mill into an apple-mill. An' everybody is hoardin' apples, Harry. It beats the Dutch."

"It's up to you to frustrate their nefarious schemes, Mr. Hawkshaw. The fair name of the Commonwealth must be preserved. I use the word advisedly. It sounds a great deal better than 'pickled.' Now, do you want me to begin a campaign in the *Banner* against the indiscriminate and mendacious hardening of apple-cider, or am I to leave the situation entirely in your hands?"

Marshal Crow arose. The fire of determination was in his ancient eye.

"You leave it to me," said he, and strode majestically from the room.

Encountering Deacon Rank in front of the *Banner* office, he chanced this somewhat offensive remark:

"Say, Deacon, what's this I hear about you?"

The deacon looked distinctly uneasy.

"You can always hear a lot of things about me that aren't true," he said.

"I ain't so sure about that," said Anderson, eyeing him narrowly. "Hold on! What's your hurry?"

"I—I got to step in here and pay my subscription to the *Banner*," said the deacon.

"Well, that's something nobody'll believe when they hear about it," said Anderson. "It'll be mighty hard fer the proprieter of the*Banner* to believe it after all these years."

"Times have been so dog-goned hard fer the last couple of years, I ain't really been able to—"

"Too bad about you," broke in Anderson scornfully.

"Everything costs so much in these days," protested the deacon. "I ain't had a new suit of clothes fer seven or eight years. Can't afford 'em. My wife was sayin' only last night she needed a new hat,—somethin' she can wear all the year round,—but goodness knows this ain't no time to be thinkin' of hats. She—"

"She ain't had a new hat fer ten years," interrupted Anderson. "No wonder the pore woman's ashamed to go to church."

"What's that? Who says she's ashamed to go to church? Anybody that says my wife's ashamed to go to church is a—is a —well, he tells a story, that's all."

"Well, why don't she go to church?"

"'Tain't because she's ashamed of her hat, let me tell you that, Anderson Crow. It's a fine hat an' it's just as good as new. She's tryin' to save it, that's what she's tryin' to do. She knows it's got to last her five or six years more, an' how in tarnation can she make it last that long if she wears it all the time? Use a little common sense, can't you? Besides, I'll thank you not to stick your nose in my family affairs any—"

"What's that you got in your pocket?" demanded Anderson, indicating the bulging sides of the deacon's overcoat.

"None of your business!"

"Now, don't you get hot. I ask you again, civil as possible,—what you got in your pocket?"

"I'm a respectable, tax-paying, church-going citizen of this here town, and I won't put up with any of your cussed insinuations," snapped the deacon. "You act as if I'd stole something. You—"

"I ain't accusin' you of stealin' anything. I'm only accusin' you of havin' something in your pocket. No harm in that, is there?"

The deacon hesitated for a minute. Then he made a determined effort to temporize.

"And what's more," he said, "my wife's hat's comin' back into style before long, anyhow. It's just as I keep on tellin' her. The styles kinder go in circles, an' if she waits long enough they'll get back to the kind she's wearin', and then she'll be the first woman in Tinkletown to have the very up-to-datest style in hats,—'way ahead of anybody else,—and it will be as good as new, too, you bet, after the way she's been savin' it."

"Now I know why you got your pockets stuffed full of things,—eggs, maybe, or hick'ry nuts, or—whatever it is you got in 'em. It's because you're tryin' to save a piece of wrappin' paper or a bag, or the wear and tear on a basket. No wonder you got so much money you don't know how to spend it."

"And as for me gettin' a new suit of clothes," pursued the deacon, doggedly, "if times don't get better the chances are I'll have to be buried in the suit I got on this minute. I never knowed times to be so hard—"

The marshal interrupted him. "You go in an' pay up what you owe fer the *Banner* an' I'll wait here till you come out."

Deacon Rank appeared to reflect. "Come to think of it, I guess I'll stop in on my way back from the post office. Ten or fifteen minutes—"

He stopped short, a fixed intent look in his sharp little eyes. His gaze was directed past Anderson's head at some object down the street. Then, quite abruptly and without even the ceremony of a hasty "good-bye," he bolted into the *Banner* office, slamming the door in the marshal's face.

"Well, I'll be dog-goned!" burst from the lips of the astonished Mr. Crow. "I never knowed him to change his mind so quick as that in all my life,—or so often. What the dickens—"

Indignation succeeded wonder at this instant, cutting off his audible reflections. Snapping his jaws together, he laid a resolute hand on the doorknob. Just as he turned it and was on the point of stamping in after the deacon, his eye fell upon an approaching figure—the figure of a woman. If it had not been for the hat she was wearing, he would have failed to recognize her at once. But there was no mistaking the hat.

"Hi!" called out the wearer of the too familiar object. Marshal Crow let go of the door knob and stared at the lady in sheer stupefaction.

Mrs. Rank's well-preserved hat was perched rakishly at a perilous angle over one ear. A subsequent shifting to an even more precarious position over the other ear, as the result of a swift, inaccurate sweep of the lady's hand, created an instant impression that it was attached to her drab, disordered hair by means of a new-fangled but absolutely dependable magnet. Never before had Marshal Crow seen that ancient hat so much as the fraction of an inch out of "plumb" with the bridge of Mrs. Rank's undeviating nose.

She approached airily. Her forlorn little person was erect, even soldierly. Indeed, if anything, she was a shade too erect at times. At such times she appeared to be in some danger of completely forgetting her equilibrium. She stepped high, as the saying is, and without her usual precision. In a word, the meek and retiring wife of Deacon Rank was hilariously drunk!

Pedestrians, far and near, stopped stockstill in their tracks to gaze open-mouthed at the jaunty drudge; storekeepers peered wide-eyed and incredulous from windows and doors. If you suddenly had asked any one of them when the world was coming to an end, he would have replied without the slightest hesitation.

She bore down upon the petrified Mr. Crow.

"Is zat you, An'erson?" she inquired, coming to an uncertain stop at the foot of the steps. Where—oh, where! was the subdued, timorous voice of Sister Rank? Whose—oh, whose! were the shrill and fearless tones that issued forth from the lips of the deacon's wife?

"For the Lord's sake, Lucy,—wha—what ails you?" gasped the horrified marshal.

"Nothing ails me, An'erson. Nev' fel' better'n all my lipe —life. Where's my hush—hushban'?"

She brandished her right hand, and clutched in her fingers an implement that caused Anderson's eyes to almost start from his head.

"What's that you got in your hand?" he cried out.

"Thish? Thass a hashet. Don't you know whass a hashet is?"

"I—I know it's a hatchet. Lucy,—but, fer heaven's sake, what are you goin' to do with it?"

"I'm going to cut th' deacon's head off wiz it," she replied blandly.

"What!"

"Yes, shir; thass what I'm goin' cut off. Right smack off, An'erson,—and you can't stop me, unnerstan', An'erson. I been wannin' cuttiz 'ead off f'r twenny-fi' year. I—"

"Hey! Stop wavin' that thing around like that, Lucy

Rank!"

"You needen be 'fraid, An'erson. I woulden hurt you fer whole United States. Where's my hussam, An'erson?"

Marshal Crow looked hopelessly at the well-scattered witnesses who were taking in the scene from a respectful distance. Obviously it was his duty to do something. Not that he really felt that the deacon's head should not be cut off by his long-suffering wife, but that it was hardly the proper thing for her to do it in public. Virtually every man in Tinkletown had declared, at one time or another, that Mrs. Rank ought to slit the old skinflint's throat, or poison him, or set fire to him, or something of the sort, but, even though he agreed with them, the fact still remained that Marshal Crow considered it his duty to protect the deacon in this amazing crisis.

"Gimme that hatchet, Lucy Rank," he commanded, with authority. "You ain't yourself, an' you know it. You gimme that hatchet an' then lemme take you home an' put you to bed. You'll be all right in the mornin', an—"

"Didden my hussam go in the Blammer ossif minute ago?" she demanded, fixing a baleful glare upon the closed door.

"See here, Lucy, you been drinkin'. You're full as a goat. You gimme that—"

"An'erson Crow, are you tryin' inshult me?" she demanded, drawing herself up. "Wha' you mean sayin' I'm dunk,—drump? You know I never touched dropper anything. I'm the bes' frien' your wife's got innis town an' she—who's 'at lookin' out zat winner? Zat my hussam?"

Before the marshal could interfere, she blazed away at one of the windows in the *Banner* office. There was a crash of glass. She was now empty-handed but the startled guardian of the peace was slow to realize it. He was still trying to convince himself that it was the gentle, long-suffering Mrs. Rank who stood before him.

Suddenly, to his intense dismay, she threw her arms around his neck and began to weep—and wail.

"I—I—love my hussam,—I love my hussam,—an' I didden mean cuttiz 'ead off—I didden—I didden, An'erson. My hussam's dead. My hussam's head's all off,—an' I love my hussam—I love my hussam."

The door flew open and Harry Squires strode forth.

"What the devil does this mean—My God! Mrs. Rank! Wha—what's the matter with her, Anderson?"

The marshal gazed past him into the office. His eyes were charged with apprehension.

"Where—where's the deacon's head?" he gulped.

The editor did not hear him. He had eyes and ears only for the mumbling creature who dangled limply from the marshal's neck; her face was hidden but her hat was very much in evidence. It was bobbing up and down on the back of her head.

"Let's get her into the office," he exclaimed. "This is dreadful, Anderson,—shocking!"

A moment later the door closed behind the trio,—and a key was turned in the lock. This was the signal for a general advance of all observers. Headed by Mr. Hawkins, the undertaker, they swarmed up the steps and crowded about the windows. The thoughtful Mr. Squires, however, conducted Mrs. Rank to the composing-room and the crowd was cheated.

Bill Smith, the printer, looked up from his case and pied half of the leading editorial. He proved to be a printer of the old school. After a soft, envious whistle he remarked:

"My God, I'd give a month's pay for one like that," and any one who has ever come in contact with an old-time printer will know precisely what he meant.

"Oh, my poor b'loved hussam," murmured Mrs. Rank. "My poor b'loved hussam whass I have endured f'r twenty-fi' years wiz aller Chrissen forcitude of—where is my poor hussam?"

She swept the floor with a hazy, uncertain look. Not observing anything that looked like a head, she turned a bleary, accusing eye upon Bill Smith, the printer, and there is no telling what she might have said to him if Harry Squires had not intervened.

"Sit down here, Mrs. Rank,—do. Your husband is all right. He was here a few minutes ago, and—which way did he go, Bill?"

"Out," said Bill laconically, jerking his head in the direction of an open window at the rear.

"Didden—didden I cuttiz 'ead off?" demanded Mrs. Rank.

"Not so's you'd notice it," said Bill.

"Well, 'en, whose 'ead did I c'off?"

"Nobody's, my dear lady," said Squires, soothingly. "Everything's all right,—quite all right. Please—"

"Where's my hashet? Gimme my hashet. I insiss on my hashet. I gotter cuttiz 'ead off. Never ress in my grave till I cuttiz 'ead off."

Presently they succeeded in quieting her. She sat limply in an arm-chair, brought from the front office, and stared pathetically up into the faces of the three perspiring men.

"Can you beat it?" spoke Harry Squires to the beaddled

marshal.

"Where do you suppose she got it?" muttered Anderson, helplessly. "Maybe she had a toothache or something and took a little brandy—"

"Not a bit of it," said Harry. "She's been hitting old man Rank's stock of hard cider, that's what she's been doing."

"Impossible! He's our leadin' church-member. He ain't got any hard cider. He's dead-set ag'inst intoxicatin' liquors. I've heard him say it a hundred times."

"Well, just ask *her*," was Harry's rejoinder.

Mr. Crow drew a stool up beside the unfortunate lady and sat down.

"What have you been drinking, Lucy?" he asked gently, patting her hand.

"You're a liar," said Mrs. Rank, quite distinctly. This was an additional shock to Anderson. The amazing potency of strong drink was here being exemplified as never before in the history of Time. A sober Lucy Rank would no more have called any one a liar than she would have cursed her Maker. Such an expression from the lips of the meek and down-trodden martyr was unbelievable,—and the way she said it! Not even Pat Murphy, the coal-wagon driver, with all his years of practice, could have said it with greater distinctness,—not even Pat who possessed the masculine right to amplify the behest with expletives not supposed to be uttered except in the presence of his own sex.

"She'll be swearing next," said Bill Smith, after a short silence. "I couldn't stand *that*," he went on, taking his coat from a peg in the wall.

Mr. Squires took the lady in hand.

"If you will just be patient for a little while, Mrs. Rank,

Bill will go out and find your husband and bring him here at once. In the meantime, I will see that your hatchet is sharpened up, and put in first-class order for the sacrifice. Go on, Bill. Fetch the lady's husband." He winked at the departing Bill. "We've got to humour her," he said in an aside to Anderson. "These hard-cider jags are the worst in the world. The saying is that a quart of hard cider would start a free-for-all fight in heaven. Excuse me, Mrs. Rank, while I fix your nice new hat for you. It isn't on quite straight—and it's such a pretty hat, isn't it?"

Mrs. Rank squinted at him for a moment in doubtful surprise, and then smiled.

"My hussam tol' you to shay that," said she, shaking her finger at him.

"Not at all,—not at all! I've always said it, haven't I, Anderson? Say *yes*, you old goat!" (He whispered the last, and the marshal responded nobly.) "Now, while we are waiting for Mr. Rank, perhaps you will tell us just why you want to cut his head off today. What has the old villain been up to lately?"

She composed herself for the recital. The two men looked down at her with pity in their eyes.

"He d'sherted me today,—abon—abonimably d'sherted me. For'n Missionary S'ciety met safternoon at our house. All ladies in S'ciety met our house. Deac'n tol' me be generous— givvem all the r'fressmens they wanted. He went down shellar an' got some zat shider he p'up lash Marsh. He said he wanted to shee whezzer it was any good." She paused, her brow wrinkled in thought. "Lesh see—where was I?"

"In the parlour?" supplied Anderson, helpfully.

She shook her head impatiently. "I mean where was I

talkin' 'bout? Oh, yesh,—'bout shider. When Woman For'n Missinary S'ciety come I givvem shider,—lots shider. No harm in shider, An'erson,—so don' look like that. Deacon shays baby could drink barrel shider an—and sho on an' sho forth. Well, For'n Missinary S'ciety all havin' splennid time,—singin' 'n' prayin' 'n' sho on 'n' sho forth, an'—an' sho on 'n' sho forth. Then your wife, An'erson, she jumps up 'n' shays we gotter have shong-shervice,—reg'ler shong shervice. She—"

"*My* wife?" exclaimed Anderson. "Was Eva Crow there?"

"Shert'nly. Never sho happy 'n' her life. Couldn't b'lieve my eyes 'n' ears. And Sister Jones too,—your bosh's wife, Misser Squires. Say, d'you ever know she could shing bass? Well, she can, all right. She c'n shing bass an' tenor'n ev'thing else, she can. She—"

"Where—where are they now?" demanded Anderson, with a wild look at Harry.

"Who? The Woman For'n Missinary S'ciety?"

"Yes. For heaven's sake, don't tell me they're loose on the street!"

"Not mush! Promised me they wait till I capshered my hussam, deader 'live, an' bring 'im 'ome. Didden I tell you my hussam desherted me? He desherted all of us—all of For'n Missinary S'ciety. I gotter bring 'im back, deader 'live. Wannim to lead in shong shervice. My hussam's got loudes' voice in town. Leads shingin' in chursh 'n' prayer meetin' 'n' ever 'where else. Loudes' voice in town, thass what he is. Prays loudes' of anybody, too. All ladies waitin' up my house f'r loudes voice in town to lead 'em in shacred shong. Muss have somebody with loud voice to lead 'em. Lass I heard of 'em they was all shingin' differen' shongs. Loudes' voice—lou'st voich—lou—"

She slumbered.

The marshal and the editor looked at each other.

"Well, she's safe for the time being," said the latter, wiping his wet forehead.

"An' so's the deacon," added Anderson. "See here, Harry, I got to hustle up to the deacon's house an' see what c'n be done with them women. My lordy! The town will be disgraced if they get out on the street an'—why, like as not, they'll start a parade or somethin'. You stay here an' watch her, an' I'll—"

"No, you don't, my friend," broke in Harry gruffly. "You get her out of this office as quickly as you can."

"Are you afraid to be left alone with that pore, helpless little woman?" demanded Anderson. "I'll take her hatchet away with me, if that's what you're afraid of."

"If you'd been attending to your job as a good, competent official of this benighted town, the poor, helpless little woman wouldn't be in the condition she's in now. You—"

"Hold on there! What do you mean by that?"

"I mean this, Mr. Shellback Holmes. A dozen people in this town have been buying up apples and grinding them and making cider of them as fast as they could cask it ever since last January. Making it right under your nose, and this is the first you've seen of it. There's enough hard cider in Tinkletown at this minute to pickle an army. See those bottles over there under Bill's stool? Well, old Deacon Rank left 'em there because he was afraid he'd bust 'em when he made his exit through that window. He told Bill Smith he could keep them, if he would assume his indebtedness to this office,—two dollars and a quarter,—and he also told Bill that he could guarantee that it was good stuff! We've got visible proof of it here, and we also know how the damned old rascal went about testing the quality of his wares. He has tried it out on the most highly respected ladies in town, that's what he's done,—and why? Because it was the*cheapest* way to do it. He didn't have to waste more than a quart on the whole bunch of 'em. Sure fire stuff! And there are barrels of it in this town, Mr. Shellback Holmes, waiting to be converted into song. Now, the first thing you've got to do is to take this unfortunate result of prohibition home and put her to bed."

Anderson sat down heavily.

"My sakes, Harry,—I—I—why, this is turrible! My wife drunk, an'—an'—Mrs. Jones, an' Mrs. Nixon, an'—"

"Yes, sir," said Harry heartlessly; "they probably are lit up like the sunny side of the moon, and what's more, my friend, if they *do* take it into their poor, beaddled heads to go out and paint the town, there won't be any stopping 'em. Hold on! Didn't you hear what I said about the case in hand? You take her home, do you hear?"

"But—how am I to get her home? I—I can't carry her through the streets," groaned the harassed marshal.

"Hire an automobile, or a delivery-wagon, or—what say?"

"I was just sayin' that maybe I could get Lem Hawkins to loan me his hearse."

Mr. Squires put his hand over his mouth and looked away. When he turned back to the unhappy official, his voice was gentler.

"You leave her to me, old fellow. I'll take care of her. She can stay here till after dark and I'll see that she gets home all right."

"By gosh, Harry, you're a real friend. I—I won't ferget

this,—no, sir, never!"

"What are you going to do first?"

"I'm goin' to get my wife out of that den of iniquity and take her home!" said Anderson resolutely.

"Whether she's willing,—or not?"

"Don't you worry. I got that all thought out. If she won't let me take her home, I'll let on as if I'm full and then she'll insist on takin' me home."

With that he was gone.

The crowd in front of the *Banner* office now numbered at least a hundred. Mr. Crow stopped at the top of the steps and swiftly ran his eye over the excited throng. He was thinking hard and quite rapidly—for him. All the while the crowd was shouting questions at him, he was deliberately counting noses. Suddenly he held up his hand. There was instant, expectant silence.

"All husbands who possess wives in the Woman's Foreign Missionary Society kindly step forward. Make way there, you people,—let 'em through. This way, Newt,—an' you, Alf,—come on, Elmer K.,—I said 'wives,' Mrs. Fry, not husbands. All husbands please congregate in the alley back of the *Banner* office an' wait fer instructions. Don't ask questions. Just do as I tell you. Hey, you kids! Run over an' tell Mort Fryback an' Ed Higgins an' Situate M. Jones I want 'em right away,—an' George Brubaker. Tell him to lock up his store if he has to, but to come at once. Now, you women keep back! This is fer men only."

In due time a troubled, anxious group of men sallied forth from the alley back of the *Banner* office, and, headed by Anderson Crow, marched resolutely down Sickle Street to Maple and advanced upon the house of Deacon Rank.

The song service was in full blast. The men stopped at the bottom of the yard and listened with sinking hearts.

"That's my wife," said Elmer K. Pratt, the photographer, a bleak look in his eyes. "She knows that tune by heart."

"Which tune?" asked Mort Fryback, cocking his ear.

"Why, the one she's singin'," said Elmer. "Now listen,—it goes this way." He hummed a few bars of 'The Rosary.' "Don't you get it? There! Why, you must be deef. I can't hear anything else."

"The only one I can make out is 'Tipperary.' Is that the one she's singin'?"

"Certainly not. I said it goes *this* way. That's somebody else you hear, Mort."

"Hear that?" cried Ed Higgins excitedly. "That's 'Sweet Alice, Ben Bolt!' My wife's favourite. My Lord, Anderson, what's to be done?"

"Keep still!" ordered Anderson. "I'm tryin' to see if I c'n make out my wife's singin'!"

"Well, we got to do somethin'," groaned Newt Spratt, whose wife was organist in the Pond Road Church. "She'll bust that piano all to smash if she keeps on like that."

"Come on, gentlemen," said Anderson, compressing his lips. "Remember now, every man selects his own wife. Every—"

"Wait a minute, Anderson," pleaded George Brubacker. "It'll take more than me to manage my wife if she gets stubborn."

"It ain't our fault if you married a woman twice as big as you are," was the marshal's stern rejoinder. "Now, remember the plan. We're just droppin' in to surprise 'em, to sort of join in the service. Don't fer the land's sake, let 'em see we're uneasy about 'em. We got to use diplomacy. Look pleasant, ever'body,—look happy. Now, then,—forward march! Laugh, dern you, Alf!"

Once more they advanced, chatting volubly, and with faces supposed to be wholly free from anxiety. The merest glance, however, would have penetrated the mask of unconcern. Every man's eye belied his lips.

"I make a motion that we tar an' feather Deacon Rank," said Newt Spratt, as the foremost neared the porch.

Anderson halted them abruptly.

"I want to warn you men right now, that I'm going to search all the cellars in town tomorrow, so you might as well be prepared to empty all your cider into Smock's Crick. You don't need to say you ain't got any on hand. I've been investigatin' for several weeks, an' I want to tell you right here an' now that I've got every cask an' every bottle of hard cider in Tinkletown spotted. I know what's become of every derned apple that was raised in this township last year."

Dead silence followed this heroic speech. Citizens looked at each other, and Situate M. Jones might have been heard to mutter something about "an all-seeing Providence."

Ed Higgins lamely explained that he had "put up a little for vinegar," but Anderson merely smiled.

The front door of the house flew open and several of the first ladies of Tinkletown crowded into view. An invisible choir was singing the Doxology.

"Hello, boys!" called out Mrs. Jones, cheerily. "Come right in! Where's zat nice old deacon?"

"Been waiting for him for nawful long time," said Mrs. Pratt. "Couldn't wait any louder,—I mean longer."

"You had it right the first time," said her husband.

"Just in time for Doxology," called out Mrs. Jones. "Then we're all going down town to hol' open-air temp-rance meet-meeting."

Late that evening, Marshal Crow mounted the steps leading to Dr. Brown's office and rang the bell. He rang it five or six times without getting any response. Then he opened the door and walked in. The doctor was out. On a table inside the door lay the slate on which people left word for him to come to their houses as soon as he returned. The Marshal put on his glasses and took up the pencil to write. One side of the slate was already filled with hurried scribbling. He squinted and with difficulty made out that Dr. Brown was wanted immediately at the homes of Situate M. Jones, Abbie Nixon, Newton Spratt, Mort Fryback, Professor Rank, Rev. Maltby and Joseph P. Singer. He sighed and shook his head sadly. Then he moistened a finger and erased the second name on the list, that of Mrs. Abbie Nixon.

"Husbands first," he muttered in justification of his action in substituting the following line:

"Come at once. A. Crow, Marshal of Tinkletown."

Compunction prevailed, however. He wrote the word "over" at the bottom and, turning the slate over, cleared his conscience by jotting down Mrs. Nixon's "call" at the top of the reverse side. Replacing it on the table, he went away. Virtue was its own reward in this instance at least, for the worthy marshal neglected to put the slate down as he had found it. Mrs. Nixon's "call" alone was visible.

He set out to find Harry Squires. That urbane gentleman was smoking his reportorial corn-cob in the rear of Lamson's store. Except for Lamson's clerk, who had seized the rare opportunity to delve uninterruptedly into the mysteries of the latest "Nick Carter," the store was empty. The usual habitues were absent.

"Did you get her home?" inquired Anderson in a low, cautious tone.

"I did," said Harry.

"See anything of the deacon?"

"No; but Bill Smith did. Bill saw him down at the crick an hour or so ago, knocking in the heads of three or four barrels. Do you know what I've been thinking, Anderson? If somebody would only empty a barrel or so of olive oil into Smock's Crick before morning, we'd have the foundation for the largest supply of French dressing ever created in the history of the world."

Mr. Crow looked scandalized. "Good gosh, Harry, ain't we had enough scandal in this here town today without addin' anything French to it?"

The only moral to be attached to this story lies in the brief statement that Mrs. Crow's indisposition, slight in duration though it was, so occupied Mr. Crow's attention that by the time he was ready to begin his search the second night after the song service, there wasn't so much as a pint of hard cider to be found in Tinkletown. This condition was due in a large measure, no doubt, to the fact that Smock's Creek is an unusually swift little stream. It might even be called turbulent.

"JAKE MILLER HANGS HIMSELF"

"Have you heard the latest news?" inquired Newt Spratt, speaking in a hushed voice. He addressed Uncle Dad Simms, the town's oldest inhabitant, whom he met face to face at the corner of Main and Sickle streets one fine morning in May. Now any one in Tinkletown would tell you that it was the sheerest folly to address Uncle Dad in a hushed voice. Mr. Spratt knew this as well as he knew his own name, so it should be easy to understand that the "news" was of a somewhat awe-inspiring nature. Ordinarily Newt was a loud-mouthed, jovial soul; you could hear him farther and usually longer than any other male citizen in Tinkletown. But now, he spoke in a hushed voice.

Uncle Dad put his hand up to his left ear and said "Hey?" This seemed to bring Mr. Spratt to his senses. He started violently, stared hard for a moment at the octogenarian, and then strode off down Main street, shaking his head as much as to say, "There must be something the matter with me. Nobody ever speaks to him unless he *has* to."

And Uncle Dad, after gazing for a long time at the retreating figure, resumed his shuffling progress up Main street, pleasantly satisfied that Newt had gone to the trouble to tell him it was a nice day.

Although it would not have occurred to Newt, in his dismal state of mind, to look upon the day as a nice one, nevertheless it was. The sun was shining brightly, (but without Newt's knowledge), and the air was soft and balmy and laden with the perfume of spring. Birds were twittering in the new green foliage of the trees, but Newt heard them not; dogs frisked in the sunshine, wagging their tongues and tails, but Newt saw them not; hens cackled, horses whinnied, children laughed, and all the world was set to music, but Newt was not a happy man.

He was not a happy man for the simple reason that everybody else in town had heard the "news" long before it reached him. For half-an-hour or more he had been putting that same old question to every one he met; indeed, he even went out of his way five or six blocks to ring the front door bell at the home of William Grimes, night watchman at Smock's Warehouse, rousing him from a sound sleep in order to impart the "news" to him, only to have Bill call him a lot of hard names while making it clear that he had heard it before going to bed for the day.

The more Newt thought of it, the more he realized that it was his duty to go back and look up Uncle Dad Simms, even though it meant yelling his head off when he found him; it was a moral certainty that the only person in Tinkletown who *had*n't heard it was Uncle Dad,—and he would take a lot of telling.

The *Weekly Banner* would not be out till the following day; for at least twenty hours Uncle Dad would remain in the densest ignorance of the sensation that had turned Tinkletown completely upside down. Somebody ought to tell him. Somebody ought to tell poor old Uncle Dad Simms, that was all there was about it.

Moved by a sharp thrill of benevolence, Mr. Spratt retraced his steps, an eager look in his eyes. He found the old man standing in the broad, open door of Bill Kepsal's blacksmith shop. The blacksmith's assistant was banging away with might and main at his anvil, and Uncle Dad wore a pleased, satisfied smile on his thin old lips. He always said he loved to stand there and listen to the faint, faraway music of the hammer on the anvil, so different from the hammers and anvils they used to have when he was a boy,—when they were so blamed noisy you couldn't hear yourself think.

Newt took him by the arm and led him away. He was going to tell him the "news," but he wasn't going to tell it to him there. The only place to tell Uncle Dad anything was over in the Town Hall, provided it was unoccupied, and thither he conducted the expectant old man. As they mounted the steps leading to the Hall, Uncle Dad's pleased expression developed into something distinctly audible—something resembling a cackle of joy. Mr. Spratt favoured him with a sharp, apprehensive glance.

"Are they goin' to hold the inquest as soon as all this?" shouted Uncle Dad, putting his lips as close as possible to Newt's ear.

Newt stopped in his tracks.

"Have *you* heard it?" he bellowed.

"What say?"

"I say, *have you heard it*?"

"Speak up! Speak up!" complained Uncle Dad. "You needn't be afraid of *him* hearin' you, Newt. He's been dead for six or eight hours."

"My God!" groaned Newt.

For the second time that morning he left Uncle Dad high and dry, and started swiftly homeward. There was the possible, but remote chance that his wife hadn't heard the news,—and if she had heard it, she'd hear from him! He'd let her know what kind of a wife she was!

Never, within memory, had he failed to be the first person

in Tinkletown to hear the news, and here he was on this stupendous occasion, the last of them all. And why? Because he had taken that one morning to perform a peculiarly arduous and intensive bit of hard work up in the attic of his wife's house. He had chosen the attic because Mrs. Spratt rather vehemently had refused to let him use the parlour, or even the kitchen. And all the time that he was up in the attic, working his head off trying to teach his new fox terrier pup how to stand on its hind legs and jump over a broom stick, this startling piece of news was sweeping from one end of Tinkletown to the other.

Never, said Newt firmly, as he hurried homeward by the back streets,—never would he do another day's work in his life, if this was to be the result of honest toil. And what's more, he hadn't even received a single word of praise from his wife when he descended from the attic and triumphantly told her what he had accomplished,—he and the pup between them—after three hours of solid, painstaking endeavour.

Mrs. Spratt had merely said: "If you could learn that pup how to split firewood or milk a cow or repair the picket fence or something like that, you might be worth your salt, Newt Spratt. As it is, you ain't."

As Newt turned gloomily into the alley leading up to his back gate, he espied the Marshal of Tinkletown, Anderson Crow, leisurely approaching from the opposite direction. Mr. Crow, on catching sight of Newt, hastily removed something from his mouth and held it behind his back. Perceiving that it was nobody but Newt Spratt, he restored the object to his lips and began puffing away at it,—but not until he had sent a furtive glance over his shoulder.

"What you doin' back here?" inquired Newt, somewhat

offensively, as the two drew closer together. "Lookin' fer clues?"

Anderson again removed the corn-cob pipe, spat accurately over the hand with which he shielded his straggling chin whiskers, and remarked:

"Do *you* see anything wrong with this here pipe, Newt?" he asked, gazing rather pensively at the object.

"I don't *see* anything wrong with it," said Newt. "Still, I think you're mighty sensible not to smoke it any place except in an alley. Why don't you get a new one? They only cost ten cents. If you got a new one once in a while,—say once a year,—your wife wouldn't order you out of the house every time you light it."

"She don't order me out of the house when I light it," retorted Anderson. "'Cause why? 'Cause I never light it till I get two or three blocks away from home."

The subject apparently being exhausted, the two alley-farers lapsed into characteristic silence. Mr. Spratt leaned rather wearily against his own back fence, while Mr. Crow accepted the support of a telephone pole. Presently the former started to say something about the weather, but got no farther than the first two or three words when an astounding conjecture caused him to break off abruptly. He glanced at the old marshal, swallowed hard a couple of times, and then hopefully ventured the time-honoured question:

"Anything new, Anderson?"

The marshal responded with a slow, almost imperceptible shake of the head. He was gazing reflectively at a couple of English sparrows perched on one of the telephone wires some distance down the line.

Newt experienced a sudden, overwhelming joy. Caution,

however, and a certain fear that he might be mistaken, advised him to go slow. There remained the possibility that Anderson might be capable of simulation.

"Where's the body?" he inquired, casually.

Marshal Crow's gaze deserted the sparrows and fixed itself on Newt's ear.

"The what?"

His companion exhaled a tremendous breath of satisfaction. Life was suddenly worth living. The Marshal of Tinkletown had not heard the "news." The marshal, *himself!*

"Well, by Gosh!" exclaimed the revivified Mr. Spratt. "Where have you been at?"

"That's my business," snapped Anderson.

"All I got to say is that you ought to be attendin' to it, if it's your business," said Newt loftily. "You're the marshal of this here town, ain't you? And everybody in town knows that Jake Miller is dead except you. You're a fine marshal." There was withering scorn in Newt's voice. He even manifested an inclination to walk off and leave the marshal without further enlightenment.

Anderson made a valiant effort to conceal his astonishment. Assuming a more or less indifferent air, he calmly remarked:

"I knowed Jake was a little under the weather, but I didn't think it was serious? When did he die?"

"He didn't die," said Newt. "He hung himself."

"What's that?" gasped Anderson, his jaw sagging.

"Hung himself some time last night," went on Newt joyously. "From a rafter in Ed Higgins's livery stable. With a clothesline. Kicked a step-ladder out from under himself. Why, even Uncle Dad Simms has heard about it. Ed found him when he went out to—wait a second! I'm goin' your way. What's the rush? He's been dead six or eight hours. He can't escape. He's down in Hawkins's undertaking place. Hey! You dropped your pipe. Don't you want it any—"

"If you're goin' my way, you'll have to *run*," called out Marshal Crow as he unlimbered his long legs and made for the mouth of the alley. He was not running, but Newt, being an undersized individual, had no other means of keeping up with him unless he obeyed the sardonic behest. For ten or fifteen rods, Mr. Spratt jogged faithfully at the heels of the leader, and then suddenly remembered that it was a long way to Hawkins's Undertaking Emporium in Sickle street,—at least an eighth of a mile as the crow flies,—and as he already had had a hard day's work, he slowed down to a walk and then to a standstill. He concluded to wait till some one came along in a wagon or an automobile. There wasn't any use wasting his valuable breath in running. Much better to save it for future use. In the meantime, by standing perfectly still, he could ruminate to his heart's content.

Marshal Crow's long strides soon carried him to the corner of Maple Street, where he made a sharp turn to the right, shooting a swift look over his shoulder as he did so. His late companion was leaning against a tree. Satisfied that he had completely thrown Mr. Spratt off the trail, Anderson took a short cut through Justice of the Peace Robb's front and back yards and eventually emerged into Main Street, where he slackened his pace to a dignified saunter.

He caught sight of Alf Reesling, the reformed town drunkard, holding conversation from the sidewalk with some one in a second story window of Mrs. Judy O'Ryan's boarding house, half a block away.

"Hello!" shouted Alf, discovering the marshal. "Here he comes now. Where you been all morning, Andy? I been huntin' everywhere for you. Something horrible has happened. I just stopped to tell Judy about it."

The marshal stopped, and gazed upon Alf with mild interest. He nodded carelessly to Mrs. O'Ryan in the upstairs window, and addressed the following significant remark to Alf:

"I guess I've got Jake's motive purty well established, Alf. You needn't ask me what I've unearthed, because I won't tell you. It's a nice day, ain't it, Judy?"

Before Mrs. O'Ryan could affirm or deny this polite bit of information, Alf cried out:

"You don't mean to say you *know* about it?"

"The rain yesterday and day before has brought your lilacs out splendid, Judy," said Anderson, ignoring him.

"I was up to your house before eight o'clock, and your wife said you'd gone out in the country to practise your new Decoration Day speech, Anderson. How in thunder did you find out about Jake?"

Marshal Crow turned upon the speaker with some severity. "See here, Alf, are you tryin' to act like Newt Spratt?"

That was a deadly insult to Alf.

"What do you mean?" he demanded hotly.

"Nothin'—except that Newt had the same kind of an idee in his head that you seem to have got into yours. Next time you see Newt you tell him I been laughin' myself almost sick over the way I fooled him,—the blamed iggoramus." Having planted a seed that was intended to bear the fruit of justification, the venerable marshal decided that now was the time to prepare himself against anything further in the shape of surprise. So he linked arms with Alf and started off down the street.

"Now, see here, Alf," he began, somewhat sternly. "I won't stand for any beatin' about the bush from you. You got to tell me the whole truth an' nothin' but the truth, and if your story hangs together and agrees with what I've already worked out,—I'll see that you get fair treatment and—"

Alf stopped short. "What in sassafras are you talkin' about? What story?"

"Begin at the beginnin' and tell me where you was last night, and *early this morning*, and where and when you last saw Jake Miller."

The marshal's manner was decidedly accusative, although tempered by sadness. Something in his voice betrayed a great and illy concealed regret that this life-long friend had got himself so seriously entangled in the Jacob Miller affair.

"Where was I last night and this morning?" repeated the astonished Alf.

"Percisely," said Anderson, tightening his grip on Alf's arm.

"In bed," said Alf succinctly.

"Come, now," warned the marshal; "none of that. I want the truth out of you. When did you last see Jake Miller,—and what was he doing?"

"I saw him about half an hour ago, and he wasn't doin' anything."

"I mean, before he came to his untimely end."

"I don't know what you're drivin' at, but if it gives you any satisfaction I c'n say that the last time I saw him alive was yesterday afternoon about four o'clock. He was unloadin' some baled hay over at Ed's feed-yard and—that's all."

"How was he actin'?"

"He was actin' like a man unloadin' hay."

"Did he appear to have anything on his mind? I mean anything more than usual?"

"Couldn't say."

"Did he look pale or upset-like?"

"I kinder thought,—afterwards,—that he did look a *leetle* pale. Sort of as if he'd eat something that didn't agree with him."

"I see. Well, go on."

"Go on what?"

"Tellin' me. Where did you next see him?"

"Oh, there was a lot of people saw him after I did. Why don't you ask them?"

"Answer my question."

"I didn't see him again until about half past seven this morning. He was hangin' from a rafter in Ed's stable. My God, it was awful! I know I'll dream about Jake for the next hundred years."

"Did he have a rope around his neck?"

"No, he didn't." Anderson started. This was an unexpected reply.

"Well,—er, what *did* he have around his neck?"

"A halter strap."

"You—you're sure about that?"

"Positive."

"I see. So far your story jibes with the facts. Now, answer me this question. When and where did you help Jake Miller write that note of farewell?"

"What?" gasped Alf.

"You heard me."

"I didn't help him write any note."

"You didn't?"

"Nobody helped him write it."

"How do you know that, sir?"

"Do you mean to tell me that Jake left a farewell note?"

"I'm not sayin' whether he did or not. You don't mean to claim that he didn't leave one, do you?"

"If he did, nobody that I know of has laid eyes on it."

Anderson smiled mysteriously. "Well, we'll drop that feature of the case temporarily. You was quite a friend of Jake Miller's, wasn't you?"

"Off and on," said Alf. "Same as you was," he added, quickly.

"What reason did he ever give you for wantin' to take his own life? Think carefully, now,—and nothing but the truth, mind you?"

"The only thing I ever heard him say that sounded suspicious was when he told a crowd of us at Lamson's one night that if this here prohibition went into effect he'd like to have some one telegraph his sister in Buffalo, so's she could come on and claim his remains."

"But he wasn't a drinkin' man, Alf, and you know it."

"I know, but he always said he was lookin' forward to the day when he could afford to get as drunk as he sometimes thought he'd like to be. He was a droll sort of a cuss, Jake was. He claimed he'd been savin' up his appetite and his money for nearly three years so's he could see which would last the longest in a finish fight."

"Was you present when he was cut down?"

"I was."

"Aha! That's what I'm tryin' to get at. Who cut the rope?"

"It wasn't a rope,—it was a hitchin' strap. An' nobody cut it, come to think of it. It was a perfectly good strap, so two or three of us held Jake's body up so's Ed Higgins could untie it from the rafter."

"And then what?"

"Old man Hawkins and Doc Brown said he'd been dead five or six hours."

"I see. What did Doc say he died of?"

Alf stared at him in amazement. "He died of being hung to a rafter."

Marshal Crow cleared his throat, and was ominously silent for fifteen or twenty paces. When he next spoke it was with the deepest gravity. There was a dark significance in the look he fixed upon Alf.

"Is there any proof that Jake Miller wasn't dead long before he was strung up to that rafter?"

"What's that?" gasped Alf, once more coming to a sudden stop.

"It's a matter I can't discuss with anybody at present," said Anderson, curtly.

"Have—have you deduced something important, Anderson?" implored Alf, eagerly. "Is there evidence of foul play?"

"That's my business," said Anderson. "Come on. Don't stand there with your mouth open like that. He's still over at Hawkins's place, is he? I been workin' on the quiet all by myself since early this morning, an' I don't know just what's been happening around here for the last couple of hours."

"He was there the last I heard of him," said Alf.

"Well, you've given a purty good account of yourself, Alf, an' unless something turns up to change my present opinion, you are free to come an' go as you please."

"See here, you blamed old hayseed, what do you mean by actin' as if I had anything to do with Jake Mil—"

"You don't know what you're doing when you're drunk, Alf Reesling."

"But I ain't been drunk for twenty-five years, you blamed old—"

"That remains to be seen," interrupted Anderson sternly. "Now don't talk any more. I want to think."

Having obtained certain desirable facts in connection with the taking-off of Jacob Miller, Marshal Crow ventured boldly, confidently, into the business section of the town. He was now in a position to discuss the occurrence with equanimity,—in fact, with indifference. Moreover, he could account for his physical absence from the centre of the stage, so to speak, by reminding all would-be critics that he was mentally on the job long before Ed Higgins made the gruesome discovery. In other words, it served his purpose to "lie low" and observe from well-calculated obscurity the progress of events.

Now, Tinkletown had not experienced the shock and thrill of suicide in a great many years. Sundry citizens had met death in an accidental way, and others had suddenly died of old age, but no one had intentionally shuffled off since Jasper Wiggins succeeded in completing a hitherto unsuccessful life by pulling the trigger of a single-barrelled shotgun with his big toe, back in the fall of '83.

The horrendous act of Jacob Miller, therefore, created a sensation.

Tinkletown was agog with excitement and awe. Everybody was talking about Jake. He was, by all odds, the most important man in town. Alive, he had been perhaps the least important.

He was the sort of citizen you always think of last when trying to take a mental census of the people you know by sight.

Once, and only once, had Jake seen his name in the columns of the *Weekly Banner*, and he was so impressed that he cut the article out of the paper and pasted it under the sweat-band of his best hat. It happened to be the obituary notice of a farmer bearing the same name, but that made no difference to Jake; he was vicariously honoured by having his name in print,—and in rather large type at that.

And now he was to have at least half a page in the *Banner*, with his name in huge black letters, double column, something like this:

JAKE MILLER HANGS HIMSELF!!!

Column after column of Jake Miller and he not there to rejoice!

Jake Miller on the front page, crowding out the news from Paris and Washington, displacing local Society "items," shoving the ordinary "obituaries" out of their hallowed corners, confiscating space that belonged to the Lady Maccabees and other lodges, supplanting thoughtfully prepared matter in the editorial column,—why, the next issue of the *Banner* would be a Jake Miller number from beginning to end. And Jake not there to enjoy it all!

Jake had been a more or less stationary inhabitant of Tinkletown for about three years. He had taken up his residence there without really having had the slightest intention or desire to do so. In fact, he would have been safely out of the village in another ten minutes if Mrs. Abbie Nixon hadn't missed the blackberry pie from the kitchen window sill, where she had set it out to cool,—and even then he might have got away if he had had a handkerchief or something with which to remove the damning stains from his lips and chin. But, in his haste, he used the back of his hand, and—well, Justice of the Peace Robb sent him to the calaboose for thirty days,—and that's how Jake became a resident of Tinkletown.

At the trial he was so shamelessly complimentary about Mrs. Nixon's pie that the prosecuting witness came very near to perjuring herself in order to show her appreciation. The dignity of the law was preserved only by Jake's unshaken resolution to plead guilty to the charge of feloniously eating one blackberry pie with never-to-be-forgotten relish. Mrs. Nixon was so impressed by Jake's honesty that she made a practice of sending a pie to him every baking-day during the period of his incarceration. But when approached by two or three citizens with the proposal that she join with them in providing the fellow with work as a sort of community "handy-man," she refused to consider the matter at all because most of her silver had come down from her grandmother and she wouldn't part with it for anything in the world.

For one who had never laid eyes on the village of Tinkletown up to the day of his arrival, Jake Miller revealed the most astonishing sense of civic pride. The first thing he did after being safely locked up was to whitewash the interior of his residence. (The town board furnished a rather thin mixture of slaked lime and water, borrowed a whitewash brush from Ebenezer January, and got off with a total cost of about eighty-five cents.) He also repaired several windows in the calaboose by stuffing newspapers into the broken panes, remodeled the entire heating system with a little stove polish, put two or three locks in order, and once, on finding that it was possible to remove a grating from one of the windows, crawled out of his place of confinement and mowed the grass plot in front of the jail.

It was then that the people of Tinkletown began to take notice of him. A few of the more enterprising citizens went so far as to consult Justice Robb about extending Jake's sentence indefinitely, claiming that it wasn't at all likely the town would ever see another prisoner who took as much interest in keeping the jail in order as he.

And when he was finally released, he obtained a job with Ed Higgins at a slight increase in wages over what he had been receiving while in durance vile.

He was a middle-aged man with a large Adam's apple and a retreating chin; his legs were so warped that a good ten inches of space separated the knees. Whence he came and why he was content to abide in Tinkletown were questions he always answered, but never in a satisfactory manner. Even the hardiest citizens soon came to the conclusion that there wasn't much use in asking questions that Jake could answer with a slow and baffling wink. He became a fixture in Tinkletown, doing odd jobs for nearly everybody in town, and still finding ample time to attend to his duties at the feed yard. Whenever any one had a job to be done that he particularly disliked doing himself, he always appealed to Jake, and Jake did it.

When not otherwise employed, he slept in the box-stall once inhabited by the prize stallion, Caleb the Second, now deceased, and you would have been surprised to see what a tidy place he made of it by tacking up two or three anatomical pictures from the *Police Gazette*, and putting in a folding bed,— or, more strictly speaking, a bed that could be folded. It consisted of three discarded horse blankets. Quite a snug little bed- chamber, you would say, and, as Jake himself frequently remarked, a very handy stall to have a nightmare in.

Twice a day, regularly, day in and day out, Jake inquired at the post office for mail, and invariably Postmaster Lamson, without looking, replied: "Nothing today, Jake."

A singular thing happened the afternoon before Jake hung himself. He received a letter,—a rather fat one,—postmarked Sandusky, Ohio. Mr. Lamson and the loafers at the store were still talking about the extraordinary event when the former closed up for the night, a little later than usual. And while they were talking about it, Jake was getting ready to hang himself.

Marshal Crow headed straight for the *Banner* office, Mr. Reesling trailing a few steps behind like a dog at heel. Quite a crowd had gathered in front of Hawkins's Undertaking Emporium across the street from the newspaper office.

"Don't foller me in here," ordered the marshal, as Alf started to enter the *Banner* office with him. "This is private. Move on, now."

"But what'll I tell the gang over there if they ask me what you're doin' about the case?" argued Alf.

"You tell 'em I'll soon have the mystery solved."

"What mystery? There ain't any mystery about it. He

done it as publicly as he could."

"Well, you just tell 'em I've got a clue, and I'm follerin' it up."

With that, he disappeared through the door, closing it with some violence in Alf's face.

Harry Squires was putting the finishing touches to a long and graphic account of the suicide. He looked up as Anderson sauntered into the back office.

"I'm glad you came in, Marshal," he said. "I hated to finish this story without mentioning you, one way or another. Now I can add right here at the end: 'Our worthy Town Marshal, A. Crow, was also present.'"

Anderson sat down. He pulled at his sparse chin whiskers for a moment or two, evidently trying to release something verbal. Failing in this, he sank back in the chair and fixed Mr. Squires with a pathetic look.

"Where have you been?" demanded Harry.

"Oh,—rooting around," said Anderson.

"Well, I'll tell you something that no one else in this town knows," said the other, pitying his old friend. "Are you listening?"

Anderson shook his head drearily. "I'll never be able to live this down, Harry."

"Brace up. All is not lost. Will you do exactly what I tell you to do?"

"I hope you ain't going to tell me to go down and jump in the mill-race."

"Nothing of the sort. That wouldn't help matters. You could swim out. Now, listen. I know why Jake hung himself; and I am the only one who does know. The whole story is told here in this article I have just written. We've been friends and foes for a great many years, Mr. Hawkshaw, and I want to show my appreciation. I don't know how many times you have saved my life. I sha'n't tell you in just what way you have saved it; I can only say that I should have died long ago of sheer ennui,—if you know what that is,—if it hadn't been for you, old friend. You have been a life-saver, over and over again. And in spite of the many times you have saved my life, I don't seem to have put on any flesh. I remain as skinny as I was when I first met you. I ought to be so fat that I'd have to waddle. But, that's neither here nor there. I'm going to save *your* life now, Sherlock. I'm going to fix it so that when you *do* die, the people of this burg will erect a monument to you that will make the one in Trafalgar Square,—if you know where that is,—look like a hitching post. Lend me your ear, Mr. Pinkerton. That's right. Take off your hat. You can hear better.

"I am going to reveal to you the true facts in the case of our late lamented friend, Jake Miller. I have in my possession the letter he received yesterday afternoon. It is under lock and key, and no one else has seen it. While everybody else was gazing at Jake and wondering how long he'd been hanging there, I—with my nose for news,—went off in search of that letter. I might have spared myself the trouble, for the last thing Jake did before ending his life, was to put it in an envelope and mail it to me. He also enclosed a short note in which he implored me to do the right thing by him and put his name in the biggest type we have on hand. That's just what I intend to do. Now, I'm going to turn that letter over to you. Instead of me being the one to tell *you* about it, you are going to be allowed to tell *me* about it. See? That's what you are here for now,—to show me this letter with all its harrowing details. Later on, when the coroner comes over from Boggs City, you can deliver it to him. Now listen!"

Ten minutes later, Marshal Crow strode solemnly out of the *Banner* office, and debouched upon the crowd in front of Hawkins's. Several erstwhile admirers snickered. He paid not the slightest attention to them. Instead he inquired in a loud, authoritative voice if any one had seen Alf Reesling.

"I'm standin' right in front of you," said Alf.

"I deputize you to act as guard during the day over the remains of Orlando Camp. You are to see to it that no one trespasses within fifty feet of it without an order from me,—or the Governor of New York. You will—"

"What the devil are you talkin' about?" demanded Alf. "There ain't no remains around here named Camp."

The marshal smiled, but there was more pity than mirth in the effort.

"All you got to do is to do what I deputize you to do," he said quietly. "Is Bill Kepsal here?"

"Present," said the iron-armed blacksmith, with a series of winks that almost sufficed to take in the whole assemblage.

"I deputize you, William Kepsal, and—" (he craned his neck slightly)—"and you, Newton Spratt, out there on the edge of the crowd, to act as guards durin' the night, until relieved by Deputy Reesling at seven A. M. tomorrow mornin'. You will permit no one to approach or remove the body of Moses Briscoe from its present place of confinement until further orders. And now, feller citizens, I must request you one and all to disperse and not to congregate again in this locality, under penalty of the law. Disperse at once, move on, everybody."

The crowd didn't move an inch.

"He's gone plumb crazy," said Rush Applegate to Uncle Dad Simms, and he made such a special effort that Uncle Dad heard him quite distinctly.

"He always *wuz*," agreed Uncle Dad. "What's he crazy about this time?"

"Come on home, Anderson," said Alf Reesling, gently. "Maybe if you took a dose of—"

"Lemme talk to him," interrupted Elmer K. Pratt, the photographer. "I had an uncle once that *died* in an asylum, and I used to keep him quiet before he got hopeless by lettin' on that he really *was* George Washington. Now, look here, Anderson, —"

Marshal Crow held up his hand. There was no sign of resentment in his voice or manner as he addressed the grinning crowd.

"I don't blame you for thinkin' that man in there is Jake Miller. I thought so myself until a couple o' days ago. That's when I first begin to suspect that he was the very man he now turns out to be. Gentlemen, if the individual that you knew as Jake Miller hadn't took his own life last night, I would have had him behind the bars today, sure as all get out. He wasn't no more Jake Miller than I am. Jake Miller was one of his alibis. He had —"

"You mean aliases," interrupted Professor Rank, of the high school.

"Or nom de plumes," added Willie Spence, the chief clerk at the Grand View Hotel, one of the most inveterate readers in town. To Willie the name of any author was a nom de plume; it didn't make any difference whether it was his real name or not.

"He had a lot of names besides Jake Miller," explained

Anderson loftily. "And he didn't have to go to high school to get 'em," he added as an afterthought, favouring Professor Rank with a withering look. "Now, disperse,—all of you. Go on now, Willie,—disperse. Everybody disperse except Alf Reesling. You stay here an' keep watch till I come back."

With that, he took the easiest and most expeditious way of dispersing the crowd by walking briskly off in the direction of Main Street. The crowd followed,—or more strictly speaking, accompanied him. He was the centre of a drove of eager inquirers. Having successfully dispersed the crowd in front of Hawkins's Emporium, he stopped in front of the post office and addressed it once more.

"All you got to do," he announced, taking a seat on the porch, "is to wait till the *Banner* comes out, and then you'll get all the news. I just been in there to tell Harry Squires about my discoveries, and he is workin' his head off now gettin' it all in shape for the subscribers to the paper. And that reminds me. He asked me to do him a favour. He says there are quite a number of cheap skates in this town that ain't regular subscribers to the *Banner*. That's why Ebenezer January's barber shop is so crowded on Thursday mornings that Ebenezer is threatenin' to stop *his* subscription. Ebenezer says there's so many customers in his place waitin' to be next with the paper that he ain't hardly got room to hone up his razors after Wednesday's work. I promised Harry I'd suggest that you all go around and subscribe today, because he says he's engaged Ebenezer to whitewash the press-room tomorrow and the barber shop won't be open at all. He says it's an outrage that—"

He stopped short to glare in speechless amazement at a familiar figure almost under his nose.

"I thought I told you to stand guard back there, Alf Reesling," he roared.

"Aw, thunder, he can't run away," protested Alf. "An' nobody's goin' to *steal* him, so what's the sense—"

"I'll give you just fifteen minutes to get back there to Hawkins's," declared the marshal firmly. "If you're not back there by that time, I'll arrest you for contempt."

"That suits me," said Alf promptly.

"Yes, sir," said Anderson, addressing the crowd, "I would have nabbed him today if he hadn't gone an' hung himself like this. He must have got onto the fact that I had him dead to rights. He knowed there wasn't any escape for him,—no chance in the world. Wait a second! Don't all talk at once,—and don't ask questions! An' say, Abner, it won't do you any good to go round to the *Banner* office, because I swore Harry Squires to secrecy. So stay where you are. Harry won't tell you a thing, even if your father-in-law is a regular subscriber. What time is it, Lum?"

On being informed by Lum Gillespie that it was later than he thought, Marshal Crow looked at his own watch and arose in some haste.

"By ginger, I got to get busy. I still got to see if I can find that letter Jake received yesterday afternoon. I wouldn't be surprised if the contents of that letter had a good deal to do with his hurryin' up this hangin' business. Like as not it was a warnin' from some confederate of his'n, lettin' him know I was gettin' purty hot on his trail. It's mighty hard to keep these things from leakin' out, 'specially when you're workin' at long range as I've been fer some time. My investigations have been carried on from one end of the country to the other. I finally got 'em narrowed down to a place out west called Sandusky, Ohio, an' I was just on the point of telegraphin' to the police out there that I had their man when this thing happens."

He was assisted in his search for the letter by a volunteer organization of about one hundred men and boys. The search was a most diligent one. Much to the disgust of Ed Higgins, the floor of Jake's sleeping apartment was yanked up by willing, excited citizens; the hay-mow was ransacked from one end to the other; the grain bins were turned inside out, and there was some talk of ripping off a section of the roof. At half past twelve o'clock, the marshal went home to his midday meal, leaving the work in charge of Lum Gillespie, the garage owner, whose love for Mr. Higgins was governed entirely by the fact that the liveryman's business interfered considerably with his own prosperity.

Secure in the seclusion of his own woodshed, Marshal Crow slyly withdrew Jake's letter from an inside pocket and reread it with great care. Later on, having fortified himself with a substantial dinner, he returned to the hunt. Advising the toilers that he was going to do a little private searching, based on a "deduction" that had come to him while he was at home, he ambled off in the direction of Power House Gulley. Half an hour later he reappeared and instructed the crowd to knock off work. He had found the letter just where he figured he would find it!

"I don't see why in thunder you didn't figure it out at breakfast instead of at dinner," growled Ed Higgins, moodily surveying the wreckage. "I've a notion to sue you for damages. Look at that box-stall! Look at that—"

"Never mind, Ed; I'll have Lum an' the rest of 'em put everything back in order, jest as they found it. Now, you fellers get to work and put things in shape around here. I'm goin' to take this letter over an' show it to Harry Squires. It proves everything,—absolutely everything. See here, Alf,—what in thunder are you doin' here? Why ain't you guardin' them remains as I told you to do?"

"I *am* guardin' 'em," said Alf. "I c'n guard 'em just as well from a distance as I can close up, an' you know it. All I got to do is to walk to the corner there an' I c'n see Hawkins's place as plain as anything. I could see it from right here if it wasn't fer Lamson's store an' the Grand View Hotel."

The marshal gave him a look of bitter scorn, and strode away. The crowd straggled along behind. Anderson stopped at the *Banner* office door and, exposing the dirty envelope to the eager gaze of the crowd, advised every one present to step in and take out a year's subscription to the paper. Then he disappeared. The crowd surged forward, filling the outer office with something like sardine compactness. The door to Mr. Squires's private office, however, closed sharply behind Mr. Crow, and for the next fifteen or twenty minutes the young lady bookkeeper was busy taking subscriptions from the disappointed throng. She got sixty-three new subscribers and definite promises from a large number of citizens who were considerably in arrears.

"You'll see it all in your paper tomorrow morning," said Anderson, coming out of the inner office at the end of half an hour's consultation with the editor. "All I can say to you now is that I have captured one of the most desperate criminals in the country. He has been wanted for nearly three years for a diabolical crime. It makes my flesh creep to think of him being loose among our women an' children all this time. Is there any one here who ain't subscribed to the *Banner*?"

Tinkletown slept fitfully that night when it slept at all. The sole citizen enjoying a peaceful night's rest was Jake Miller. A singular circumstance connected with the broken rest of three-fourths of the people of Tinkletown was the extraordinary unanimity with which Jake became visible to them the instant they did drop off to sleep.

Bright and early the next morning, the *Banner* appeared with its gruesome story. Jake was in very large type, but not much larger, after all, than Marshal Crow. The whilom Mr. Squires, revelling in generosity, gave Anderson all the credit. He held forth at great length on the achievements of the redoubtable marshal, winding up his account with a recommendation that a movement be inaugurated at once looking to the erection of a memorial statue to the famous "sleuth." The concluding sentence of this bold panegyric was as follows: "Do not wait till he is dead! Do it now!" And appended, in parentheses, the statement that the *Banner* would head the list of subscribers with a contribution of one hundred dollars!

In the body of his article, Mr. Squires printed in full the contents of the letter received by Jacob Miller on the afternoon before his death,—the letter which had been recovered, after the most diligent and acute search by Marshal Crow, at the bottom of an abandoned well in Power House Gulley,—the letter which so completely vindicated the theories and deductions of Tinkletown's most celebrated son.

Jake's letter was from his brother in Sandusky. It warned him that the authorities had finally located him in Tinkletown and that officers were even then on the way east to "pinch" him. They had run him down at last, despite the various aliases under which he had sought to avoid apprehension; brotherly love impelled him to advise Jake to "beat it" as "quick as possible." Moreover, he went on to state that if they got him he'd "swing" as sure as hell. Brotherly interest no doubt was also responsible for the frank admission that the "family" had done all it could for him, and that if he had had a grain of sense, or had listened to his friends, he wouldn't have married her in the first place. And if he hadn't married her, he wouldn't have been placed in a position where he had to beat her brains out. Not that she didn't deserve to have her brains knocked out, and all that, but "you can't go around doing that sort of thing without getting into trouble about it."

In short, Jake—(by any other name he was just as guilty)—had slain his wife, presumably in cold blood. At any rate, Mr. Squires, sustained by the information received from Marshal Crow, (who had gone deeply into the case), stated in cold type that it had been done in cold blood.

Apparently Jake had decided that he was tired of dodging the inevitable. It was quite clear that he could not endure the thought of being "swung" for his diabolical deed.

The account also stated that Marshal Crow had at once advised the Western authorities by telegraph that he had their man, but regretted to state the scoundrel had anticipated arrest in the manner now so well known to the readers of the *Banner*, long recognized as the most enterprising newspaper in that part of the State of New York.

A day or two later, after the inquest, an officer arrived from Sandusky. He was a spectator at the funeral of Jake Miller, whom he readily identified as the slayer of Mrs. Camp, and was afterwards a most interested listener to the recital given on Lamson's porch by Marshal Crow, who, described with considerable zest and surprising fidelity the manifold difficulties he had experienced in "running the criminal to earth,"—one of the most puzzling cases he had ever been called upon to tackle.

The astonished officer walked over to the Grand View Hotel with Harry Squires. From time to time he passed his hand over his brow in a thoroughly puzzled manner.

"I don't mind telling you, Mr. Squires," he blurted out at last, "that we hadn't the faintest idea that this fellow Camp was as desperate a character as all this. We looked upon him as a rather harmless, soft-headed guy,—but, my God, he turns out to be one of the slickest all-round crooks in the United States. No wonder he managed to give us the slip all these years. It only goes to show how even the best of us can be fooled in a man."

"That's right," agreed Harry. "It certainly does show how you can be fooled in a man."

"When I get back home and tell 'em at headquarters what a slick duck he was, they'll throw a fit. Why, by Gosh, we all thought he was a nut,—a plain nut."

"Far be it from me," said Harry, "to speak ill of either the living or the dead."

"It's a wonder he didn't up and blow the head off this old Rube when he found he was about to be cornered."

Harry took that moment to relight his pipe, and then abruptly said "Good night" to the gentleman from Sandusky.

As he rejoined the group in front of Lamson's, Marshal Crow was saying:

"I'm mighty glad Harry Squires had sense enough not to say in the *Banner* that as soon as Jake Miller found out that the jig was up, he took the law in his own hands, and lynched himself."

THE END

Lightning Source UK Ltd.
Milton Keynes UK
UKOW01n2300311017

311951UK00003B/292/P